"*Echo Lake* is more than just a good debut novel. It is the coming-out party for Letitia Trent, the new poet-queen of neo-noir."

—KYLE MINOR, author of *Praying Drunk*

"In *Echo Lake*, Letitia Trent, with deceptively simple, beautiful language, creates a small American town slowly self destructing under the weight of its secrets. Trent illuminates the mystery of family and community, the pain of loss, all the while spinning a tale of murder and suspense. It's at turns a lovely and bone chilling read."

—PAULA BOMER, author of *Inside Madeleine*

"In *Echo Lake*, Trent's small town characters guard their secrets, and warn their children away from the mist-covered lake. Dark, ominous, and lyrical, *Echo Lake* is a beautiful exploration of loss, and the menace of deceptive surfaces."

—KAREN BROWN, author of *The Longings of Wayward Girls*

"Trent's debut novel combines a ripping good scare with prose as rich as dark verse. Her characters wear the imprint of the past like livid bruises, the bravest among them untangling their distorted histories to discover truths about the nature of community, family and self."

—SOPHIE LITTLEFIELD, author of *House of Glass*

"Trent's years as a poet serve her well in this heavily atmospheric novel, which deftly conjures up both evil and a small town's complicit reluctance to face its past."

—*KIRKUS REVIEWS*

D0092287

DARK HOUSE PRESS

ECHO

ECHO LAKE

PART ONE

1

Where are we going? Emily asked, and she heard her voice smaller and higher in her throat than it had been in years. She looked at her hands, white and smooth. She didn't have that scar at her knuckle where she'd cut herself on a broken glass at the bottom of the sink, the cut she'd needed stitches for her senior year of college. On her feet were plastic jelly sandals, purple ones, her skin dusty between the crosshatching.

Her mother Connie drove with the windows down and was young again. She wore a sundress, and her hair was gathered in a high ponytail. Her blonde hair whipped around her face—the driver's side window was opened just a crack and made a loud, sucking sound.

Her mother hummed and kept her eyes on the road.

But I'm thirty and my mother's dead, Emily thought. She could not let herself imagine that life was otherwise. Even in dreams, she was not able to let go. She wished she could, but she knew: I am only dreaming. Connie was really dead. Emily was no longer a child. Everything was much worse than it looked right now.

Where are we going? Emily asked again, this time speaking over the sucking sound from the window.

Her mother turned to her and smiled, her cheeks bright, but her lips pale and dry. Connie never wore soft shades of lipstick, never had the soft feathered hair or chalky pale eye shadow of the television mothers in the eighties, the mothers Emily had so wished for as a child.

We're going to Heartshorne, her mother said. We're going home.

Emily sat up looked out the blue-tinted window. The road before them was flat and empty of cars. They passed a ranch where the cows stared dully at the very edges of a thin, wire fence, chewing and chewing on what? The brown grass? Emily didn't know. Her small body made her afraid to ask questions. She imagined that she might accidentally reveal to her mother what she knew—that Connie had died in two thousand and four of lung cancer. That Connie really hated Heartshorne. No matter how bad it is here, it's better than where I came from, she'd tell Emily while awake late at night, pacing the living room while Patsy Cline sang on the tape from the tinny little boombox on the kitchen counter or cleaning until she was so exhausted she could only lay in bed smoking cigarettes.

Why are we going there? Emily asked. Connie rolled up the car window and the sucking sound stopped. She heard only the muffled inside sounds of the car now—the road rolling underneath their wheels and the sound of the wind trying to get in.

Why? Emily asked again. Connie kept her eyes on the road. They were coming up to sharp curves, some hills even, and though the grass was still brown, the trees were taller and houses scarcer. They were entering the country, not the rambling, long stretches of flatland but the closer, secret hollows of forest.

Because you can't stay away from home for too long, she said. It makes you crazy. You can't just leave. You have to understand why.

Listen, Emmy, she said, using the name that Emily had always wanted to hear whenever her mother was in one of her rare moods of happiness.

Emmy, you'll be going home soon, she said. Make the most of it.

She touched Emily's knee where her jeans had faded from playing in the dirt with her buckets and dolls and collections of dirty stuffed animals she treated as pets or children, depending on the game.

Emmy, I'm taking you home.

2

Emily woke at five thirty. The light outside was at the soft angle she loved but rarely got to see anymore. She used to stay up with Eric until five, after his gigs that lasted until well after midnight, days when she would go straight from gigs being with him to her early-morning work in tech support, her hair reeking of cigarettes and the hem of her dress smelling of gin where Eric had spilled his drink. Now, she worked a proper day job that required pumps and stockings, her hair arranged in some semblance of order, and a professional wardrobe of blacks and neutrals. They had health insurance now. They had moved into a larger apartment, closer to downtown Columbus, which didn't mean much anymore. Downtown was dying, the malls empty of stores and people, the restaurants with service staff who spent more time on break than at work. But still, it was a central location and she could catch the bus from there.

She was alone in bed, the covers kicked onto the floor. She sat up, goose bumps traveling down her arms and legs in a wave. Her phone lit blue in the still-dark room. Eric had left a message at three—he had crashed at John's after the gig. He'd be home sometime the next day. Love.

He'd used the word crashed like they had when there were just out of college, young enough to get carded and to stay up until dawn smoking cigarettes on the porches and steps of clubs or apartments.

Five years. Thinking about how long she'd been with Eric made her tired. She missed those early mornings, everything hatching, even the light weak and new, and being young enough to feel that you weren't hurting anything or wasting any time by being awake when others were still sleeping.

Now, it pained her to stay up too late. So much of the next day was wasted.

Emily rose—she couldn't go back to sleep now—and put the bed back together, tucking the blankets and sheets in tight. Her feet and hands were stiff with cold, but she couldn't stand the look of an abandoned, messy bed. Her mother had never been much interested in made beds, washed dishes, or outward signs of order. Emily had developed that habit on her own. As a child, she'd made her bedroom an oasis of order and calm, her dresses organized by color, her toys displayed or tucked away, never on the floor. She had learned how to contain herself tightly in small spaces, like trailer bedrooms and corners of studio apartments.

At eight AM, still an hour and a half from when she had to clock in for work, she decided to bring Eric breakfast—she'd leave it at the door, of course, not barge in and disturb them. It would be like old times, when she used to go out in the clothes she'd slept in to buy juice and bread to soak up the night's leftover alcohol.

The man at the bakery counter didn't recognize her. It had been years since he'd seen her two or three times a week at ungodly hours, stumbling in with her skin and hair greasy from being in a close, hot space all night. She dressed differently now, too. A slim, pencil skirt, heels clacking. But she looked otherwise the same, she hoped. Same dirty-blonde hair, same thin lips and big eyes, same long, oval face. Had she become noticeably older? Probably. She wished she could see what the man at the counter saw, but his eyes swept over her face, uninterested.

Beautiful morning, he said.

She remembered the dream then, her mother driving, how she'd known that she was dreaming and hoped that she wasn't all at the same time. In that car with the cracked window, the hissing, sucking sound, it had looked like a beautiful day then, too. Not a city beautiful day with its walkers and light streaming between buildings. It had been a beautiful day empty of people, all light and all sky from window edge to window edge.

It is, she said. She smiled at the man and walked out, enjoying the sound of her shoes, the feeling of her dress fabric whisking, the chill in the air that made her face cool and red.

She hadn't intended to look through the window before she knocked on the door. It was only because the windows were wide, large as a double-door, curtainless, and because the white screen of a computer was on, casting its blues onto a couple on the floor. They lay on the opened insides of a sleeping bag, naked. It was Eric and a woman. Or a girl, more like it, blonde and small, her hands folded under her head like a child taking a nap. One breast fell out on to the floor, flattened and sad.

Emily left the coffee and bagels at the doorstep. She wrote a note on the receipt and went to work, her hands shaking.

Fool, she thought all day at work as she filed documents and made phone calls and input numbers flawlessly into a computer program. You've been a fool.

She was surprised at herself, the calm she felt below the anger, which roiled and sickened her, as she knew it should, but where did it come from? Below the tumult, she was still and small, a receding pool. She should be devastated, throwing plates at the walls as people did when angry in movies or books: coming home early to beat Eric's chest, clawing his face, doing something more than feeling sick to her stomach and knowing that this would go away soon enough, and that when it was away, there would be hardly any trace of him.

•

Eric packed up all of his clothes, his instruments, and half of the music collection, though Emily had bought the Pixies and Velvet Underground boxed sets and protested when he packed them.

They were gifts, he said, his voice stuck in a permanent whine. He had cried when she told him what she'd seen, that she wanted him to leave, which had surprised her and then disgusted her when it happened again, after she insisted that yes, it was over, and he had to leave by the end of the week. She'd been crying, too, but he did not seem moved by her tears. She had been ready to be upset, to crawl into bed and stay there for days, to fall into a depression from the anticipation of missing him, but he had saved her from that. He so annoyed her with his attempts to make her feel responsible for his sadness that she couldn't feel anything but anger toward him, which she liked. It was good to be angry, enlivening, even. It wasn't a feeling she had indulged in before she'd found him naked, holding that girl on the floor.

It wasn't just the girl, she realized as the tears and shouting unfolded. It was their entire life together. He had made her his wife. She was responsible for everything, and he was free to live as he liked on the back of her work. She wasn't willing to do it anymore.

She refused to help him pack, refused to do anything but give him time and space to disentangle his belongings from hers.

Fuck it. Take anything you want, she told him, too tired, after almost five years of bending her desires to his, to argue. Leaving it all to him was a relief. He could choose to throw away what he wanted. When he finally left, she'd get rid of the rest.

Emily left him with his boxes, took a towering pile of mail from the kitchen counter, and stood at the end of the block where the walk sign blinked on. She didn't cross the street. She leaned on an empty newspaper box and closed her eyes. She imagined he'd be in the kitchen, fixing something alcoholic, ready to assail her with his moping, the only thing he could do with much skill or gusto (he was only a mediocre guitarist, she secretly thought, and an execrable songwriter), when she returned.

Emily sat on the stoop of the tattoo parlor by the apartment and opened the day's mail in the light of its fluorescent signs. Inside the shop, people were getting things stamped on their bodies—the names of lovers and children, bands and brands and flowers and pin-up girls. She could hear the whirr of tattoo guns from outside, the buzzing like a dentist's drill.

She set aside everything addressed to Eric except for the things that she paid that happened to be in his name (so he could build some good credit to counteract the bad debt of old parking tickets and long-ignored student loans). It was mostly his mail—bills, fliers for gigs and bars, magazines for cigars and music. At the bottom of the pile, there was a letter addressed to her by hand from Oklahoma. The envelope was thick and heavy, the paper fine. She opened it carefully along a narrow edge. This was the most beautiful letter she'd ever received. Even the ink was rich and black, furred slightly at the edges where it sunk into the veiny fibers of the paper.

Eric was in bed by the time she came back inside, the television and stereo quiet, the bedroom door closed. She pushed a week's worth of magazines and scarves and jackets onto the floor and lay on the couch without getting a pillow, sheet, or blanket. Usually, she took the room and he took the couch, but tonight she didn't want to try to wake him from his boozy, red-eyed sleep.

The letter from Oklahoma was nestled in her purse like a golden ticket.

3

The lake was not clean. The bottom went down farther than anyone could see. What would they find there if they could swim down the bottom and look? Was there even a bottom anymore?

Connie sat on the wooden dock next to her, looking much as Emily remembered her before she grew sick and thin.

Look, Connie said. There's a whole town under there.

Emily imagined people swimming to work, the underwater grocery store with melons and apples floating in the air above their bins, the vacuum packs of sandwich meat spinning.

What do you mean? Emily looked down at her hands and saw that they were her adult hands—scarred in three places, older than her years, a few dim, silver rings.

You'll find out, Connie said.

They sat for a while longer, not speaking. Emily wanted to reach out to her mother and hug her. It seemed like an appropriate time—a sunset, a lake, the air warm and without even a shift of cold in its wind—but she was afraid. What if she hugged her too close and dropped them both into the lake? What if they fell down into the lake town and nobody knew them and they were not welcome?

4

She couldn't place the accent of the man on the telephone. His voice was quick, the inflections sharp. He shouted, but without anger. It was simply the way he spoke.

It's good to hear from you—we prayed that we had the right address and that our letter would find you!

Thank you. Emily wondered if they really had prayed or if it was only an expression.

You never know with them, she heard her mother's voice, gravelly between mouthfuls of smoke (she never inhaled, only filled her mouth with smoke, a habit which had not saved her from cancer). *They'll pray for most anything. Pray you find a parking spot. It's a way to make you beholden to them and their prayers.*

But that wasn't such a bad thing, was it? Maybe what she needed were some prayers.

Emily pushed the thoughts aside. The voice was open and kind. It was her escape.

So what are the next steps? She asked.

Emily took a notepad from a stack of yellow pads that Eric had left. On the first page, he had started a lyric:

Black fingers break
the lake gray and hard as a nickel

She ripped the page free and crumpled it into a tight ball. She didn't even feel a twinge of guilt, though she had to admit these lyrics were better than his usual grade-school rhyming couplets. She made her list, clean, simple, and freeing. Better than any of Eric's lyrics had ever been.

She had been rootless before the letter. Sure she wanted to leave Eric and Columbus, but she was unsure where to go. She had no family that she knew and had few friends that were not his friends, too.

She was unused to doing things on her own. In the last five years, she'd hardly driven more than half an hour by herself, had not seen a movie alone or eaten dinner alone at a sit-down restaurant, had never thought of her money as her own, only our money. The only significant time she'd had to herself was when she had visited her mother in the hospital, early on in their relationship. She had relied on Eric to be the one who introduced her to the world. He was good at it. His big, open face and easy talk invited people in, not to mention his music. She had once been like this, too. She'd been popular in college, had even played drums in a band, that's how she'd met Eric, but during her years with Eric, she'd forgotten how to be the object of other people's attention.

He had made her the responsible one, the boring one. Or she had let him do this. Or, more likely, she thought, she'd done it to herself. She couldn't blame him, really. They had created a system, and she had not stopped it. She had even taken comfort in it for a while, in the lulling rhythms of everyday life and her clear role in it.

But all of that was over now. She'd received the letter from Oklahoma, where her mother had grown up, where her mother's side of the family had lived for decades. And her mother had come to her in her dreams and said she was going back home, finally, and Connie hadn't been angry or sick or thin in those dreams— she was the woman Emily had loved in the few times when she'd loved her mother purely without the complication of fear and dislike that was so familiar in their relationship.

The Connie in her dreams was the mother she had wanted and had seen only sometimes, like when Connie was dancing in the kitchen, or putting up Christmas lights, or when she'd pull Emily into her arms and unpin her hair and brush it straight around her shoulders before bed.

Emily knew now that she'd had a great aunt in Heartshorne the entire time. Connie had said that nobody was left there, that everyone had scattered, and good riddance to them, too, but she'd been wrong: Frannie Collins had remained. And if a great aunt had been there all of this time, there might be others. Maybe she would meet her family.

She'd wanted to meet them so badly and had asked until her mother shouted and told her to give up.

I don't know where they are, Connie had said, and they don't know where I am, and that's how I like it.

Emily would finally see the place she might have grown up, if her mother hadn't left. She had a house waiting for her, paid in full, her inheritance for being Connie's only living relative.

•

After two weeks of anger at Eric and the realization of the years she'd wasted, Emily finally felt nothing but a muffled annoyance and tenderness toward the remnants of her old life.

Her lack of anger surprised her. She felt not only calm, but triumphant, as though she'd done something to be proud of, though she'd done nothing but be the last surviving member of a broken family and a woman who had the courage to leave a philandering man who had never committed himself to her to begin with. Still, it was something—she had somewhere to go. She'd never been the one going, the one with a direction out. Eric would be in the same city, under the same rain and clouds, walking past the same gutters clogged with leaves and potato chip bags and ripped posters of bands who would never get anywhere beyond Columbus, and she'd be somewhere else, starting afresh.

She helped Eric pack the last of his books and his half-dozen identical black boots and drove him to John's house, which was shared by four other men in their late twenties or early thirties, all musicians, all broke. She remembered the young woman in his arms as she looked at that bay window but felt nothing but sadness. So much wasted time for both of them.

She kissed him on the forehead like a mother leaving her child on his first day of school. He seemed confused by the kiss and nodded goodbye. She'd told him she was leaving for good, but he didn't seem to believe it.

See you around, he said.

Sure, she answered.

At work, she gave her two weeks' notice.

But why? Her supervisor, a middle-aged man who wore an enormous jade ring on his pinky finger like a gangster, though he was otherwise pale and bespectacled, gave her a pained look. He was probably imagining all of the paperwork he'd have to do to find a new employee, the weeks of training, the professional development required. Are you pregnant? He asked.

Emily realized she was smiling, probably blushing, probably glowing.

Oh God, no, she said. She hadn't told anybody from work that she had left Eric or that she'd received the note from Oklahoma. They didn't know that she was going to leave everything behind. She wouldn't know how to begin to tell them. She didn't have work friends, really, just people that she spoke to in passing. They knew her exteriors—her heels, her boyfriend in the parking lot waiting to pick her up, how she never ate cake during noon birthday parties because the icing made her sick. But they didn't know anything else about her. If she told them where she was going, she'd have to tell the whole story of how and why.

Just looking for a change, she said.

She bagged up her work clothes and gave them all to Goodwill, those thick knits and stockings with runs down to mid-thigh where she'd stopped them with clear nail polish. She gave away every pair of slacks, rows and rows of pleated, folded blues and greens and blacks. And winter boots, too, were unnecessary where she was going, like chains on tires or antifreeze or snowsuits. No more dirty snow after months and months of it piled up like modern art made of cold and mud.

•

The trip to Oklahoma took two days, most of which she spent driving. When she absolutely had to, she'd eat at the counter at cafes and truck stops. She didn't sleep for more than six hours at a time, too excited in the mornings to stay in bed and try to sleep when her body told her to get up. No, excited wasn't exactly right. Excitable. Nervous in her stomach. She drank coffee with cream at restaurants, not black like she took at it home. She didn't take photographs along the way, though her camera lay in the glove box, the batteries charged, the memory card empty after she'd deleted the last photos of Eric.

She drove across the Midwest through a series of thunderstorms that filled the wide expanse of sky with clouds that churned black in the middle and moved in mottled colors, though the sky remained cloudily unbroken as a pot lid above her. She had never imagined there could be as much sky as there was from horizon to horizon in the middle of Nebraska, the corn whipping heavy heads together. She stopped at one-story motels, each little room a box within an L-shaped arrangement of identical boxes, the televisions and lamps bolted to the tables, each bed covered by the nubby white blankets that let the cold in through the visible webbing of weave. These rooms always smelled the same, like carpet-cleaning fluid and pine. She watched cable television and laughed when the people laughed on screen. Usually, she couldn't stand sitcoms and canned laughter. What a good idea, she thought for the first time, to have laugh tracks. She now understood how it worked: It was uncomfortable to laugh when you weren't sure you were supposed to laugh, particularly in a room you didn't know that smelled of pine and was always too warm or too cold.

Outside, cars went past all night. Even when she woke up at two in the morning, cars still passed.

They were all going somewhere, just like her. She imagined herself driving away like those cars and somebody else watching her from a window, wishing they had such direction.

•

Oklahoma is OK! Each license plate gave the same lukewarm recommendation.

I'm going home, she thought, though the landscape continued to look like Kansas for miles—flat and green, the sky neverending.

Emily stopped at Tote-A-Poke convenience store on the outskirts of Tulsa, mostly because of the name. She couldn't understand it as a command, as a pun, or as a description of a place. It sounded vaguely sexual, like a country euphemism, but inside, the Tote-A-Poke it was like any other convenience store: pumps in the front and rows of junk food flanked by magazines and overpriced T-shirts for tourists inside. She bought a *Vogue*, a map of Oklahoma, and a *Tulsa World* newspaper.

What road should I take to get to Heartshorne? Emily asked.

The man at the cash register looked upward, past the bill of his cap. He might have been Emily's age or much older. He looked as though he'd spent much of his time outside, his cheeks and nose reddened and slightly chapped. He wore a t-shirt with the name of a football team on the front and jeans. He took so long to answer that she wondered if he had heard her or if she'd have to speak again, more slowly.

Hmm, he said. Heartshorne. Near what?

I don't know, Emily said. Just Heartshorne. Had her mother ever mentioned the big town, the place they went to get groceries? What was it called?

We went to Keno once a month to stock up on frozen French fries, ham, big tubes of bologna, and enough toilet paper to keep us from having to buy it for a dollar-fifty a roll at Jimmy's.

Keno, she said. It's somewhere near Keno.

He nodded. Let me see the map. I went to church camp at Keno. Beautiful place. He looked up at her and nodded. Beautiful country.

She smiled. So it would be beautiful. She hadn't known that it was beautiful. Connie had never said so.

Lots of forests, lakes, even mountains, he said. Not much country like that around here. You're in for a treat. Some people call it God's country, he said, but I think everyone calls a place they love God's country, so that probably doesn't mean much. Still, it's a pretty place to visit.

He spread her map out on the counter and highlighted one long stretch of road. She watched his hand move down the map.

Take this road, he said, pointing to the thickest blue line. It went straight through the middle of the state until it veered a sharp right and disappeared into Texas. You just take it all the way until you see Keno. Get off there and ask for the easiest way to Heartshorne. I can't help you from there, he said, shoving his cap back on his head in a gesture that Emily recognized from young men in movies, though he wasn't a young man. But I bet the signs will help.

She took the map to the car and highlighted that road all the way down to Keno, a small dot on the map, but not the smallest dot, meaning it was a big town or a small city. Heartshorne didn't show on the map at all, like Chester, Harrisburg, or any of the other places her mother had mentioned when talking about her childhood. Whole clusters of little towns filled those empty expanses between dots, towns that had their own Elementary and High Schools and rival basketball teams, their own churches and houses in rows, all conducting the business of life. She was, momentarily, shocked by the map, the great white gaps of it, and how many people lived in those gaps.

The Chester kids all came to Heartshorne when they failed.
Connie had said. Harrisburg always beat Heartshorne in
Basketball, but we beat them in Quiz Bowl.

Her mother had spoken about her childhood and early adolescence more than any other time in her life, mostly of things that had seemed insignificant to Emily at the time. Connie retold the same stories over and over as though they meant something more than she was saying, something that Emily could have figured out if she'd only listened hard enough. She liked to tell about the time that Reggie brought firecrackers to school and set them off in the bus barn, which resulted in an enormous fire. *The fire truck had to come all the way from Keno,* Connie had said, smoking furiously, her eyes wide. *And the black smoke filled the school, but we couldn't go outside, it was even worse, and so we lay on the floor under our desks and covered our mouths with wet brown paper towels from the bathroom.*

Emily remembered this story more vividly than the others. She'd had nightmares about it as a child, as though it were her own memory of a fire and not her mother's. In the dream, she was trapped under a desk, black smoke stinging her eyes. Her mother was under the teacher's desk opposite Emily's, though its bulk of wood kept anything but her eyes and red fingernails from showing.

•

If you blink you'll miss it, the old man behind the counter at the gas station just outside of Keno had said, and he was right. There, Emily had bought a *Heartshorne Star*. Heartshorne had its own paper, though it served all of the little towns between it and Keno, or "The City," as people called either Tulsa or Oklahoma City, depending on which direction they were going to or coming from.

HARRIS TWINS STILL MISSING

The headline dominated the front page, and under it, there was a photograph of a boy and girl, dark-haired, smiling in bathing suits at the rocky edge of a lake.

The closer she got to Heartshorne, the wilder and emptier the landscape became. The highway narrowed to only two lanes with a wide, pebbly shoulder. Dead animals and pieces of metal and rubber littered it. She passed her first armadillo, its armored back on the ground, the pink pads of its feet turned up to the air.

She passed through Chester (a bait shop, a Pentecostal church, the sign reading A ORTION STOPS A BEATING HEART, and a gas station with picnic tables outside and a microwave to cook frozen burritos and pizza pockets) and soon entered Heartshorne. It almost didn't seem worth it to separate the two towns, but somebody had.

Here, the trees grew closer together, dense and tall. Emily couldn't see through the stands of trees that lined the highway, the blocks of pines that stood out in dark, wet green against the otherwise sun-faded leaves and grass. Sometimes a mailbox leaned into the road at a small opening in the trees. That opening meant that a house was at the end of a path, but Emily couldn't see it. The trees ate the path and only the mailbox stood as the only sign that there was something human beyond.

Mountains rose up before her and as her small car climbed them with difficulty. Some of the only mountains in Oklahoma, the man at the gas station had told her. The only scenic view in the state. Her mother had mentioned the mountains, too.

They surrounded Heartshorne like a wall. It was hard to get in or out past them.

Emily liked the mountains. It reminded her of living in Virginia, in the hollows between mountains, in little towns tucked away from immediate view. She liked how overwhelmingly green it was, how it was almost a shock to the eye. It was a comfort to be rolled up in so much darkness.

Her cell phone stopped working soon after she entered the town.

Heartshorne proper began with Echo Lake, a man-made lake still new enough that the dead trees, their branches blackened, broke through the surface of the water. Emily's mother had hated the lake. *Slimy bottom, dirty, filled with snakes, branches so sharp they could rip a hole in the bottom of your boat.* She'd told stories of teenagers jumping from the reservoir tower on dares and impaling themselves on trees still standing deep underwater and how in the summer, the lake released a yellow fog like condensed poison.

We weren't allowed to swim when it fogged up like that.

An ugly place. Cemeteries and trailer houses and animals all down there at the bottom.

But the sky was blue as Emily drove, almost completely clear, and the lake reflected back that light. A man and a woman wearing battered, brown cowboy hats, sitting in bright red lawn chairs, threw their fishing lines over the bridge's wide shoulder. The signs said to slow to thirty miles per hour, and then twenty. She was the one car on the road at six AM, besides the occasional log truck or semi.

Emily spent an hour and a half meandering down back roads, past whole spools of wire fence, which seemed a flimsy and slim barrier between the road and the cows that stared dully out at her when she passed. She'd been given directions on the phone, but she realized now they were meant for somebody who knew their way around; a right at the fork, a left at the creek. Some of the roads lacked signs, and all had been changed to a numbering system, though the lawyer had given her roads with names. She couldn't get any cell service to call the lawyer back for clarification.

Emily drove slowly, looking for road signs or even mailboxes with names she remembered from her mother's stories— *Gilbraiths, Nix, Coulter, Harrington.* She ended up back on the

main road, stopping at Tony's Swap Shop, which sold rebel flag t-shirts, plastic lighters decorated with American flags, and other Southern kitsch, though Emily didn't think of Oklahoma as the South. The young woman at the counter, who must have been her age or younger—though her dark eye-makeup and bleached hair made her seem older—said that Wells Road was back the way she'd come from, just barely past the lake, between the bait store and the *Cut and Tan*, which had been shut down because the owner didn't actually have a beauty school license.

It says here take a turn at the flower place, Emily said.

The woman sniffed. That place ain't been there for years, she said. They sell flowers over at the little store by the Baptist church now.

Emily nodded.

The road starts out paved then, *boom*, it's dirt, not but a half-mile down it, the woman said, moving shards of ice from her soda cup around in her mouth. That's how you'll know it's the right one—most roads go right to dirt off of the main one.

Thanks, Emily said. I'm new around here.

Huh, the woman said, cracking ice between her teeth. You got family around?

Not anymore, she said. Not that I know of.

Emily imagined there had to be someone around, though. She planned to find them, if there were any left. She'd take a thin Claymore County telephone book and call all of the last names she could remember from her mother's stories and ask them if they knew of any Collins and where they'd gone.

Best forget the whole rotten bunch, her mother had said. *It's not like they can do anything for you that I can't.* Emily had stopped asking about the absent family by the time she was a teenager. She convinced herself that she liked being alone, she liked having no family photographs. It made her mysterious and different, even if nobody noticed but her.

I don't know anyone who moves here without family or an oil or logging job or something, the woman said. She leaned on the counter, her forearms flat, hands folded together.

It's a nice place, she said. Good for kids. They get outside and everything, or at least they used to, before this summer. She shook her head and sighed. No gangs, at least. You have any kids?

Emily shook her head. She thought *I'm too young for kids,* but of course, she wasn't really, not anymore.

ECHO LAKE

31

I've got three, the woman said, each of them a handful. She leaned forward across the counter, her elbows rustling in a pile of Heartshorne Stars. It's even harder now that we can't let them play outside. She pointed to the newspaper headline, the two children missing.

She shook her head. Her dark hair rioted with the platinum. It looked as though her scalp bled ink.

The world is different than it used to be when we were kids, you know? She said. Can't even protect your children.

True, Emily said, that's true. She wondered, though, how true that was. She remembered the faces on the back of milk cartons, stories about cults on Geraldo, and learning about good touches and bad touches in school. Everybody had been afraid then, she remembered. But maybe it was worse now. Maybe parents hovered by the window, hoping that their children would make it home every afternoon after school.

Thank you for your help.

The woman nodded and stood up straight, patting the newspapers back into a neat stack.

Good luck, she said. Holler if you need help.

Emily nodded, but she didn't think she'd want help. She was free. She had the key to her own house in her pocket. She had five boxes and a loose pile of clothes already on hangers balled in the trunk. She could do it on her own.

●

The house was set far back from the road, beyond a wide, deep lawn, left un-mown for several rains and infested with dandelion and dark patches of clover. It was obscured by trees and heavily shaded. She parked her car in the driveway and walked up to the door, watching the cicadas jump away from the dirt path as she stepped. The grass rattled dryly under her shoes and she imagined it would be hard and cutting under her bare feet. Before the door were three concrete steps and a stoop. On it, a stained Welcome mat and one newspaper rotting in its bright orange plastic bag greeted her.

The house was nothing spectacular: one-story, the roof sloping upward slightly and meeting itself at a dull peak. It was covered in a standard white aluminum siding, grimy from rain, and the windows were small and infrequent, but she wasn't disappointed. She had expected so little that an intact house, only cosmetically ugly, was a relief. The lawyer had told her little about the house but that it needed few repairs, was small, and that she could move in as soon as she got there. He seemed eager to be done with it.

She'd learned her low expectations from her mother, who had always had a glimmer of hope at every new place, though she had been disappointed over and over again. Emily had learned that hope was exhausting.

She held the key in her hand. It looked like any other key, a generic copy from a hardware store key machine, the edges serrated. She clutched the key and stood on the first step, occasionally looking behind her out into the driveway when something rustled or a car threatened to come closer from the distance.

What if she were wrong about the house, if the lawyer had been wrong and this very minute was on his way to take the key away and turn her back, to tell her that somebody else, a closer family member more in need of a home, had been found?

But she didn't have anywhere else to go. She saw herself getting down on her knees in the dried weeds to beg the lawyer not to make her leave. She imagined the feel of the grass beneath her knees, how even the crickets would jump away from her.

He'd look down at her without understanding.

You can't be alone, he'd say, looking at her with the contempt that the loved try to hide from the unloved. That's impossible. You are thirty years old. Go to your family. Go to your friends.

The front door opened into a dark, empty room. She almost tripped on piles of letters and pamphlets piled before the front door—a mail slot was placed knee-level in the door. Emily stuck her fingers into the slot, making the hinge squeak.

She gathered the mail and shut the door behind her. The small living room had one large window which revealed a square of the backyard and the woods that surrounded it. The light dappled sparsely through onto her dry backyard, which was grown up and completely empty of anything but a coil of old water hose, disconnected from a spigot and cracked where the plastic had been curled.

She hadn't lived somewhere so secluded since she'd been eight, when they had lived in a trailer in rural Virginia and Connie had tried to make a living as a reiki healer. She'd set up shop in the trailer, in what should have been Emily's room, after a weekend reiki training and retreat which had cost them an entire month's worth of utilities money.

In those days, they'd eaten their dinners of canned beans and wheat bread out on the porch, it being more comfortable outside than in the trailer, which caught and held heat like the inside of a car in summer. Emily remembered tossing and turning at night, the sheets sticking to her body and her sweat waking her with its tickly slide down her face.

The only people they'd seen on the roads then were the mailman and teenagers looking for the backroad way to the lake and sometimes a police officer trailing a swerving pickup. Connie's few clients would arrive and immediately be whisked away to her office. It smelled of incense and little bottles of essential oils that pooled and stained the wooden countertops. Connie had placed soothing things in the room, like Aloe Vera plants, crystals, and photographs of various spiritual teachers. Emily had hated the room. All of the smells made her eyes water.

As a child, living so far away from everything had made her feel isolated. She had hated it. Now, she felt safe tucked away from the road and other houses. She could dissapear if she wanted to.

Emily flipped the light switch in the kitchen and set the mail down on the kitchen counter: Three Wal-Mart circulars, a printed advertisement for a high school Indian Taco dinner, and a pamphlet from Heartshorne Free Will Baptist Church:

Welcome to Heartshorne!
We hope that you will join our church family

in worshipping hte Lord and serving our community.
Sundays: 9:00 to 11:00 AM and 5:00 to 6:30 PM
Wednedsays: 6:00 TO 7:30 PM
Fridays: Community prayer and remembrance, 7:00 to 8:30 PM

This was the only message that was meant for her—*Welcome to Heartshorne!* How had they known so quickly? The typos were charming. She imagined the church secretary, ancient and unfamiliar with computers, hunting and pecking her way through the announcement, probably counting spaces to center the document. She placed the mail neatly in a pile on the kitchen counter.

She walked from room to room, turning on every light, touching each doorknob, examining the walls for marks of the previous inhabitant, great-aunt Fran (a name that made Emily think of spunky older women in cozy mysteries, though she knew nothing about the real woman). The walls, though, were clean and white and she could smell the faint poison of new paint. The two bedrooms were small, and one windowless, but this was still far more room than she was used to having. Being here wouldn't be like living with Eric, who took up all of the space with his instruments and his sheet music and his piles of Buddhist philosophy books, the first chapters filled with earnest highlighting and dog-eared pages, the rest clean and unread.

Downstairs, she'd been left with a refrigerator, range, plastic counters, and a rickety kitchen table with a gouged plastic tabletop. She slid her fingers along the deep grooves.

Probably from knives cutting through apples or tomatoes.

The kitchen's enormous, deep steel basin could hold every pot and dish she'd brought with her, and the water came out strong and hot, though a small stream flew ninety degrees from the faucet, spraying her shirt with water when she turned the water all the way up. Lighting came from an uncovered, low-watt bulb above her, a metal-beaded string hanging down.

The living room was clean, with only faint, whiter spaces on the freshly painted walls where pictures had been removed and a plate-sized stain darkening the maroon carpet just below the window. The lawyer said there had been few things of value in the home, and they had either destroyed or sold some pieces, according to her will. She had donated any money from the sales to the local Baptist church. Fran had left Emily a few basics; a refrigerator, range, couch, and a bed.

She sat cross-legged on the carpet and looked up at the still ceiling fan, its dust collected in strings, the strings moving slightly.

This is my house. I own it. She said it aloud to the house, which absorbed the words without an echo.

Her great-aunt Fran had been dead and buried for four months before the Claymore county courthouse had tracked Emily down. Frannie had left the house to Connie or her survivors. The lawyer had asked Emily if Fran and Connie had been close. Emily had not known how to respond, the idea of Connie being "close" to anyone so foreign to her.

When Emily had heard her mother's name spoken by the man on the telephone, she'd had a strange moment of fear: what if he knew that Connie had died a difficult, lonely death and that Emily had been grateful when she finally stopped breathing completely? Of course, he knew nothing about it—nobody did. Connie had been, as she usually was, completely alone when it had happened. The man on the telephone had merely given his condolences and moved on to business.

Emily got up from the floor and started to move boxes from the car to the living room. She set her teakettle and dishes in the cabinets, folded her clothes in a neat pile in the back bedroom, and put away the little bit of food that she'd had left over from the trip and her infrequent stops at convenience stores.

After two hours, she'd all but finished, and it was still morning.

I should nap, she thought, but she wasn't sleepy, despite getting only five hours of sleep the night before. She felt a humming inside her body, the same kind of excitement she'd felt in those first years with Eric, when she'd see him mount the stage and think *he is mine. That's my boyfriend.*

She examined each room in the house carefully, kneeling to into the gaps underneath and behind the refrigerator and stove for anything Frannie might have left behind—a loose shopping list, a leftover piece of junk mail indicating what charities she gave to, if she gave to any at all—to indicate who she'd been. What kind of woman would choose such a red carpet? Why hadn't she planted flowers? And the white boxes on the walls—what pictures had they held? What did a woman without much family have on her walls? Did she collect art?

Emily was on her knees, trying to peel back the carpet in

the living room to see what kind of floor had been covered up underneath it, when the door rattled with a knock—it was loose in its frame and a slice of light came through the edges.

She had the thought, again, that this must be the wrong house, not hers at all. What if the real owner wanted to come in?

She stood up, smoothing her clothes. It's fine. Just somebody knocking, someone who wants to say hello. The house was hers.

But there was still that nagging feeling that she did not belong.

Emily touched the key in her pocket, that proof of her belonging, and opened the door.

The man at the door wore a neatly ironed blue-checked shirt, the colors of sky and snow. His face was round and abundant without being fat—boyish cheeks below crow's feet that indicated he was older than he looked. He smiled and held out his hand. Emily was distracted by his metal watch, the enormous face which was sparsely populated with slim roman numerals, the kind of watch you could barely read, it was so minimal.

Hello, Ma'am, he said. I'm Levi, Pastor of the Heartshorne Free Will Baptist Church. You might have seen our flyer.

Emily held out her hand to him and hoped that her handshake was firm enough—clergymen made her nervous. She imagined that they were always weighing her for possible sins, gauging how much prayer might be necessary to make her whole.

Emily Collins.

He smiled, dropping her hand. The light glared down on his watchface, making it expand into a star of light.

I heard from Cheryl down at Rod's that you'd made it in, he

said. We heard somebody was taking over the place. I thought I'd come down and welcome you to our little town.

Emily nodded. Thank you.

So what brings you here? Do you have family in the area?

Fran was my great-aunt, Emily said. She left me all of this. She motioned toward the room behind her.

He didn't speak, though his eyes widened slightly.

Did you know Fran at all, Mr...?

Call me Levi, he said. Or Pastor Richardson, if you prefer. I knew her a little bit—she wasn't a frequent visitor to the church, but she was well-known in our community. I'm sorry about your loss, he said. Lovely woman. The first of many tragedies we've experienced here in Heartshorne. He looked up at her from behind his eyelashes, his head bowed slightly.

Emily nodded. She had the urge to say amen, but didn't. She didn't know what he was talking about.

I didn't really know Fran, she said, but thank you.

Whether you knew her or not, her death was a shock to everyone.

Emily searched her mind for what might have been a shock to anyone about an eighty year-old woman's death. He continued to shake his head. She'd have to say something soon—she wasn't sufficiently shocked for his taste, she could tell.

But why shocking? She asked. Very sad, of course, but I wasn't shocked, once I heard her age. I thought she was eighty.

He looked at her, frankly confused this time.

You don't know?

She shook her head. Tell me, she said.

She hated moments like this, when bad news she should have known was still mysterious, still beyond her reach, and she looked like a fool for not knowing.

You weren't told how she died? He shook his head. They should have told you, especially before you came all the way down here with your things.

I've hardly been told anything, she said. I got my key in the mail and I have to meet with, what's his name, George, George Sawyer, to sign the papers tomorrow—Levi's vigorous head-shaking stopped her. She felt a quick, jabbing pain in her stomach. Her happiness couldn't be over so soon, already. Levi was going to ruin everything. The house wouldn't be hers anymore after he said whatever he had to say. Or it would be hers and she wouldn't want it anymore. She'd been greedy in taking what wasn't hers from a person she did not know, and now she'd be punished with the very thing she had wanted.

She waited, clutching the edge of the door.

I'm sorry to the be the one to tell you this, he said. This was supposed to be a friendly visit. He made a sound between his teeth, as people do when touching something hot.

Emily stepped outside and shut the door behind her. She should have invited him in, but she didn't want to hear what he might have to say in her new house. The words might catch in the curtains and wallpaper like cigarette smoke and remain there, hanging in the air.

Tell me, she said. It's better to know.

He looked down at his black shoes. The sun, now high above their heads, shined down directly on them through the scant trees. Emily felt her cheeks and forehead redden. His silver watch gleamed.

Fran was murdered, he said. They found her with her throat cut. He swallowed and leaned against the siding, which buckled slightly under his palm. She'd been dead for days when they found her—she didn't have many visitors, no family around here anymore, not for years, and so the home-health nurse found her on her scheduled visit.

Emily held her hand against her throat. Do they know who did it? Levi shook his head slowly. No. They figure some meth heads. Some kids trying to rob her. They didn't take anything. Probably because she didn't have much to take.

Emily saw a quick, involuntary image of a blade sliding across skin, the skin separating like lips, the blood pouring out.

How did they come in?

The police say the killer came right through the screen door, killed her, and walked away, Levi said. She left her door unlocked, like many people around here do.

Emily noticed her own hand around her throat and lowered it. She leaned back, touching her fingers against the doorframe. The house behind her had changed. She imagined something growing inside it, a pulsing, moving something.

You all right, Ma'am? Levi asked. He squinted at her and ran his hand across his forehead. He was sweating visibly.

Emily nodded. Is it safe? I mean, do the authorities think it's safe to live here?

Well, he said, that I can't say, Ma'am. Nobody feels safe right now, with Frannie's death, the children missing, and the others—

The others?

Other deaths in the area—mostly people who were mixed up in things like drugs and drinking, younger people. He shook his head. But if you're asking what I think, I don't think this house is more dangerous than any other place. It was a random crime, that's what the police said. Nowhere is safe anymore, is it?

Emily nodded again, though she wasn't sure if she agreed. He had not answered her question, but she felt too tired to push him.

Thank you for telling me about Fran, she said. She looked at the man, sweaty and well-meaning, squinting up at her against the sun.

She walked back up onto the steps.

Please, she said, opening the door to her house, please come inside and have some tea.

•

After Levi left, Emily turned on all of the lights and shut the windows, despite the damp heat that invaded the living room and made her discard her clothes as soon as he'd left. She wore only her bra and underwear and walked around the still-empty rooms, sticky and uncomfortable, jumping at shadows on the walls.

She'd agreed to go to a community pot-luck at the church. She cursed herself for not thinking.

It isn't just a Free Will Baptist thing, Levi had assured her. We invited all the churches. We even put an ad in the paper. It's a good way to get to know your neighbors!

She'd wanted to say no, but the idea of being with people appealed to her in that moment. And she felt she owed him something: he had given her news that nobody else would. She was nervous about accepting; she saw, poking from his breast pocket, a red-edged tract, which she was sure he would pull out at some point, or perhaps leave in her bathroom. When she'd lived in Virginia, she remembered that the religious kids used to bring stacks of them to school, convinced after a particularly exciting summer of church camp that they were meant to spread the gospel. The desire never lasted all that long, but when they were in the heat of it, she'd find multiple tracts stuck just inside her locker every afternoon. Even then, she was a well-known unbeliever, her mother's disdain for organized religion having rubbed off on her. It was, Emily quickly realized, an easy way to shock people, at least, even if it made her an outcast.

At one point, he did offer her "some literature," which she turned down, kindly.

I do understand about your beliefs, she said. They just really aren't for me.

He nodded, sighed and dropped the subject.

Eventually, after a few more words about community and friendship, she agreed to go. She promised to bring cookies.

I'm sorry to turn down your materials, she said as he left, waving her hand to the neat, front pocket of his shirt. I have my own beliefs, she said. I understand what you are preaching and all, but I'm just not interested.

He had only nodded, smiling tightly. I understand, he said, and I appreciate your honesty. I can only pray that you'll change your mind.

Her aunt Fran, according to Levi, had kept to herself (meaning she wasn't a member of a church, Emily assumed, not sure what other community activities there were to be part of), but had been *a good woman*, a phrase that Emily didn't know how to define.

There used to be lots of Collins's around here, Levi said. But you probably know more about that than I do.

Emily thought he might want her to tell him more, to explain how an eighty-year old woman happened to be left alone without any family in a remote house, miles down a dirt road. But Emily had nothing to say. Her mother had left Heartshorne before Emily was born and had given Emily only her stories about her childhood and her distaste for the place. Emily had simply shrugged in response. It didn't seem like the right time to launch into personal stories.

Now that she knew how Fran had died, Emily walked through the house again, examining the walls and carpets and cabinets for evidence. What could have possessed somebody to murder such an old woman, a woman who owned little of value? Did Aunt Fran have a hidden heroin stash behind a false wall or a cache of machine guns under the shag carpet?

Nothing had been stolen, according to Levi, and no messages left. Surely it wasn't a suicide—Emily imagined that cutting one's own throat was impossible, though she had heard of some people who wanted to die so badly that they stabbed themselves in the chest or set themselves on fire.

She forced her mind away from the image of her aunt seated in a recliner, running a knife around her own throat, and instead touched the pencil lines that marked the doorframe inside the small, windowless bedroom. A mark to indicate a child's growth? But as far as she knew, Fran had had no children. If she had, then they'd be living here instead of Emily.

The rooms, though plain and bright, seemed cast in a reddish glaze now. This was the scene of a crime, no longer a normal house. Where had they tied the yellow police tape?

Funny how all of the things that had been done in the house—making coffee, sleeping, arguing, presumably sex—were swallowed up by this one event, this event that probably had taken less than a few minutes. The murderer had come in and slit her throat as she slept, that's what Levi had said. Maybe she hadn't even woken up, and instead just drifted from a shallow sleep to a deeper one, her skin faintly wet, her throat itchy, and then gone into whatever unconsciousness or different sort of consciousness happened when you were no longer breathing.

Had she been afraid, though? What if she'd woken up, confused by her own blood, trying to call to somebody before realizing that nobody was close enough to hear and her voice no longer worked? Had she wished she wasn't alone?

Emily walked back downstairs. The small upstairs rooms made her feel claustrophobic with their sloped ceilings and leftover furniture. Downstairs, she put on her shoes to walk across the red carpet. She'd have it pulled up and replaced. Surely you couldn't get blood completely out of a carpet.

She was certain that she should feel more afraid. She lived in the middle of nowhere, and her aunt had been murdered in this house. Plus, the pastor had mentioned other murders in the area. She felt jumpy, electric, but not afraid. Curious, but not afraid.

Emily touched the walls of her new house, and walked to the window, avoiding the stain. The yard was impossibly green in the afternoon light and she sun glinted through the cracks in the green, little commas and triangles of yellow light.

It was beautiful.

She would call the police tomorrow and ask, demand, in fact, to know what they knew. And if she was not in danger, she would stay.

But isn't everyone in danger of something? And Emily wasn't an old woman, asleep in her chair with her front door open. She locked her doors out of city habit. She woke at any strange sound in the night, or even unstrange sounds, like the television's creaks and shifts in the humidity or the click of the ceiling fan. She was careful. Maybe she'd buy a gun.

She opened the front door and made her way to the backyard, where the grass had grown up past her ankles, though it was sparse and infested with thick, hardy weeds that made the ground sharp under her feet. The yard made a neat semicircle around the back end of the house, ending in narrow passages through which Emily could circle back to the front yard and the dirt road. She pushed the dry hose aside with her feet and a small animal—a toad or enormous grasshopper—hopped away and into the woods.

The forest gathered around her, green and heavy. It pulsed with the sound of cicadas. She watched the wall of green rustling with the wind. The grass crunched as she walked toward the forest, the dandelions and thick, thorny plants crackling under her heels.

It was sweltering even under the overhanging trees, which bent down, caging the heat, fanning it lightly onto her head and bare arms.

She didn't know how much of the woods beyond the house were hers—the deed had said, and the lawyer had told her over the telephone—but she couldn't remember the exact amount. More than five acres but less than ten. A number that had surprised but not astonished her.

It seemed like such a responsibility, to own a piece of the woods. Maybe she would put up a fence.

Her land was at the far edge of Echo Lake. If she walked straight through those woods (she didn't know her directions well enough to know straight in what direction, but straight, the man had said, referring to the deed's untranslatable lawyerspeak), she'd make it to the shores of Echo Lake eventually—after five minutes, ten?

She stepped toward the woods, where the trees overran the lawn and the lawn dissolved into a mishmash of leaf and dirt. Something rustled in the grass and she stepped back, afraid of snakes. She had read the North American wildlife guide about Oklahoma and found at least five poisonous native species, the copperhead and cottonmouth being the most common. She'd memorized their various markings, their diamonds and stripes, their enormous, venom-heavy heads, and knew which appeared in the lake and which in the woods. She stepped carefully across the yard, examining each piece of ground before she let her feet touch it, her heart beating hard and her mind telling her fool, you can't stay here. You can't even walk barefoot without being afraid.

•

That night, Emily slept with the nightlight on in the upstairs bedroom. She cracked the window, despite her worry—she'd locked the windows below and deadbolted the door, surely nobody could climb to the second floor window. The sound of cicadas, first muffled by the glass, spilled into the room. The sound swelled and sunk, swelled and sunk, and what was at first soothing soon made her feel choked, the sounds pulsing in the empty room like an alarm. She turned on the fan, its constant, mechanical hum drowning the cicadas out, though she worried it would keep her from hearing if somebody got into the house through the front door or a broken window.

She listened to the fan's steady clicking and whirring and waited for sleep.

Emily closed her eyes and played back everything her mother had ever said about Hearrtshorne. She extracted one positive characteristic, something Connie had said when she was drunk, happy, dancing around the kitchen with the clock radio tuned to a classic country station, the kind of music she only listened to when feeling very good or very bad.

When something happens to one of their own in Heartshorne, they do something about it.

5

PARANORMAL OKLAHOMA:
THE TOP FIVE PARANORMAL HOTSPOTS

A well-kept secret to most, the Sooner State is a great place to raise a family, own an affordable home, or just get away at one of our hundreds of man-made lakes and state parks, but did you know that it is also a hotspot for a real-life paranormal investigation? Read our "What to Take on Your First Ghost Hunting Expedition" checklist and then check out these five paranormal destinations for your next ghost hunting expedition:

1. Crying Woman Creek, Anadarko: Visit out this creepy destination in the outskirst of Anadarko at midnight; legend has it that if you park your car on the bridge and keep it running, your lights will go out spontaneously at the stroke of midnight and you might hear scratches on your car door. This sight lists number one due to the sheer number of reports we've received, so this destination is a must for Okie paranormal researchers.

2. The Girl Scout Camp, Talequah: This town, home of the Cherokee Nation, is also known for one of Oklahoma's greatest unsolved cases: the Girl Scout Murders of 1973, when three Girl Scouts were kidnapped from their tents and found dead the morning after, just feet away from their tent. If you visit the sight of the old Girl Scout Camp, just off of highway 20 near Emerald Lake, you might just hear the voices of those lost girls calling through the woods for help.

3. Spook Light Road, Quawpa: Take Spook Light Road (also known as Roosevelt) right up to the county line at night and get your camera ready to catch the many light orbs that come out in the early morning hours. Stick around after 1 AM for the highest likelihood of catching something paranormal on camera (click here for Spook Light Road shots submitted by our readers).

4. Crying Baby Creek, Pryor: The creek, supposedly the sight of a tragic toddler drowning in the 1960's, has been plagued by paranormal reports ever since. Researchers and townsfolk alike report hearing both a baby crying and the shouting of grieving parents. Check out the parking spot and picnic table by the bridge over the spillway for the best possibility of EVP or photographic evidence.

5. Echo Lake, Heartshorne, Oklahoma: This man-made lake, created in 1945, is one of the more unusual paranormal destinations in Oklahoma. Legend has it, every few years, the lake releases a poisonous green gas of mysterious origin that can cause illness.

Some say that it is due to chemicals leftover from Old Heartshorne, abandoned and flooded to create the lake. Others claim it was a Native American curse. Others say it is ghosts of people murdered in Old Heartshorne, a famously lawless town located just thirty minutes South of Robber's Cave National Park, a well-known hideout for criminals such as Billy the Kidd and Belle Starr.

6

Emily slept late and woke sticky, the blankets wrapped around her chest and legs like bandages. She had dreamed of the house, of the red carpet and Frannie knocking around somewhere in the walls like a mouse, but she could recall nothing else. It was hot in the upstairs room and Emily kicked her blankets off and shut the windows. It seemed cooler to keep the air out, as it was windless and when the wind did blow, it felt like a hair dryer in her face.

Emily drove to Keno, the biggest town in Claymore county and the location of Wal-Mart, the only place Emily could find to buy what she needed for the pot luck.

The Wal-Mart in Keno was in the process of expanding its already enormous spread across a flat, once-grassy field. Bulldozers and crews had already laid concrete across a stretch of weed-tangled green space next to the existing store. When she entered the store through the sliding glass doors, the air conditioning hit her and dried the fine layer of sweat on her face. An elderly man in a blue vest standing by the rows of interlocking parked carts smiled and asked her how her day was. He offered her a cart, which she turned down, and he ushered her forward with his wrinkled hands. When the sleeve of his button-up shirt slid up, she saw the tail end of a dragon tattoo grown pale and greenish with age.

Emily navigated the narrow, overstuffed aisles to find a bag of cookies. People pressed against her with their shopping carts, children cried in the aisles, and women hefted 100-pack toilet paper rolls into their car-sized carts. The sheer excess was difficult to resist. The paper towels seemed so clean and fresh in their packs of eighteen, the six-packs of underwear folded neatly against their cardboard backing, and even pre-packaged food, like those soft oatmeal creme cookies, seemed wholesome and frugal when they came in boxes of fifty.

She managed to leave with only a few groceries and a pack of chocolate chip cookies. They rustled dustily in the bag as she walked to the car and hoped that she wouldn't look like a fool bringing something marked *IMPROVED TASTE!* to a pot luck. Was a faux-pas not to cook your own dish, even if you knew nothing about cooking and had only brought a skillet and a saucepan to heat soup? Would people look at her and her bag of cookies and immediately understand that she didn't belong? She didn't know enough about Heartshorne to even know how exactly to worry.

•

She passed the church and had to backtrack. Levi had told her that if she hit the Quick Trip she'd gone too far, and she had quickly passed the yellow sign. On her way back, she found it: squat, with a purely decorative belfry atop, partially hidden by arching trees.

Inside, a man in starched, tan overalls, the fabric thick and inflexible like tarp, led her through the sanctuary, which was plain, all-wood paneling. He took her behind the pulpit, where a single painting of Jesus hung on the wall, and through a small door which led to a maze of turquoise-painted hallways that reminded her of one of her elementary schools with its dappled white ceilings and rough-surfaced walls above yards and yards of dull carpet.

The church dining room was decorated with pink and purple fake flowers—wild roses and impossibly hued daisies—their fabric and wire stems tangled together in the bellies of dusty glass vases. Emily touched the plastic, clover-sprigged tablecloths and ran her fingernails over the flimsy material and the places where the white cotton poked out. These cheerful, shabby decorations made her think of other people's mothers and grandmothers and dinners at her childhood friends' houses. She had not minded the shabbiness then.

She had wanted to live in those houses as a child and would have, if offered the opportunity through some fairy-tale means, changed herself into one of those girls. She could have slipped into their lives smoothly without as much as telling her mother goodbye. Then, she'd been in a constant state of embarrassment at the smallness of her mother's life and their holidays celebrated alone over dinners that they'd be eating for days and days afterwards.

In the dining hall, long, school-style tables were placed end-to-end in rows, chairs lined on either side. Most people had already claimed their seats by setting down their purses and Bibles.

As a child, she had wanted nothing more than a community, family, friends, big groups of people meeting at long tables to eat together. But she'd gone too long without it, and now, she didn't know quite how to act in such a place. People spoke to each other in the tones of resumed conversation. She stood in the doorway, her arms crossed. She wished then that she had Eric with her. At least he was somebody familiar. She could turn to him and speak and people would think she was normal.

All of the Bibles worried her. It was a church, of course, but Levi had said it was a community event, that everyone was invited. But had that just been something he'd said to make her come and assure her that she wouldn't be spending the night fielding offers of prayer?

As she scanned the room for empty seats, for people who looked sympathetic to strangers or better yet, strangers themselves, she noticed that she might be the only single woman over twenty-five—the people her age were clearly coupled, their chairs pushed close together, their fingers entwined while waiting in the food line. Some had children old enough to toddle or even walk, and some had babies strapped into highchairs who whacked their fat hands or spoons against the plastic tables.

Groups of teenagers clung together, some wearing t-shirts featuring pictures of a pale, blue-eyed Jesus, either alive with a glowing heart or nailed to the cross, gaunt and bleeding from the forehead. The girls were as flush-faced and nervous as any other teenage girls in the presence of boys. The boys wore clean jeans and t-shirts and had short hair. No earrings or tattoos, or at least none that she could see.

Hello, sweetheart.

Emily jumped and looked down to find the source of the voice. An old woman stood at Emily's elbow. She reached out with crepey hands and touched Emily's shoulder. She smelled delicate and well-preserved, like a dried prom corsage.

Are you new to our church family?

The woman was small and impossibly fragile, her hair gray and thick, braided down her back. Her knitted shawl swallowed her shoulders. Her face, small-boned but fleshy and lined, gave an impression of beatitude.

Oh, no, Emily said, I'm just here for dinner. She closed her eyes as the old woman's hands moved down her arm and enclosed her fingers.

Levi invited me, she said. He said it was a community event, open to everyone, she explained, as though defending her right to be here. She tried not to move away from the woman's hands. It was wrong to be afraid of the elderly, the imperfect. She'd be elderly someday, too, clawing at people for attention despite the skin that hung from her bones, thin and spotted. But Emily was afraid of the woman, afraid the woman would say something incoherent or cough until she bled or trip and break her bones in her presence and that she'd somehow be held responsible.

That's good, the woman said, that's good. She patted Emily's hand. So many young people don't come to church, she said. So many doing dreadful things to their elders. To their children. To each other. The woman shook her head.

Emily!

Emily turned, though the woman kept hold of Emily's hand and didn't turn.

It was Levi. Or Pastor Richardson, as he was called here.

Emily! He said again, his hand extended. He wore another flawlessly pressed shirt and pair of slacks.

I see you've met one of the true angels of our congregation, he said, our sister Colleen. He beamed down at the old woman.

She's our oldest member, and she still comes to Sunday school and helps out with the children's Fall Carnival.

The old woman dropped Emily's hand and nodded. We have a carnival for the children so they don't have to celebrate Halloween, she said. So they don't have to be part of the occult influences. Levi swept out his arm and Emily followed its arc to the very end of the first table, where an enormous, red-leather Bible lay next to the mismatched silverware.

Come sit with me after you've gotten your food, he instructed her.

Emily took off her sweater and marked her place with it. She nodded, grateful for direction.

She wished she hadn't come— people were starting to look at her, to smile wide at her in a way that all but guaranteed that they'd be coming up to her later for a conversation. What if they thought she was Levi's much younger girlfriend? Could Free Will Baptist pastors even have girlfriends? He didn't wear a ring and had mentioned no wife. Oh Christ, what if that's what they think?

Emily stood in line for food, which was laid out across one long table at the front of the room. Her bag of cookies sagged at the end, lumpy and unopened. She spooned lasagna, salad, hard dinner rolls, and a slice of quiche onto her plate. She avoided the dessert and didn't touch the cookies. Maybe nobody would know that she'd brought them if she didn't open them and pretended they weren't there.

Emily sat down by Levi's Bible and sipped at the pale, reddish drink she'd picked up from the drink table. Fruit punch. She hadn't had fruit punch in years. The sweetness hurt her teeth.

Colleen sat down next to Emily. She'd gotten soup in a Styrofoam bowl and a piece of chocolate cake. She blew on the soup and fluttered her hands around the steaming bowl.

Colleen attempted to put the soup spoon against her lips and quickly drew it back.

It's so hot, she said. Why'd they make it so hot?

Emily turned when Levi sat back down. The old woman continued blowing and murmuring.

Thank you for coming, he said. It's good to have a new person here. He looked around the tables. It seems like I've known everyone here since they were a baby or since I was a baby.

Emily wondered what that felt like, to know a group of people all of one's life, to see them get older, smarter, richer, or fall more and more into some kind of decline.

That sounds beautiful, she said. To have a community of people you've known all your life like that.

It is, he said. I'm very blessed.

Nobody had started to eat yet, so Emily didn't eat either. As everyone seated, the room grew quiet. When the last seat was pulled back and the last plate settled down on the plastic tablecloth, Levi put his hands together.

Let's thank the Lord for this meal, Levi said, his voice elevated. The hands around her made steeples and each person closed their eyes. Emily pressed her hands together and closed her eyes, too.

Dear Lord, he said, his voice filling the room. We thank you so much for this wonderful bounty. And we thank you for community. You've brought hard times on us, Lord.

Some people murmured amen.

But we thank you for the hard times and pray you'll help to see us through them, Lord, and we know you will. We thank you for struggle and the strength that comes from struggle, and we pray you'll bless those families who have lost loved ones. We pray especially for the missing little ones, that you'll guide them back home to us safe and sound. Amen.

She remembered the children in the newspaper, the brother and sister in bathing suits, their hair slicked back from their heads. The Harris twins.

The crowd said amen in return. Emily opened her eyes.

Colleen touched Emily on the shoulder. So where do you live, sweetie? Over near Keno?

Emily tried to spear a piece of slippery, butter-soaked brocoli on her fork. Oh no, she said. I live here in town, in Heartshorne. I live in Fran Collins' old house.

The old woman looked at her with watery eyes.

Fran? Over at Frannie's house? The woman's eyes grew wide. But Frannie's gone, she said.

Emily hoped she hadn't frightened the woman. Maybe she was senile.

I'm her great-niece. I guess that's what it's called. She was my great-aunt.

The woman stared at her. You're a Collins, she said, almost accusingly. A Collins from around here.

Emily nodded. My family's from here, yes. But I'd never been here before yesterday. Levi seemed to sense some confusion and leaned over Emily's plate. His hair smelled clean, like citrus.

Colleen, this young lady just moved into Frannie's old house, isn't that nice? He spoke loudly and slowly. Emily was embarrassed for the woman. What was it like to not be able to hear, to not be able to think straight, to have your body no longer move and work at your own command?

Colleen nodded. I knew Frannie. Good woman. Don't let nobody tell you different. She nodded at Emily, her face hardened as though she expected an argument. She wasn't like the rest of them, Colleen said. She didn't leave.

Emily began to reply, but Colleen returned to her soup, which she spooned up to her mouth methodically.

Did you know Fran well? Emily asked.

Colleen shook her head. I didn't know her that well anymore. She kept to herself.

Emily nodded. The woman looked down at her soup and

finished it quickly, lifting her bowl to her lips to drink the leftover broth. Levi touched Emily's shoulder, turning her away from the woman, and made small talk, asking how the house was, offering to send men from the church over for repairs. Emily said it was fine, absolutely fine, and that she needed no help. Truthfully, she had already hired men from Keno to come tear out the living room carpet and restore the original floor. They exchanged pleasantries until Emily felt Colleen tug at her sleeve.

I'm afraid I'm tired, she said. It was nice to meet you, but I must get home. I've worn myself out. She leaned forward, past Emily's eyesight, to catch Levi's eye.

Pastor Richardson, I'm worn out, she said. Can one of these young men take me home?

The woman turned to Emily, her eyes cast downward. I'm sorry to have to leave so soon, she said. Don't mind me tonight, she said. I'm just tired.

When Emily was finished eating, after she'd shaken hands with and introduced herself to dozens of people, each of whom pressed her hand and thanked her for coming as though she were an honored guest, she found Levi and told him she was going to go.

I have to unpack, she said.

This was a lie. She didn't have to do much of anything, which was a strange feeling. She had a bottle of cheap wine on the counter at home. She wanted to get into bed with it and a book and drink and read until she fell asleep.

Can you stay just a little longer? He asked her. He looked out toward the front of the room, where the tables full of food had already been pushed aside by the men. An old-fashioned classroom projector now reflected a blank screen against the white wall.

We're going to have a community meeting, he said, about the recent tragedies.

You mean those children missing? And Fran?

Oh, there've been more. He closed his eyes and shook his head. Four deaths so far.

Jesus, Emily said. Oh, I'm sorry, she said immediately, covering her mouth. Levi smiled. Have a seat, he said, please. As a favor to me. It won't take long.

Emily nodded. She made her way to the back of the room, brushing against knees and skirts, the corduroy fabric of her pants making a zipping sound against the other fabrics.

Piety made her nervous. Being in a church remineded her of when she had accidentally stumbled into a chemistry class her freshman year of college. She'd sat down, even started to take notes, before she realized that she didn't understand anything that the professor was saying. It had seemed so normal at first — students scribbling in notebooks, an enormous textbook with onionskin-thin pages on every desk, a teacher at the front writing things on the board. But the words coming out of people's mouths hadn't made any sense to her.

The overhead projector buzzed like a bug-zapper. Emily remembered that sound from High School — it meant a video about drugs or sex or the composition of a cell. The reflection it threw on the white wall was blurry at first, but one of the teenage girls fixed it by turning a knob slightly until it sharpened and revealed words, lines, a chart.

I had to do this for the fourth graders when I helped out in Miss Channing's class, the girl at the projector said. She had braces and frizzy hair barely tamed under a french braid and a shiny slathering of gel. She wore a t-shirt featuring Jesus' bloodied face, the thorns pressed into his forehead.

Emily felt for her—the girl probably loved church because each person had to listen to and love everyone else. God said so. Not like at school, where a girl like her, not savvy in the ways of making oneself worth notice, was probably ignored by everyone. Emily had been like that. Unspectacular, untalented with makeup and clothes. Smart, but not so smart she got noticed in good ways or bad ways. The girl watched them all with hunger, waiting for their acknowledgement that she was at the front of the room, doing something useful.

Emily smiled at the girl and squinted at the image projected . It seemed to be a timeline, and her Aunt's name was on it. She was the last, after the names Shannon Dawkins, Christopher Jenkins, and Lillian Cosgrove.

It was a timeline of all the dead. The Harris children were on the chart, too, though a question mark hung next to their names. They were the most recent. Levi stood up. Thank ya'll for coming, he said. The room quieted and stilled. We're here to discuss something that people around here are afraid to talk about—these deaths, why they've happened, and what needs to be done to take back our community for the Lord. That's our focus tonight: seeing what we've done that might have removed God's protection from our little town.

Amens rose, some whispered and some said aloud. People nodded, their heads bobbing in the silvery light the projector threw out.

I think it's our job, he said, hooking his thumbs on the waistband of his pants, to try to figure out what might be lurking in our community. Who else cares? Do the police care?

The audience shook their heads. No, they said, no.

So we have to be the ones who care, he said, nodding. We have to use our heads. We have to look at the world around us and see what we can understand.

Now, we all know evil here, don't we? Even those of you not from this church family know evil—we know what The Book says is evil, and we also know what's so evil that anyone, unbeliever and believer alike, can know it. What's happening here is that simple evil, an evil so great that even a regular sinner can see it.

Amens rose.

But we know, as believers, that great evil can come from the more subtle evils that only we can see.

Amens again, this time louder. Emily was glad then that she was in the back, out of most everyone's line of sight.

Some people might say these deaths, aside from the little ones and our sister Frannie, aren't important. That they were good for nothings, the kind of people who get themselves killed all the time. But remember this: Jesus tells us that what we do for the least of these, we do for him. Some of these folks were what we might call "the least"--they were poor, they had problems with drugs and drink, they didn't have the love of family or the support of a church family.

Nods all around, though the room was quiet.

If we care about them like we should, we would want to figure out what makes people get into these situations. What makes people turn from the Lord? What makes them turn to things outside themselves to fill that hole that only the blood of the lamb can fill?

The amens were deafening. Levi had started to pace as he spoke, and his forehead glistened. He took out a handkerchief and mopped his forehead, then folded it up neatly again and placed it in his pocket.

Now, we know a few things. First, our community has been plagued with drugs. Meth. Oxycontin. Pills of all sorts. I know you folks have experience that yourselves. I've counseled many a family and teen on this very topic, as you well know, church family. The church needs to open up to people in need. We need to find the people who've let Satan into their lives through addiction and help them to break his grip.

Now, some of you have been asking if there's any other reason why our little community is being hit so hard with the judgment of God. I can't say that I know for sure. I do know that a few new elements came to town right before the Harris children went missing and then the murders. Levi held up his hands as a police officer would while directing traffic, indicating that a car should stop. Not that I'm saying there is any connection, he said. I'm not making any accusations here. I'm only noting because I want my church family to be aware when I come across things that make me sit up and take notice. And by church family, I mean the whole family of Christ, wherever you choose to attend.

The crowd murmured in response. Yes, they said. Yes.

God gave us minds to use them, Levi continued. And so I'm here now, using the mind God gave me, and making connections. Levi held a wooden pointer, something a mid-century schoolteacher might use to tap against a chalkboard, and aimed it at a house-shaped drawing below the timeline, right where the line began.

In July, he said, a new store called The Garden moved to the outskirts of Keno, just outside of Heartshorne, by the highway. It was in the town before, but now it's practically on our doorstep.

Some of the audience began to shake their heads, though the drawing seemed simple and sweet, a child's house with big windows above a skinny door.

As some of you might know, this is what you might call a head shop—they sell all sorts of drug paraphernalia, Levi said, pronouncing the word paraphernalia precisely. But that's not all—they sell incense, candles, Tarot cards, books about the occult. Basically, anything that might distract and cloud the minds of our youth, they've got it.

We shouldn't underestimate the power of the occult, he said. The witch of Endor was able to conjure ghosts. God didn't give her that power, but the power existed, and she conjured something real, even if it was a demon, a creature summoned up from the lower places.

Emily shifted in her seat. She owned a pack of Tarot cards,

round cards from the 70s with pictures of goddesses and earth mothers and rotund women dancing naked in rainshowers. The deck soothed her. It made her think of her mother, a thought that didn't usually make her feel anything but anxiety. But Connie had been her most loving with her cards. When she was in a good mood, after a string of clients, a good day at work, or on the first warm day of spring, she'd take out the cards and lay them out for Emily, telling her the future. The future was always good. No disasters waiting for her, no unhappiness. Just pictures of women dancing or gardening or giving birth.

The crowd made sounds of clicking and humming. Apparently, they knew the Witch of Endor. It didn't sound like a real name to Emily. It sounded like a Tolkien villain.

Next, he said, sliding the pointer across the surface of the wall, we got the herbal store, Levi said, the place that sells all those teas. But they don't just sell tea—they sell books about herbal medicine. Nothing wrong with that by itself, but I looked around, and it isn't just medicine. Potions to make you feel better, potions to make your anxiety go away—

Jesus is the only cure for anxiety, an old woman called out, one almost as old as Colleen, wrapped in a fleece blanket. The people around her said Amen.

Amen to that, sister Florence, Levi said, picking up his rhythm again. This place sells potions to make you more beautiful, potions for almost anything. I even saw "herbal abortion" potions in these books—mixes of herbs that would make the child die inside a woman's body.

Now, let me say this again—I'm not saying these establishments have anything to do with the murders. I'm just saying we need to understand what has happened to our town, what has happened to this beautiful place that we all love. We need to see the snake in the garden. God doesn't like it when we stop trusting him, when we rely on potions and the occult to understand our lives. And when we choose those things over him, he withdraws his favor.

He tapped the wall with the pointer. Two new places of business, both built around non-Christian principles, both just months before the murders began. He turned. It's something to think about, he said.

He turned the projector off, and the room was momentarily dark. Emily heard the faint, raspy breathing of the older women, the scuffing of a teenager's shoes.

Turn on the lights, Levi said, and the room was lit with greenish florescents. Emily blinked.

We've been looking for answers, he said. Some of you have come to me asking me to pray, to use my spiritual discernment, to find out what the Lord wants us to know about these murders, what we need to learn.

He closed his eyes and clasped his hands behind his back, as Emily had done as a child while reciting the pledge of allegiance.

Truthfully, I don't know what to tell you, church family. I've had no word from the Lord, no small still voice. All I know is that we need to protect ourselves from anything that might lead us astray. And so, I'd say stay away from these places. Stay away from what might lead you astray. And be careful.

The room again filled with Amens.

Pastor Richardson, do we know if any of the victims had any interest in the occult? A woman asked this, a woman approaching middle-age with a child in her lap. Her hair was white-blonde and cut into a perfect cap of curls.

Well, Levi said, we have no way of knowing. But I suggest you keep an eye out. Watch your children. And the wonderful teens in our youth group, you need to be leaders. You have to be examples to your friends and protect the younger ones.

The group of teenagers, who sat together, all nodded.

Report to me if you see any occult behavior, any increase in interest. Let your peers know that they need to put on the armor of God in every aspect of their lives.

The teenagers nodded grimly, armed with purpose.

7

Billy woke in the dark, the television the only light in the room. Everyone who'd slept over after the party lay on the floor, snoring. Claire lay next to him, curled up with her knees against her chest.

His head throbbed. It was going to split. He imagined it cracking, a seam of blood running from forehead, down his nose, down his lips. He shook his head to get the image out and the pain grew with the movement.

Fuck, he said into the dark, and tried to stand up. He had to piss. It was almost worse than the pain.

Fuck, he said again, and made his way to the door, which was opened. Only the screen door kept out the bugs that whipped against the mesh, trying to get to blue television light.

On TV, a black and white movie about war played, the sound turned all the way down. Two men huddled in the mud behind a barrier, their faces too clean, their hands wrapped around their guns.

Billy stepped outside and went around the back of the trailer where nobody else would stumble out and find him. It wasn't his place. It was John's trailer, a rental place his folks had left for him when they'd retired and left town for Florida. John lived in Keno but kept this place for parties—you could do whatever you wanted out here in Heartshorne. No cops. Even if they came, you could get out of things easy. All John would have to do was flash his smile and say his father's name, and they'd be golden. Unless they killed somebody or something like that, they were untouchable.

Billy lived in Keno now, but he had come out here as a kid for camping. Now that he was an adult, he only came out for John's parties. These woods gave him the creeps, though he, too, nodded when people said *such pretty country, nowhere like it in Oklahoma.* That, at least, was true.

He zipped up his pants and leaned against the wall.

Just through the woods, down a trail, was Echo Lake. Billy wasn't a big fan of lakes, particularly not lakes the way they were out here—no lifeguards, no buoys to tell you where the water got too deep. He was not a fool, not like the others. Sometimes, after a few beers and some weed, they all went out into the lake to swim, but Billy stayed onshore. He'd seen water snakes one night at dusk, their pale heads held above the surface of the water, and now he couldn't step into the water without thinking of them slinking just below the surface. Plus, he still remembered when he'd cut his lip open as a child on an underwater branch here at Echo Lake—it had snagged him like a hook in a fish's mouth. His mouth and nose had filled with water as he pulled and pulled and felt his skin tearing before his mother splashed out into the water and extricated him from the branches.

The air was thick, foggy. The day had been unseasonably cool, but the night was humid. His head felt worse after he had pissed. Now, the pain had room to make itself known.

He looked behind him: he heard branches snapping, the sound of something coming toward him. He saw a faint flicker of flashlight.

Hello? He called out.

Maybe one of the girls had stumbled out of the trailer and was confused, he thought. Too drunk or high to remember where she was.

Hello. It was a woman. She shone her light on Billy's face and aimed it downward again when he held his hands up to guard his face.

Come here, she said, motioning towards herself with the flashlight. He couldn't make out her face behind the light. Could you help me? She asked. I don't feel so well.

Me neither, Billy said, and wondered if he were dreaming. Maybe he'd smoked too much—years ago, when he'd taken a big hit of hash laced with something much more potent, he'd felt time slowing, dripping from events like honey from a spoon, and he'd spent the night in the fetal position in some kid's bedroom, starting at the Hannah Montana posters as they gyrated on the wall. But he'd never thought a dream was real before. That was a new one.

Come here, she said. The light shone at his feet and he followed it until he reached the woman. Up close, he could finally see her. She was older than thirty, thin, her hair blonde. She wore a nightgown that reached just below her knees. She took his hand. Come on, she said.

She took him down the trail to Echo Lake. He wasn't afraid and thought it strange that he was not afraid. Surely their heavy steps would scare the snakes away, he thought. She wore no shoes.

When they reached the beach, she shone her light on the water.

Look, she said.

Across the surface of the lake, a yellow fog rose. It billowed from the water as though the water were breathing. It was thick, darker than the air around it.

Shit, he said, watching it pulse and movie its almost physical bulk. That's fucked up.

She nodded. It's making me dizzy. She stood on her tiptoes and breathed in heavy and hard, as though trying to catch a smell high in the air. Then she laughed. The more you breathe it in, the funnier you feel, she said.

Billy nodded. He could feel it entering his nose and mouth. It

LETITIA TRENT

tasted faintly like oil and metal. His stomach hurt and his headache widened. He was all pain from ear to ear. He imagined the smoke invading his lungs, hooking his blood vessels (he wasn't quite sure how oxygen got to the blood—that part of high school had flown right past him), making his whole body feel heavy and fogged. He looked across the water, where power lines were strung along the roads with lights at the top of the posts, dotting the bridge. The trees below it made a jagged mass of black.

Come on back to my house, she said. She was quick and light, happier now than she had been when she first met him. He wondered how she could be so cheerful in such thick, suffocating air. He could almost feel the fog rising from the lake, the mass of it carrying a physical force. He had the quick, paranoid thought that if it wanted, it could knock him off of his feet. He took her hand to steady himself and found his feet following her along the edge of the river and down another path. He followed her light, not sure now where he was—he hadn't gone by foot much farther than the path from John's to the river and then up the road to the gas station that sold Bud Light and Kool-Aid colored bottles of wine coolers.

I should go back, he called, but she didn't turn or acknowledge him. Without her light, he wouldn't be able to find his way back. He followed behind her, though his head pounded with each step, with each swing of his arms through the air.

It's right up here. She turned and the light shone in his face.

She lived in a trailer much like John's—flimsy, but neat, the skirting in a design of white hatching. She sat on the front steps and motioned for him to sit beside her.

His head throbbed. I'm going to die, he thought. I'm going to die right here in front of this woman I don't even know. My skin is going to split and my tongue will tear from my mouth and then my heart will stop.

Please, he said, kneeling on the ground. Can I use your light to get back? I'm sick. I'm sick with something.

The woman stood over him. You're just not used to the fog, she said. Or you're hungover. Why don't you come inside?

He shook his head, on his hands and knees. His right knee leaned against something sharp—a baseball-sized rock with a tip like an arrowhead. He pushed the rock out of the way and let his knees sink down in the mud. He couldn't think through the pain.

She knelt down close to his face. She smelled of sweat and shampoo and of the fog rising from the lake, vaguely salty and poisoned.

Hey, she said so loudly the sound echoed in his head, in the hollows of his face, and the pain crowded in behind it.

Please don't shou—

What? She leaned close to his ear. I can't hear what you're saying. Can you hear—

The sound of the rock against the back of her head was sharp and quick and satisfying. She made small sounds, her mouth against the ground, and when he hit her again, her head collapsed slightly beneath the rock, she made tiny, jerking movements, one arm reaching up to slap the ground and then go limp. Her hair blackened in the light. The white dress was mud streaked, the collar splattered with blood.

He waited on his hands and knees until the headache faded enough for him to stand. He took the flashlight and the rock and went back down the path, back down the edge of the lake, where he stopped to throw the rock out into the water and wash his hands. The rock made a heavy, fleshy sound against the water and he imagined the lake swallowing it up and letting it rest down at the bottom, where the yellow fog came from.

He walked back up the path to John's without any trouble. Inside, the room was just as he'd left it. How long had he been gone? He didn't know how far it had been to the woman's house, how long he'd stayed. Already, his memory was fading. The headache was like a buzzing television, a sound that drowned out his memory of the events or images. He remembered the rock, sharp against his knee, and how the smooth side fit perfectly in his hand.

The television was still on, but now it showed an infomercial for a bottle of pills. A number flashed across the screen and a man with teeth as bright as the concentrated light of a flashlight (how did he get the one in his hands? Billy thought) smiled and his mouth moved. Billy lay back down in his spot, curled his body into a ball, and fell asleep.

Shannon Dawkins was found four days later. She was a loner, a little strange, people said, and had been missing from work for three days before anyone came out to see how she was. She lived in the country, far out even for Heartshorne, and her parents were used to not hearing from her for long stretches of time. She'd had trouble with drugs when she was a teenager, and she hadn't been quite right since then. But she was quiet and kept to herself and worked at the Dollar Tree fifty hours a week from Monday through Saturday.

The sheriff found her in the front yard of her trailer. He had to shoo away the birds, who'd ripped holes in the thin white fabric of her nightdress and had pecked holes into her scalp, leaving her hair scattered across the lawn.

By the time her body was found, John and his friends had cleared out. Billy had seen blood underneath his fingernails when he woke that morning.

Fuck, he said. How much did I drink?

John laughed. You had your share.

I think I must have scratched myself in my sleep, he said. Or maybe that girl, Judy or Claire or whoever, the one I was sleeping next to.

He remembered dreaming of a woman in white who had led him down to the edge of Echo Lake and had tried to drown him in yellow, soupy water.

8

Emily repainted the walls a softer white than the bright bluish white they'd been before and had the carpet torn up, revealing real wood floors that needed only to be polished and finished. When the carpets were gone, Frannie seemed gone, or at least the image of her death had faded. Emily was glad she had never met the woman—it would have been that much more difficult to live in the house if she'd had a face to match with the name.

She had called the police station and inquired about Frannie's death. It was unsolved, but deemed a random act of violence, unrelatd to any of the other recent deaths.

The other ones are probably drug-related, the woman who had covered the case said. And Ms. Collins' death could be related to drugs, too, though not by any fault of her own; sometimes meth heads, looking for money or drugs or simply out of their minds, do things like this. It isn't common, but I'd get your locks re-done, your windows secured, all of that. Otherwise, I'd say you are in no more danger than anyone else.

The news didn't comfort Emily, but at least she knew what to do about it. She had the windows reinforced, the locks changed. Every night, she shut the house up tight except for her second-floor bedroom window.

Despite what had happened there, the house was becoming hers. And she had to make it hers, had to stay, because she had nowhere else to go. She'd considered leaving after the church meeting, had told herself that she'd just go back to Columbus, where at least she had friends from work, or more accurately acquaintances that she had once called friends. Maybe she could get her old job back if the position hadn't been filled already. She imagined herself going back to the office after buying a new black skirt and button-up shirt from the thrift store, explaining that she'd been wrong to leave, that it was an error, that she'd had nothing waiting for her where she'd gone and that she wanted nothing more than to slip back into the life that she'd abandoned.

But it wasn't possible. She had only a small amount of money saved to tide her over until she found a job. Having no rent helped, but she was still running out of money—food, gas, home repairs, and electric bills were slowly picking away at her savings. She had enough for four months, tops. She couldn't make the two-day trip back to Columbus with no place to go, no job secured. Renting an apartment and paying the first month plus deposit would take out the equivalent of four months food budget here in Heartshorne. She was here for good, despite her fear after learning of how Frannie had died, despite the fact that (she had to face this, it was true) she didn't feel much in common with the people she had met here so far, at least not the ones at the church meeting.

She felt unkind to even think it, but there was a gap between her and the people she'd met so far. She'd been to college, she had lived in a city, she had lived with a man for almost ten years, yet had no children with him—these were all relatively rare things in Heartshorne. She had realized that at the church service, where questions about her job, her children, her family, had all fallen flat. So Emily was a rare and strange creature, somebody that they didn't know how to categorize, exactly. And she, too, didn't know where she fit.

For now, being alone was a welcome change: she could walk around in her underwear and lie on the floor to read in the middle of the day, nowhere to go and no-one to please, but she could already feel that the freedom would soon weigh on her. Too much of nothing to do had never suited her well, and she knew she'd grow tired of it and look for something—a job, a friend, a lover—to create those limits and edges that would push her into some shape. She'd looked in the Heartshorne Gazette for jobs, hoping for something administrative. She could file and type and answer phones, at least until something better came along. But there was nothing administrative, which made sense—there were few offices in the area until you reached Keno, and the people who already had desk jobs probably held on tightly to them. She circled jobs that she never would have imagined herself taking: car hop at Sonic, waitress at the Keno Kitchen diner, stocker at Wal-Mart.

Though objectively she understood that she'd have to take some kind of job—and soon—it didn't feel urgent. She had lost the drive that she'd had her whole life, the feeling that she had to be doing something, anything, no matter how little she liked it or how little she understood its purpose. Now, she found herself satisfied to do nothing, and it frightened her. She woke up in the mornings and ate her breakfast at the kitchen table, the windows opened out into the damp backyard, trees and underbrush rustling with the movement of animals she couldn't see. She'd waste hours just listening to how the house filled with sound as soon as she opened a door or window into the outdoors: the cricket-filled silence after dark and the daylight sounds of faraway car noises and the damp stickiness of her legs against the vinyl of her kitchen chairs or her feet slapping against the newly revealed living room floor. In Columbus, she'd been afraid of being still, of not moving forward, not moving forward was a kind of death. But how had she been moving forward while supporting Eric, moving up slowly in the ranks of a job she could hardly remember just a month after leaving it? She sometimes tried to think back to the steps she'd had to take every morning for four years at her previous job, which had involved typing new information about clients into computer accounts. She'd done this thousands of times, but she now she could only remember clearly two things: the blue border around the program she had used to input statistics and numbers and the curious ping sound that the program made when she typed something in incorrectly. This was how her days had been filled, and she couldn't even remember how it felt or exactly what she did. Emily was alone, but not lonely.

Living as she did in Heartshorne felt like camping. She drove to town every other week for toilet paper and weekly groceries and drove back and loaded up her refrigerator so she wouldn't have to go to the convenience store and subsist off of hot pockets and chicken strips. She was alone with herself and sometimes so bored that she read books she hadn't cracked since college: the essays of Montaigne, *The Confessions of Nat Turner*, and *The Catcher in the Rye*, which made her miss being young enough to be charmed and not annoyed by Holden Caulfield. The days were long and warm. And her house, not yet cluttered with the things that she would inevitably buy to fill it, was all empty spaces and bare corners. She hoped she'd never fill the space. She practiced being there in all of that empty, in lying down on the living room carpet and staring at the white ceiling until she could memorize the stipples of paint and cracks. So much had passed her by in her previous life. She wouldn't forget so much now, she decided. She wouldn't be the kind of person who couldn't remember what she had done everyday for years or exactly how the places she spent her time had looked.

She hadn't met many people in Heartshorne yet, aside from the church meeting. She wasn't quite sure where people lived. The main roads and highways were all but deserted, dotted only with infrequent houses and convenience stores and churches, but each afternoon a schoolbus full of children passed her. She'd driven her car down the dirt road that went past her house until it branched off in two smaller dirt roads, each labeled with a direction and a number: SW 56, NW 305. She supposed all of the houses were there, but where did they go? Did the roads even out and widen and become pavement again? There were mazes of roads and houses beyond hers, she imagined, but she feared getting tangled up, her car stuck in a muddy ditch miles and miles from a house or phone. Her cell phone didn't work out here—didn't work until Keno, where she didn't much need it anyway, there being nobody to call. She had called Eric once, when she arrived, to let him know where she was. He had said little when she called and she heard the faint sound of music in the background. He asked her how she was, but she could hear the boredom in his voice, so she'd told him that she had a job interview to go to and hung up. But she knew Cheryl at Rod's Swap Shop, and often visited, making excuses about having to stock up on supplies, though there truthfully wasn't much there she had any use for. She could only use so many beer cozies and wind chimes and American flag flip-top lighters.

How do you do it? Emily had asked Cheryl one day when visiting to buy an umbrella and plastic cups. How do you manage to stand here for eight hours a day? You don't even have a chair!

Cheryl shrugged. I'm just standing here, she said. It's not rocket science. I mostly have to keep myself from falling asleep. That's the hardest part. Cheryl chewed gum when she spoke, a habit that reminded Emily of being a teenager. Chewing gum and sitting in your room, the smell of nail polish and magazine perfume samples, watching television for clues about how to be an adult and worrying deeply about how well a particular boy liked you, a boy who you would probably never see again after high school. They'd all be gone, all of your friends, probably, scattered. Those were the beautiful years before you understood how temporary other people can be.

Do you know anything about the Free Will Baptist Church? Emily asked. She hadn't gone back since the meeting, but felt she should do something to return Levi's kindness.

Cheryl nodded. Everybody knows them—nice, but hoity-toity, you know? Think Heartshorne's their town. They look down on people who show up to church not dressed to nines. My Momma used to go to the nondenominational church up in the Painted Hills. Cheryl pointed vaguely towards Arkansas, where a jagged but short range of mountains interrupted the highway. They didn't look down on nobody for how they dressed.

Emily nodded. I went there the other night, to the Free Will Baptist church, I mean. They had a dinner.

Cheryl removed her gum and put it back in the foil wrapper.

That's how they get you to come—all friendly at first. Then they come to your house and want you to commit yourself to Jesus and come to their church. She shook her head. Once they came to my door. I told them I worship Jesus in my own way. She looked up at Emily, suddenly, her eyes wary. It was such a swift, clear change that Emily was afraid that she'd somehow offended. Are you big into church? Cheryl asked.

I've never been to a church service, Emily said, not before this one I went to, and it wasn't even a service, really. My parents didn't have a religion. I guess I'm an agnostic. Don't really believe in any of it.

Connie had believed in astrology and in the presence of evil, free-floating and capable of showing up in anyone, anywhere, and that was about all. She checked the paper every morning for her own horoscope and Emily's and read them aloud, scoffing the entire time.

This isn't real astrology, she'd say. *You have to know the time of birth, the moon sign, the houses, all of that.*

Cheryl sniffed. Well, I believe in God and Jesus and all, she said. I just don't think I gotta be in church all day, you know?

Emily liked Cheryl because she need only be asked a question and she'd be off, rarely pausing to ask Emily her thoughts on the subject. Emily liked this. She didn't want to talk about her thoughts right now.

Cheryl talked about her children, all three in consecutive grades at Heartshorne Elementary School. She talked about the man she was dating who had just gotten a ticket for driving with an open beer can in his truck, even though he wasn't even drinking the beer. She talked and Emily listened, happy to hear the sound of anyone's voice but her own echoing in her head.

Sometimes, Emily drove to Keno for amusement. Keno had a decent library, a cafe, and a few restaurants. Heartshorne had a library, too, a tiny place where teenagers came to check their e-mail on the two old computers and flip through fashion magazines. Emily kept her reading to classics and mass-market novels—Stephen King, Daniel Steele, and some pocket classics like *Tess of the d'Urbervilles* or a smattering of Dickens novels in crumbling hardback. She'd taken home *Tess*, *Carrie*, and *It*. They'd all given her nightmares. And there was The Garden, the occult shop. The week after the church meeting, she visited for the first time. She didn't expect to find anything but incense and water pipes and books about chakras and yoga mats. The Garden was just outside of Keno, before the *Welcome to Keno* sign proclaimed its name and the famous citizens who had hailed from there—a country singer who had won the second season of American Idol and a professional football player. The store had only a small hanging sign outside of an otherwise normal one-story house, the house notable only becuase it wasn't a trailer or a crumbling one-story with a yard full of waist-high weeds, car parts, or children's toys bleaching in the sun. The land between Heartshorne and Keno was not just empty, but emptied-out, as though everybody who was able had picked up and left together, leaving behind only what they had broken or objects too large to take along—cars with flat tires and children's playhouses. The land flattened and emptied as Emily drove north, the stretches of space covered in scraggly, dried grass. It was like the surface of the moon for stretches, rocky and with no sign of human life aside from the road she was driving on and the trash that littered the edges of the highway. And then, The Garden's sign appeared, so small she had to squint to make sure it was the right place.

Emily pulled in to the driveway, which was newly laid with bright, white and gray pebbles. The door made a vague, hollow bump. Wooden wind chimes.

Hello. The first thing that Emily thought when she looked up was that this was the first man she'd met in Oklahoma that she could be persuaded to sleep with. His hair was close-shaven to his head, the chosen haircut of balding men. She envied his eyelashes, the thick and black kind that women try to achieve with mascara. Can I help you with anything? He asked.

No, she said. Just looking. Thank you. She looked away from the register, where the man resumed leaning on the counter, a laptop opened before him. She focused on the bookshelves, which were stocked with the usual—books by the Dalai Lama, Starhawke, and Eckhart Tolle. The incense ran the usual gamut of scents, from sandalwood to midnight, a smell that reminded her of soap in a public bathroom.

Is this your first visit?

Yes, she said, examining the poorly-made hemp bracelets.

How did you hear about us?

She laughed. Actually, I heard about you from church. I was warned this was an occult establishment.

He nodded. Yeah, we get that a lot. He stood up straighter and crossed his arms. You here to tell me about how I'm luring people to hell via incense and tarot readings?

No, she said, no. I'm not really concerned about hell. You do tarot readings here? She asked. She'd never gotten a reading from anyone but her mother before, and she suspected her mother

We're offering reduced-price readings, if you're interested, he said.

I'm not sure if I'm interested in knowing the future.

He shook his head. I'm not interested in the future either, he said. It doesn't exist anyway.

She didn't know what he meant—wasn't that exactly what a Tarot reading was for? Now she was curious.

How much?

20 for fifteen minutes. 30 for an half-hour.

How about a half hour? Emily said.

The man behind the counter smiled and rose. Excellent, he said.

Claire! He called, and from a door adjacent to the cash register, a woman emerged. She was young, younger than the man or Emily. Her dark hair flew free when she shook it free from a clip and gathered it back up on her head again. Emily felt her stomach tighten. She wished she could back out, now, seeing this girl who seemed so sure of herself. You could tell just by the way she twisted her hair expertly on top of her head that she did not spend her days alone in an enormous, empty house. Emily didn't want this girl knowing anything about her present or her future.

Can you take the register? He asked. I've got a client.

Okay, the girl said, glancing quickly at Emily and then away, seeing nothing worth noting, Emily thought. Emily had wanted hair like that as a teenager—black and wild and everywhere. Instead, her hair was smooth and straight and unassuming. She was tall, and the long, straight hair lent to that, so she scrunched her body in strange angles to accommodate rooms or people, arms pretzeled or hips slanted to make her smaller.

Come back here with me, the man said, and opened the door.

The back room was small and dim, the shelves filled with books, boxes of incense and candles. In the middle of the room, a small wooden table was covered with a piece of white silk, strangely clean and bright in such a place. A cedar box sat in the middle of the table.

Sit down, the man said.

I didn't know you were the reader at first, Emily said. The man wrestled a folding chair from behind a stack of boxes. I mean, I've never heard of a male tarot reader before. He didn't answer. She'd offended him, she thought, or maybe he thought the comment too stupid to bother answering. The room was windowless and the bright boxes of incense seeped a dusty smell through the air. He wrested the chair from the behind the boxes and unfolded it across from her. She kept her hands folded in her lap.

Sorry about all that, he said, opening the wooden box. A clean scent of cedar drifted out. Inside, it was only cards wrapped in a silk hankerchief.

I have to admit that I don't get very many readings, he said.

It isn't the usual thing around here. So I hadn't set up ahead of time. He held the cards between his hands as if to warm them and looked at her, his gaze disarmingly steady. She looked down at the cards, avoiding his eyes. You're right, he said, there aren't that many male readers—at least not my age. He smiled. He was normal. As normal as a man who read tarot cards in a windowless closet could be.

She was surprised by her own relief: she'd let the church meeting spook her.

What's your name? he asked, setting down the cards in a neat pile before him.

Emily. What's yours?

Jonathan. He bowed his head slightly. Nice to meet you.

Nice to meet you, too. She looked down at the cards. He began to shuffle again, and as he shuffled she looked at the shadows of his face and how his hands separated and joined the cards over and over and remembered that she was alone and that she didn't even have a cat back at her small house. He stopped shuffling and made eye contact, which she slid her gaze away from.

I recommend not asking about the future, he said. Like I told you, it doesn't exist. He placed one hand to the side of his mouth as though to shield his speech when he said the last part, as if somebody were there to hear him give away a trade secret. Emily nodded.

Can I ask you something personal, just before we begin? She asked. Her throat seemed chalk-filled as she spoke and she felt her color rise, which surprised her. She was growing unused to speaking casually with people. She'd been in the woods too long. She remembered this feeling of sudden embarrassment at existing from her elementary school years, her blood and sweat rising up to show whoever she was speaking to that she was only an animal, all blood and water like everyone else, nothing to be afraid of.

Sure, he said. Shoot.

You live around here? She asked.

He nodded.

How long?

I grew up in Keno, but I lived in the city for a while.

Emily laughed. Which city? In Heartshorne, Keno's the city.

Oklahoma City, he said. I lived in one of the ugliest, most dilapidated apartment buildings you can imagine. I think the paint was laced with lead and there were three outlets in the entire place. We had to unplug the refrigerator to use the toaster. I loved it there, though. I never thought I'd come back.

Why did you? She asked.

He jerked his head toward the closed door. My parents are getting older. They had this shop in Keno, but they couldn't keep up. My sister and I moved the inventory to this new location and they retired. He shrugged. I came back because there wasn't any reason not to, he said. Nothing in the city. I began to wonder why I'd stayed away. After years of living in the city, I left and there was hardly anyone to say goodbye to that mattered.

She watched him resume his shuffling. The cards did not move so smoothly in his hands now. She wondered if she had asked him something too personal, but his face didn't reveal anything.

So, you're a local, she said. You're from here.

He smiled at her. I grew up here, but I'm not a local. But after ten years away, I don't know what I am. Some people remember me. Most people don't. He stopped shuffling and set the cards down. He looked at her and she looked down at the table's smoothed-down grain. Are you from around here? He asked.

I just moved to the area, she said. My family was from here. My mother, grandparents, all of them. He nodded, picking up the cards again. He's probably bored, she thought. Probably wants me to get on with it already. She knew what she wanted to ask about. Her family of course. That was what she didn't understand.

I have a question, she said. A tarot question, I mean.

Go ahead.

What do I need to know about my family history? In order to live here, I mean. What would be helpful?

He closed his eyes and shuffled. She was able to watch him without worry when his eyes were closed. He had a puckered earring hole in each lobe, a patch of graying hair just above his left ear, and a slight cleft to his chin. When he finished, he gently slapped the pack of cards down against the table to straighten them and then set them down.

Take the cards, he said, sliding them across the table to her. Cut the deck. She took a third of the deck from the top and slid it under the other two-thirds.

He laid out five cards and named each as he put it face-up on the table. The cards were bright and roughly drawn, cartoonish almost, like illustrated medieval woodcuts. Past, he said, and laid down the first card: The Tower. People fell from the Tower, which had been broken open by a bolt of lightning. Below the fire and rubble, people prayed, their hands upraised to the angry, red-streaked sky.

Jesus, Emily said aloud. He didn't respond.

Near-past: Eight of Swords. A woman, blindfolded, her arms bound, was surrounded by a circle of swords.

Present: The Hanged Man. Upside down, a man bound at the ankles hung from a jutting tree branch. His eyes were closed, his hair surrounded by a halo of light.

Near-Future: Six of Swords. A couple crossing a black, choppy sea, swords bundled at the back of their tiny boat.

Future: The Fool. A young man—or woman, the sex wasn't clear—was steps away from the edge of a cliff, a flute pressed against his mouth as a dog nipped at the edges of his coat.

She looked at each card, and then the whole scene together, the weeping, the uncertain destinations, the cliffs. She couldn't help but speak aloud: This looks grim, she said.

Let's figure out what we are looking at first, before we decide if it's grim or not, he said. What jumps out at you first? Which card, which image?

The Hanged Man, she said, the Hanged Man as my present. And the Tower. That building crumbling, the people on their knees.

He nodded. He looked down at the cards, silent, a fist balled under his chin. He didn't speak.

Is it bad? She asked. His seriousness made her nervous.

He laughed. None of the cards are bad.

Even this one where people seem to be jumping from a burning building?

Even that one.

She looked at The Tower until she could imagine the scene on the cards moving, the figures falling from the tower, the people below shielding their eyes from the brightness and screaming.

He pointed to The Tower. Your family history has one enormous, life-changing upheaveal in the past, something that defined the lives of your family members and possibly affected your life—does that mean anything to you?

Emily shrugged. I don't know much about my family. My mother left Heartshorne when she was a teenager.

So you don't know why they left? She shook her head. He touched the card. She noticed that his fingernails were long and ragged; he didn't cut them, but chewed them.

What happened was out of their control, he said. Something out of the blue that could not be avoided, like a natural disaster or an event that somebody else initiated. I imagine it was something that made the papers, if you're curious about finding out exactly what it was. The Tower is always something big. He touched the card with the bound woman. In the near past, you or somebody close to you—maybe your parents—have felt trapped by this past event, unwilling to change or move past it. This card is about pain in movement. Moving past this thing will be painful, there's no doubt, but the movement has to happen. She's surrounded by swords, but she can't stay where she is, blindfolded. She needs to use a sword to cut herself free.

He pointed to the Hanged Man. This card means that you—definitely you, not anyone else—are experiencing an intense, probably painful period, but you have to let it happen. Hang there.

Let myself be hanged, Emily joked, but Jonathan said nothing.

And look at this, he said, excited, look at the near future. The Six of Swords. There will be some kind of journey—often, it literally means crossing the water, but it can also be metaphorical. There will be some kind of passage across difficulty. You'll be safe, in the end. He pointed to the Hanged Man. Coupled with this card, I'd say that the martyrdom won't be too bad: it's something you can take, because it will end well. You will come across the difficulty.

It looks to me like the waters are choppy, she said. Like the boat might sink.

Well, you might lose somebody from the boat. But not everyone. You'll remain, at least. You'll make it.

She felt sudden pinpricks under her eyelids at his words. You'll make it. She had not known how much she needed to hear those word and believe them. Don't cry, she told herself, and bit her lip, squinting her eyes in what she hoped might look like intense concentration.

And what about my future, she asked. Though you say it doesn't exist. The Fool. It doesn't sound good.

He picked up the card and handed it to her. What do you think is about to happen to the Fool?

He's just about the fall off the cliff, she said automatically. She had not looked deeply at the card, being too distracted by the brush of his rough thumb against her palm as he passed the card.

She tried to look again at the card closely, as he had instructed. She liked the way that the fool wasn't looking where he was going. He looked instead in the opposite direction, at where the music flew from his instrument, not at something so banal and obvious as his own feet.

He won't fall, she decided. I take it back. He'll notice the dog tugging at him.

Jonathan nodded. I like that, he said. You have a new start when this is over, when you've found out everything you need to know. You will feel foolish and embarrassed at first, it might even mean throwing away what you've started and beginning something new, but you will do it. And you won't fall.

He set the cards down and sat back in his seat. He crossed his arms and nodded at the spread. Any questions?

She looked at the images, her past and present and future, bright and fixed within the gold borders of the cards.

So the Fool isn't bad?

Nope.

It doesn't mean I'll fall over the cliff, or make a fool of myself?

Well, you might make a fool of yourself, he said. But that's a strange thing to be afraid of, isn't it?

She nodded. Surely, at this point, she'd gone over her half hour. As if reading her mind, he pulled his cell phone from his pocket to check the time.

Our time is up, he said, but remember what I said; the future doesn't even exist. The cards are only a guess at one possible future. He swept her cards up, shuffled them back together, and placed them in the box. Then he ushered her from the tiny room. Out of the room, she took a deep, clean breath. The smell of incense was in her nose and on her clothes, making her sneeze when she stepped out into the cleaner air of the store. Her head swam and ached vaguely, as it did on mornings when she woke with a slight hangover from drinking bad wine in bed out of a Styrofoam cup. It was hard to tell exactly how much wine you actually had when drinking it out of a Styrofoam cup. She rubbed her eyes as Jonathan rang up her reading and the little bag of dried sage she had picked impulsively from the incense display.

Driving out some bad spirits? Jonathan nudged the baggie of sage toward her hand.

Maybe so, she said. She looked up at him. Can I come back for a follow-up reading, if I want to know more? Jonathan put his hand in his pocket and pulled out a business card. Give me a call, he said.

She looked at the card. His name and number and a small, crescent moon in the corner. Thank you.

And give me a call anyway, he said, if you want somebody to show you around town. We don't get many new people, at least not brand new ones. Just people like me who leave but can't stay away.

She paused, holding the card in her hand.

Really, he said. I would love to show you around.

Thank you, she said. I'll give you a call.

I'm being completely serious, he said. He leaned forward on

the counter, his elbows on the table. Please call. I get lonely with only my sister and my parents. It's hard to meet people here, as you've probably figured out.

She nodded, both happy to hear the words and distracted. Behind his shoulder, the sun slanted low—it would be dark soon, and she wanted to be home before dark. Sometimes, when she entered the house, she had the feeling that she was entering a place that had just been filled with voices.

9

Emily had learned in the last few weeks that she enjoyed driving. In Columbus, it had been a chore to get from stoplight to stoplight, to dodge men in dirt-streaked jackets holding buckets and squeegies asking her for money for an unnecessary windshield cleaning. She had stopped once and given five dollars, which had made the man (who wore a bloodspotted, filthy bandage around his head) inexplicably angry.

Is that all? He'd shouted into the car, the alcohol on his breath mixed with rot and sweat, the smell of the street. It made her feel guilty to drive down those streets, angry that the cars in front of her wouldn't move faster, angry at the stoplights that kept them all from barrelling through the street, angry at the people who weaved between cars, angry at the stolen grocery carts full of aluminum cans that sometimes stood in the tiny parking spots where homeless men and women rooted in the university trash barrels, angry at being angry at people who could find no other way to keep themselves fed, angry that she had been reduced to fear and self-loathing and loathing for those who got in the way as she drove to places she didn't really want to go anyway.

Here, she could drive for miles without encountering a streetlight or a stop sign. The highways here were beautiful, particularly these sparsely-used highways, long stretches of pavement between towns that truckers used to get to Texas from anywhere East and South. She passed enormous trucks hauling water and logs and Hostess snacks and bread and metal cars full of cattle that pressed their soft noses against the holes and sometimes their black, lashed eyes. She also saw trucks full of chickens, their dirty feathers sticking out from the cages, sending a cloud of dusty scat and feathers and stink behind them. She had the road to herself and she could drive ten miles above the speed limit. The official speed limit was 45, but nobody did 45 on this stretch of straight, empty road. She'd learned this in the first week, when she had been passed in a no-passing zone by car after car, some honking at her as she did the speed limit. There were no sidewalks, no pedestrians, and scarcely any houses—just trailers and one-story houses set far back from the road, the mailboxes heavy-headed above the ditches that marked the place between road and ground. Here, poverty was hidden, not like in the city, where it stretched out on the street or shouted in clothes with a real bodies and voices.

In her early days of trying to find her way home from Keno, she'd found a back road lined with slumped trailers set far away from the road, most flanked by blackened burn-piles of trash, wrecked cars and trucks in various stages of disrepair, and beige laundry hanging on lines that extended from the edge of a trailer to the closest tree. She'd driven slowly past, trying to find her road again, and saw a woman emerge from the front door of one of the trailers with a bucket full of water. She made eye contact with Emily and, without changing her face to acknowledge the presence of a strange car, threw the contents of the bucket out into the yard. The bucket was sudsy, the water black, and it arced up with the force of her throw and beat against one of the cars without tires.

On her way home from The Garden, Emily passed the Swap Shop, where Cheryl was surely inside, trying to keep herself upright until seven when the shop closed and she could go home to cook her children dinner and watch television or play games on Facebook, her favorite new activity, she'd told Emily. Now, whenever Emily checked her e-mail at the Keno library, she found her inbox full of e-mails asking for boards, nails, cows, flowers, gems, and other things that Emily did not understand or know how to give her, she so rarely checked her Facebook and never played games. Emily passed the Free Will Baptist Church, which was lit up. It was Wednesday night, another church night for the faithful. Then came Echo Lake, calm and black, its branches still, people in shadow lined along the piers and bridges, their poles cast into the flat water. She pushed the gas lightly as she grew closer to Wells road.

When she turned the last sharp corner before home, past the last pier that jutted out into the water, Emily saw pieces of rubble strewn along the road—a long, ragged strip of rubber torn from a tire, an unidentifiable piece of pipe covered in rust and dirt, and a pool of shattered glass. She slowed down. The objects gathered shape until she recognized a car lurched over so that its underside showed, belly-up in the late-afternoon sun. In the ditch and brush by the side of the road, water bottles, clothes, and discs of light that must have been cds spread out on the grass. The accident was just yards from the bait shop that boasted live crawlers and minnows. It was closed now, though, since it was past 6:30, the absolute latest that the old man that ran it kept the place open. Once, she'd went into the shop, curious, and found walls of fishing lures, each as elaborately strung and decorated as a designer earring. If you lifted the makeshift lids of grimy, plastic tubs that lined the wall near the check-out counter, you could see the minnows or crawlers inside, writhing in the murky water together. The man had watched her the entire time, suspicious. She didn't visit again. There were no other houses on the road, not until past Wells road. She might be the only person to pass for the next five or ten minutes.

Emily slowed and parked on the shoulder. An arm, white and unhurt, splayed out, the fingers lax. It was a woman's hand. Dark brown hair covered the woman's face. The hair was thick, tarry with blood, which had splattered on the bit of bare shoulder she could see. No, not a woman. A girl. The girl wore a sweet, summer dress, something in light, white fabric with sparse blue flowers. She was free of the car, unpinned, and so must have been flung from an open window or open door before the car had crashed. Emily picked through the grass, avoiding the plastic cups, smashed cd cases, and one women's sandal, the thin strap snapped. The girl lay twisted, her right arm under her body, her left flung out and stretched upward in an angle that must have torn her shoulder's hinge. Emily kneeled next to the woman. The whole scene smelled like something burning, and heat came from the car in waves. She touched the swell of the girl's hip—she didn't dare touch her head, afraid of that tarry blackness of hair. The girl's hip was soft and she didn't move or twinge when Emily pressed it. Her body seemed heavy on the ground. She was dead, she had to be, or something close to it—the puddle of blood beneath her and her hidden face, pavement down, almost assured it. Emily reached out and touched the pale hand, turning it over to reach the wrist. She put her fingers on the blue-veined pulse lines. She felt nothing moving, and the skin was damp and somewhat cool. Emily stood up, her stomach aching. She wanted very badly to run in the opposite direction of this woman, but her mind would not let her. She felt ashamed of the weakness in her knees. To distract herself, she felt her pockets for her phone, but then remembered that she'd left it at home. Since it hardly worked anywhere but in Keno, it had become a useless acecessory, good only for checking the time and setting a morning alarm.

She saw the man when she walked around to the front of the car to survey the damage and get away from the girl. He sat against the vertical bumper, his head hanging down, his hands on his thighs. His legs were stuck out straight before him as though he'd been posed there, a rag doll with stiff knees. Emily thought at first that he, like the girl, had been flung back up against the car he'd been thrown from, somehow, and was dead. But she heard, faintly in the rising sound of crickets in the lakeside trees that clustered beyond the shoulder, that he was mumbling to himself. She knelt down as close to him as she dared—she was afraid of him, too, but didn't understand why. She didn't want to be the kind of person who ran from suffering. She knelt by the man and listened to his whispers. He was breathing normally.

Hello, she said, and he looked up, revealing a wide, deep cut across his forehead. It streaked blood down his face from brow to chin.

I didn't mean it, he said, the blood sticky in his teeth. I didn't mean it. I wanted to scare her.

Do you need help? She asked, setting her hand down on the wet ground to balance. He shook his head and a new, thin line of blood came down from his forehead. He pressed his hands into fists and pushed them against his thighs. He didn't meet her eye. I only meant to scare her. He looked at Emily carefully, his eyes narrowing. Do you know me? he asked. She shook her head. I'm not a bad person, he said. The kids love me. They love me like a father. I'm not a bad person. I tried to stop and help her, I tried, but I flipped the car and I'm afraid I...He stopped and began to rock back and forth, his hands flat on the ground to keep him from falling over. Emily stood.

I'll get an ambulance, she said, backing away from his rocking and the blood that now dripped from his forehead to his khaki pants, making big, sticky splotches of reddish-black on the fabric. Emily was backing away, trying not to see the girl on the ground, when a truck pulled up in front of the wreck, its big wheels grinding into the soft dirt of the ground.

Are you all right? A man stepped from the car. His t-shirt was bright orange and had the name of a sports team on the front in black letters. It's not me, she said, shaking her head and pointing. There's a man here, he's hurt. And a girl. I think she's dead. At her words, the man leaning against the car began to wail in a low, broken voice.

I don't have my cell, she said. Can you call?

They don't work here, the man said. He peered down at the man leaned against the car, walked around the back, shook his head at the girl's body, and came back around again.

I'll go call the police, the hospital, over at my house, she said. The man with the truck knelt down by the man with the cut in his forehead. The man with a cut moaned. They seemed to know each other: the man with the truck spoke low, familiar, like a father to a child. Emily could not make out what he said, but when he rose, he seemed unshaken.

It's fine now, the man said to her. I live just right over here. He gestured out to his left in an indeterminate direction. It'll be quicker if I do it. Why don't you just go on home?

Are you sure?

He stood up. Yes. It's best if you go home. You don't want to get in the way.

This convinced her. She had always been afraid of getting in the way.

After she came home and crawled into her bed with new sheets and blankets, her walls still smelling of paint, she wondered if she had done the wrong thing in leaving. Weren't people who came upon accidents supposed to stay at the scene to tell what they had seen? Wasn't she supposed to call somebody?

She woke in the morning early, having forgotten to undress or brush her teeth before bed. Her mouth felt thick and dirty. Emily had expected a phone call, a knock on the door, something. She had not called the police. Wasn't it illegal not to call? Emily found the thin yellow phone book that had materialized in her mailbox the week before, a faded picture of a stream on the cover. The county sheriff's office phone rang three times before anyone picked up.

I saw the accident yesterday, she told the operator, the one with the young girl and older man, over on Wells Road, around Echo Lake.

The woman on the other end of the line seemed distracted. Emily thought she could hear chewing.

Yes, operator finally said. So you saw the incident happen?

No, I was there after, after everything happened.

We'll take your name and number, the woman said. If we need you, we'll call.

So I shouldn't come down?

Don't bother, the woman said. Just come if you're called. Emily nodded and gave her address and phone number.

I don't get my cell phone calls out here, she said, so it might be hard to get ahold of me that—

It's fine, the woman said. We'll get you if we need you. And then she hung up.

She spent the weekend after the accident cleaning, disinfectng every surface. When she was done, the house smelled as chemical as a hospital and bore no traces of tobacco and cabbage, which she had smelled faintly in the drapes and other porous surfaces of the house before. She had scrubbed the past away, and now all that was left of the past were the measurements in the doorframe, which would not come away without taking the paint with them.

She dreamed about the girl in the accident. In her dreams, the girl turned her head. She wasn't dead, but damaged beyond repair, her face bloodied and misshapen. I'm alive, she said to Emily, her broken arm flapping against the ground, held down by the snapped bone. Don't just walk away.

•

Emily sometimes bought the weekly necessities that she inevitably ran out of—toilet paper, toothpaste, coffee, milk—from Jimmy's store, where one roll of toilet paper cost three dollars and the coffee was dusty on the shelf, an off-brand vacuum-packed for freshness probably years ago. But it was better than driving all the way to Keno, and sometimes she'd drink too much wine to even contemplate the ride. Other people, too, shuffled in to buy things they'd forgotten in qualities and quantities less than what they otherwise would stand for: paper towels stained yellow with age, cans of beans with torn labels and bent sides for full price. She was in Jimmy's when she saw Colleen.

Colleen was reading the Heartshorne Gazette at the counter,

holding the front page close to her face. On it was a photograph of the girl from the accident. Emily had seen it as soon as she came in. She hadn't seen the girl's face that day, but she knew it must be her: the black hair, narrow shoulders. It must have been the girl's senior picture, since she wore her cheerleading outfit and smiled before a fake background of autumn leaves. She stood with her hands on her waist, one knee bent, her sneaker balanced on a basketball. Colleen turned, the paper in her hand, and saw Emily. Emily smiled and nodded.

Hello, she said. How are you doing, Colleen? The woman's eyes didn't change, though her mouth crept slightly up at the edges.

I'm Emily Collins, she said. Related to Fran, you remember? I live in her house now.

The old woman continued to stare, clutching her paper tighter.

We met at the church dinner? Emily said, smiling wider.

Colleen finally nodded, closing her eyes. I know you, she said. I remember you from church. Did you see this? She pointed at the front page of the newspaper. Did you see what happened to this little girl? She held the newspaper so tightly that it wrinkled beneath her hands. She held the page up, inches from Emily's face. The girl's teeth were white and unbroken, her hair one black mass. Emily remembered how difficult it had been to tell her hair from the ground, both were so darkened with blood.

Yes, she said. I heard about it.

Colleen lowered the newspaper. It's a shame what can happen to young girls, she said. She looked up at Emily. Did your mother ever tell you about why she left here, about what happened? Emily shook her head.

She didn't tell me much about living here, Emily said. I was hoping to learn more from anyone who knew her.

Colleen pursed her lips and shook her head, disagreeing with whatever Emily might have said, not listening to the actual words.

Whatever she told you, Colleen said, she didn't tell you everything. Emily opened her mouth to speak, but Colleen interrupted her. She didn't tell the whole thing, Colleen repeated. Girls don't usually tell everything. They keep secrets. Not like boys, all out in the open.

Emily's stomach lurched. She tried to speak quietly and calmly, as she would to a skittish animal.

So you knew my mother? She asked. And why she left? Colleen had to be in her seventies. She would have been a young woman when Connie was a teenager. How old had Connie been when she'd left? Emily couldn't remember exactly. Her mother never told the stories straight. She'd gone to high school in the Midwest, though, Emily remembered that much, those stories of flat planes and farms and trucks parked in cornfields as a backdrop to her exploits smoking pot and failing geometry. So she'd left with her family during or before high school.

I knew her a little bit, Colleen said. Everyone did. All the Collinses were wild. Colleen looked down at the floor and clutched the paper to her chest. Shame they all left, though, she said. It's a shame when anyone has to leave.

But why did they have to leave? Emily asked.

Colleen looked at Emily, her eyes wet and unsteady. We like to keep our people close, she said.

Col! The young woman behind the counter called, standing on tiptoe. Your burger's ready.

Colleen walked away without saying goodbye. Emily stood with her roll of toilet paper and half-gallon of milk in her hand, not sure what to do. She could follow Colleen and demand answers— finally, somebody who had known her family, who might know what had happened—but the old woman had seemed agitated, and now she hurried from the door, not looking back at Emily as she got into the backseat of an already-running car. One of the young men from the church was in the driver's seat.

Emily tried to imagine her mother as wild. She had been paranoid, secretive, but never wild as an adult. She told high school stories about driving cars through cornfields and smoking weed, but she seemed to have been genuinely uninterested in true wildness. Despite her problems, Connie hadn't been an alcoholic—she didn't like to be out of control, to be made stupid, and so she limited her drinking to her rare nights out at bars with a boyfriend or a glass or two from a bottle with a screw cap, which she'd keep in the refrigerator for months. Her only major vice was smoking, which she did alone in the living room while watching television or reading horror novels, which she liked because they helped her to understand human behavior.

Everybody is secretly like the people in these books, she'd tell Emily. She'd point to the lurid cover, a figure in black against the red backdrop of a sunset or a hatchet in relief against the paperback page, the title of the novel in letters formed from splatterings of blood.

Wild. She'd never been wild.

Jonathan had said that Emily's family history in Heartshorne had started with the Tower, with some event like lightning that had sent her family flying from their place of security, an event that had dashed them to the ground and left them below, praying for it all to be over. Emily picked up a copy of the local newspaper and placed it on the counter with her milk and toilet paper.

And I'll take a pack of Marlboro's, too, Emily said, imagining all of the possible towers that her mother might have lived through to make her the woman she had become.

10

The quiet around her house was a quiet she had never heard before. No human sounds cut through the dark, but the night was filled with as much noise as any city street during rush hour. The cicadas made their usual steady hum with a spikier cricket accompaniment. Sometimes birds erupted from the trees, roused by a sound or movement she couldn't hear or see. Small animals rooted in the dry leaves. They crunched away when she clapped or threw a rock into the tangle of bushes. She was spooked by their noise, though she knew she shouldn't be afraid. The only dangerous animals were cougars or mountain lions, and those walked heavily through the woods and screamed like a woman.

She'd listened to a recording of a mountain lion scream on YouTube, a keening, enormous sound that announced itself immediately. She had grown used to the sounds and kept a flashlight and pile of rocks on the porch to throw at the woods or road if she was afraid. She knew that the rocks probably didn't help, but they relieved her fear for a moment, and that was all that she really wanted. She smoked her Marlboros on the porch, one per night, just to be safe from the perils of addiction, and imagined the ways her life might turn out now.

Maybe she could go back to church, make it a habit; it wasn't so bad to have something to organize your life around, even if you couldn't believe in it completely. She'd meet a young man. She'd let him move in—after they married, of course—and they'd have a baby. The baby would cry in the small kitchen as she fed it mush from a tiny spoon. He would be tired and would smell of sweat and come home wanting nothing but quiet and the sounds of beer moving in his mouth. She would cry in the bathroom as he strenuously avoided seeing her tears. She knew this pattern from her mother's life—the tears and the boredom, if not the marriage, which Connie had been smart enough to avoid. Or maybe she'd be like Frannie, alone until she died by herself in her living room, nobody with her in her last moments but the cats licking her blood until somebody found her body. Or she could be like Jonathan and his sister, running an occult shop, living at the edges of completely acceptable society. But there were other options. She could become an artist, an eccentric. She could make art out of deserted cars and trash she found in the ditches between the pavement and the woods.Or she could devote herself to some cause: orphans or pit bulls or recycling.

It occured to her that by now, she should know better the kind of person she really was.

She finished her cigarette and sat in the dark, listening to the bugs and the animals. I won't be afraid, she thought. This is where I live. I belong here. Whatever I choose to do, I belong here.

She threw a rock into the dark. It bounced dustily into the underbrush, scaring away something small and light, a bird, maybe. She went inside, taking her pack of cigarettes and flashlight with her.

She decided to call Jonathan.

Jonathan didn't ask her why, which she appreciated. It was the kind of thing best to explain in real life, preferably over something involving alcohol.

Of course, he said. Of course I'll help.

•

Emily sat in Jonathan's car, stiff by his side. Now that she had actually called and they were together in his car, she wanted to sink into the sticky plastic fabric of the car seat. She had been forward. She had asked him to do something silly and he probably regretted giving her his phone number.

I'm sorry, she said, to ask you to do this. I know you don't know me very well, and this isn't—

It's fine, he said. It sounds fun, even. He wrapped both of his hands around the steering wheel. He was a careful driver, good at navigating the roads. I wouldn't have given you my card if I didn't want you to call, he said. She looked away when he turned to look at her.

Thank you, she said. When you showed me that Tower, during the reading, I wanted to know more, but I figure I need help.

I met a woman when I was at that church thing in Heartshorne, she told him. She knew my family. She hinted that something had happend, something that had made them leave. It made me think of what you said, that whatever it was had probably shown up in the papers.

He nodded. We'll see what we can't find. If it's something as big as the cards say, then we should be able to find it.

So the cards might be wrong? It might not be that big?

He shrugged. Please don't take me too seriously, he said. Really, they're only cards. They've helped me before, but they're just paper.

The library was one of the oldest buildings in town, flanked by the courthouse and an old hotel, all made of the same white stone. Inside, the woman at the periodicals table motioned them toward the back, where the enormous encyclopedias and reference books sat on sharp metal shelves, rust eating away at the corners, a lightswitch on each shelf that turned on a row of ancient flourescents above the books. As they walked past rows of books, dust-covered and untouched for years, the woman at the periodical desk switched on the lights just above them. They kicked on gradually, growing into their full light only after

Jonathan and Emily had passed on to the next row. Each light made a small humming sound: together, they reminded Emily of the sounds throbbing around her house every night.

Back here, the woman said. She pointed to a door, unlabeled, windowless. That's where we keep the microfilm machines, she said. Hardly anyone uses them, so we got them off of the floor to make room for computer stations.

They were at the very back of the library now, far from the bright, new tables in the fiction section or the plastic-covered magazine stand between two aging leather couches, the old skin cracked. Two rows of cubicles lined the back wall, each with a hardback wooden seat. One was occupied by an older man, his hair gray and yellowing at his temples. The table around him was covered in balls and scraps of paper. On the floor around his feet were grocery store bags full of something, though Emily couldn't tell what. His hands were red and peeling. He must have spent most of his time outside in the sun or the cold. He held a pencil in the fist of his left hand and wrote hurridly on a yellow legal pad. When they passed him, he moved the pad closer to his chest and bent his head, hiding his work from them.

Every library has them, women and men writing their manifestos or novels or letters of grievance to people dead or alive, real or imaginary, important (the president, God) or mundane (their fathers, mothers, daughters, men or women they have loved). They hunch over their words, afraid that other people might take them or see them and understand and use that knowledge against them.

Emily and Jonathan followed the woman into the small room. She switched on the lights. The room contained four enormous machines, all clearly from before the digital age, featuring enormous knobs and convex screens that reflected them back distorted, their midsections doubled and their heads small.

The microfilm is over there, the woman said, pointing one red nail at a wooden cabinet shoved against a wall. It used to be a card catalogue, but now it kept the boxes of microfilm and micofiche, each fragile, yellowing envelope of film separated by year and periodical.We have the Harshorne Star from 1935 to 1990, the Keno Gazette, too, the librarian told them. She looked up at the ceiling, wiping her hands on her navy skirt. The room as dusty, and each time she touched the surface of a machine or cabinet, dust stirred and coated her hands. I think we have some tribal papers, too. The Choctaw paper. And some from the City, of course, and Tulsa, but we keep them out there on the main floor.

Jonathan switched on one of the machines. It made a whirring, heavy sound, like an animal kicking inside the plastic box that held the machinery. A light illuminated the screen.

Let's get started, he said. The librarian left them alone and Jonathan turned to her. How can I help? Emily's head hurt from the dust and she felt small and stupid, as foolish and the man out in cubicle writing books that only he would read. The room was so small and shabby, the task so boring.

I'm sorry I brought you here, she said. She saw him in the dim room, his hands in his pockets, and imagined him gritting his teeth, balling his hands into fists hidden in his pockets, hating her politely. This isn't any way to treat somebody who has been so—

He laughed. Jesus, it's ok, he said. You don't have to apologize. I'm the one that gave you The Tower. It's my fault. He pointed at the cabinet. It's interesting anyway, right? Who knows what kind of crazy shit we'll find. The murders and the scandals and the accidents. And we'll go somewhere else next time, he said.

He walked over to her and touched her shoulder. Hey, it's okay, really, he said. Next time, it'll be my turn to choose.

She nodded, unsure what to do with his hand. Ok, then. I'm officially done apologizing, she said. He slid his hand down and touched her elbow. He wore a gray, long-sleeved shirt with holes in the cuffs where he had pushed his thumbs through the fabric. In the small room, she could smell his aftershave, something cold-smelling, like mint.

Really, I'm happy to help, he said. I don't go where I don't want to go. She nodded and gently turned out of his touch.

That's a rare thing, she said. Most people go where they don't want to go all of the time.

He took '50 to '65 and she took '66 to '85 of the Heartshorne Star. In 1965, her mother had been thirteen years old. She had been beautiful in that wholesome, cone-breasted way that girls had been in the fifties and early sixties, before women allowed their hair to fall down relaxed. Emily had seen pictures, the few that her mother had. The oldest picture was Connie at sixteen, taken with a polaroid. The edges had peeled up, the metal and plastic between the white sealant exposed. It was at home, in a pine box, along with the other things that Connie had left as a hint of what her life had been before Emily was born: a tarnished silver heart necklace (so cliché, so sweet in its simplicity, that it could be nothing but a love token), a birthday card that said "To Connie from Paul" with a bouquet of roses on the front and the words "Happy Birthday" in a calligraphic scrawl. The card had to be at least twenty years old. Emily didn't remember a Paul. Her father's name hadn't been Paul. His name was Charles, and he lived in Troy, New York. She had never met him or tried to meet him: he had made a choice thirty years ago and Emily figured she had no right to take the choice away from him and force herself into his life. Now, she would be easy to find if he wanted to find her. She didn't think much about it. After her father, Connie had dated a succession of men with names like Bill or John or Bob, mostly working-class men that Connie had met through friends or work, men that she invariably left because they lacked something: ambition, a sense of self, a spiritual side, something ineffable that she was searching for in other people but could never find.

That had been her mother's problem, Emily thought. She always thought what was missing was in somebody else.

As she fed the microfilm into the machine, Emily felt the old twinge of shame that she always felt when she breached her mother's deep love of privacy. Emily had had a desperate curiosity about her mother's things—what she kept in the battered shoe boxes in her closet, the fancy clothes she kept under plastic in the closet, her jewelry boxes and stacks of letters still in their envelopes--but Connie's anger teetered on the verge of violence whenever she found Emily in her things or even suspected that Emily had rifled through them.

Get out of my things, she'd shout. Stop snooping. Once, she had slapped Emily the face when she found her standing in Connie's closet, a tube of red lipstick just touching Emily's lips. Connie would be upset at what Emily was doing now, combing through the past, bringing along a stranger to help. That would be the worst part. Emily could almost imagine her mother coming through the door along with the smell of spearmint Certs and hairspray, her shoes hard and clicking, coming to shout at her for *snooping*. For *bringing somebody else into her business*. Emily fed the spool microfilm through the machine and the screen shouted a headline: *Echo Lake Flood*. A grainy newsprint of a flooded

street was directly below the headline, and nothing more, the picture sufficient for the explanation. Below it, she read that the Heartshorne High School Bears had defeated the Broken Arrow Warriors and had taken their place at the state championships. A photograph accompanied it, the ink faded down to a uniform gray. A group of young men in shorts gathered around a plaque. One held the ball against his hip. It was March 15th, 1966. They were all old now, some maybe even dead. She tried to see the details of their faces: which boy was handsome, which was plain, which was pockmarked and which had a weak chin or protruding ears. They all looked the same, though—their hair short, their faces white without variation. She flipped through the paper, skimming the small tragedies: housefires and car accidents and inclement weather. That spring, a tornado had gone through the heart of

Keno, throwing trailer houses and sheds and cars aside as it rolled down to the valley and exhausted itself just before Echo Lake.

Hey. Jonathan leaned back in his seat, the old wood creaking. I found a Collins in the paper. Look. She hung over his shoulder, squinting to see the print on the screen. His newspapers were even fainter, the pictures more grainy, rubbed down to shade. It was an article in the *Births* section of the paper, wedged between weddings and obituaries.

Mr. And Mrs. Edward Collins welcomed a baby girl, Constance Beth Collins, on November 21st, 1952.

That's my mother, Emily said. That's her birthday. Emily stood, aware she was breathing close to Jonathan's hair, her chin almost brushing his shoulder.

Edward. That must be my grandfather's name, she said, excited.

You didn't know him?

No. I didn't know anyone but my mother. And I guess I didn't know her very well, either. I didn't know her middle name was Beth. Emily remembered the bracelet around her mother's arm at the hospital, the "B" initial that she'd never thought to ask about, not at that point, when it was too late to ask anyway. Emily took a pad of paper from her pocket. I'm writing down all of the names, she said. Edward Collins, Constance Beth Collins. I wish they had my grandmother's name here, a picture, something.

Emily went back to her slides, scrolling through days and days of records that proved that events had passed, events important enough to be marked down in ink and kept, though the people that had experienced them were old or dead. Emily was happy to see babies as she scrolled through the births sections. At least the babies were still alive, maybe, and proof that what the newspapers said was attached to something real.

11

Christopher walked at night along the dirt roads near his parent's house, down the same roads he'd walked as a kid and would probably walk until he died, just like that old man who lived down by the high school who had died in his house, slumped onto the kitchen counter over a bowl of soup. He faced this matter-of-factly, without anger. He wore a headlamp, the kind hunters used to spot deer, so he wouldn't be surprised by a dog or bear. When cars passed, he jumped down into the ditch by the road. Everybody knew him—they waved from their cars and sometimes sounded the horn. He nodded, but rarely waved back. He kept to himself.

In high school, he had been a fixture, neither loved nor hated, just one of the people who had grown up in Heartshorne, who had always been there and always would be. He remembered his high school years fondly, though imperfectly. He remembered everything being easy: schoolwork, the mostly friendly and familiar people around him, the teachers in their seats at the front who didn't ask much of him but his presence.

He lived in his parent's basement and had since graduation, when he decided that life didn't need to move forward. If he stayed where he was, in the same room, the same house, things could remain as they had before. And they did. Not completely, of course. He had a job. He worked at the lumber yard just outside of Keno. He drove there in his truck every morning, usually before the sun was just a haze at the horizon, and came home well before dinner, exhausted. He took a nap until hunger woke him and he wandered upstairs to see what his mother had made for dinner. He'd come back down afterwards and listen to music or watch television. He liked shows about traveling and food. The best shows were about both traveling and food — about the strange things people ate who lived in other countries. Bugs or organs or animals that people here used as pets. Sometimes he went fishing or drinking with buddies from high school, other young men who had stayed in Heartshorne, men who lived in the low-income housing just outside of Keno or with their parents, creating lives that echoed the smooth hum and movement of a school day. He had a girl who drifted in and out of his life: she didn't seem to expect much, and he liked it that way. She'd gone to visit family in Tulsa and he didn't miss her, but he knew that he'd be glad to see her when she showed up at a party or called him up to meet at a bar. She didn't ask anything of him that he wasn't willing to give. It was just like in high school, only they could drink legally and she'd sleep with him almost any time he wanted. School, he decided, had been the best time of his life. He hadn't realized it then, but now he knew the secret that adults didn't tell: it wouldn't get any better after graduation. Life had never resumed that delight of daily expectation — the bus arriving in the cold at the same time each day, lunch on a regular rotating menu, and that beautiful hour of waiting for the last bell to ring to go home again. It had been so simple.

In school, you were always moving forward to a higher grade, a higher status, until graduation, when everyone recognized that you had achieved something. How could you move forward working in a lumberyard? You could go up to manager, of course, but there was only one of those. Sometimes you got stalled along the way, and at some point, there was nowhere else to go. There was no more up. You mostly just went along doing the same thing until your hands got shaky and you had an accident—crushed fingers or a broken elbow or, this was the worst, something to do with the machines, which would almost certainly mean losing a finger.

It was late July when Christopher decided to walk to Echo Lake, farther than he'd walked in a very long time. He used to ride his bike there, back in elementary school. The road must have been smoother then, because now it was impossible by bike. It was scarred with deep grooves that filled with mud when it rained and most of the gravel had washed away into the ditches. It was barely dark, but already the air had that peculiar damp, heavy scent that it carried on summer nights. He turned on his headlamp. The path before him was laid out brightly, the shadows around it darker in contrast. But he wasn't afraid. He'd lived here for twenty years now, twenty years of nothing much happening except a copperhead in the garage or a cat dying under the house. People died here, of course, but usually from doing stupid things, like jumping from the water tower into the lake or driving drunk in the mountains, hill hopping their way into the bumper of another dumbass who was hill-hopping, too. There were urban legends about the lake being poisonous, ghost stories, and the occasional panic about prisoners escaped from the maximum security prison outside of Keno, but most of that was nonsense. His cousin had been in prison up in Keno for a year and said it was nearly impossible to get out, not worth the trouble.

He passed a trailer, wrecked, probably empty. He shone his headlamp on it briefly, surprised by the corner of turquoise siding that had flashed in his lamp's proximity. The yard around the trailer was overgrown, the driveway covered with low brush. Two windows had been broken and were covered with cardboard from the inside. He wasn't sure how long the trailer has been there; he hadn't been out this way in years.

He kept walking. He'd be close to the lake soon: already, he could feel the damp, the mosquitoes thick in the air. Soon, the road would dead end and a path would lead out to a small beach, the shore rocky, the water first shallow then deepening at a sudden drop. It wasn't a safe place to swim, but he had swum there since childhood, so he knew where the drop was. The light on the water highlighted the darkness around it. It was still, only slightly lapping at the shore. Christopher regretted coming out all this way once he had finally reached the shore. It had seemed like the right place to go, fitting somehow for his mood, but now that he was there, he was bled by bugs and jumpy at the rustling sounds in the leaves. The lake put off a fog, too, a damp air that hung above it. It smelled like salt and reflected back his headlamp, blinding him.

•

The woman in the trailer had not slept for days. When she woke, she lay collapsed in the bathroom, the one room that still had glass instead of cardboard in the window. The man had left her hours ago and taken everything but the broken, blackened lightbulbs and foil and one lighter with him. The light from the bathroom window shone into her face from the road. That's what woke her up. She'd been dreaming that she was playing with her daughter at the old trailer, the place where she had lived when she was happy and had a good job at the feed store, before she met him, before she got thin and forgetful and found herself walking with a trail of blood around the store, hardly noticing that a piece of broken glass had gashed her bloodless palm and was told to go home, go home until she was feeling better. She did not feel better, and no amount of time at home had helped. Alexis lived with her grandma and father now: they'd taken her away one day a few weeks or months ago. When they left, she'd torn at her hair until somebody made her stop and she woke with bloody spots on her pillow. The last time she'd tried to visit the child had cried and Glenn, that bastard, had said *just look at you — have you looked at yourself? You hardly look alive. You aren't fit to raise her.*

When the woman woke the light shone on her face and she was afraid. She wasn't supposed to be here: she was supposed to be home. If they found her here she'd have to go back to jail. Her mouth and throat were dry. She climbed up the sink, supporting herself on the cracked plastic basin, and turned on the faucets. Nothing came out. The light shone again in the window. She wanted to lie back down on the floor and go back to sleep, but she was afraid, and her mouth was dry. She bit her tongue hard to make blood or salt come up in her mouth and moisten it. She had to find water.

•

Christopher tried to skip rocks on the surface of the lake, something his father had taught him as a child. The rocks, though the right size, the right flatness, plopped straight down into the water.

Who? It was a shout, a one-word question. Christopher turned, his headlamp still on. It was a woman. She held up her emaciated arms and hands against her face.

Turn it off! She shouted. She was covered in cuts, most scabbed over. She wore cut-off shorts that ended in hanging threads mid-thigh and a bathing suit top, both filthy. Her hair was in a ponytail, matted and ragged around her head. It was impossible to tell how old she was: between 25 and 40. She was so thin, so dirty.

Sorry, he said, sorry about the light. I forgot I had it on. Christopher took the light from his head and placed it on the ground, where it send out a spreading triangle of light on the lake and into the bushes. A small splash broke the surface of the water. A fish or a frog jumping from the shore into the water, thinking it safer there than here on the beach with these two humans and their shrill light. Christopher turned back to the shore, where the woman now kneeled down at the edge of the water, drinking the lake from her cupped hands.

You think you should drink that? The woman didn't look up.

Thirsty, she said. No water up at the trailer. She continued to drink. Her bony knees ground into the sand, her bare feet, hard and cracked, depressed him. It bothered him that he couldn't tell how old she was. What if she was his age? What' if he'd gone to high school with her and he just couldn't remember?

Do you need help?

The woman had finished drinking and now sat at the edge of the water, her head hanging, her hands flat on the shore. She looked up.

I don't need no help. I'm good now. She breathed heavily.

Are you sure? Christopher asked. I can help you—

Don't tell no-one where I am, she said. No-one needs to know.

Are you going back to that trailer back there? Do you need help back? Christopher was alarmed by her gravelly voice, by the stale smell of her.

Sometimes, people don't know they need help until you extend your hand, that's what the pastor had said last time he made it to church, when his grandmother insisted he come along for a special sermon, given by one of the leaders of the Southern Baptist Convention of Oklahoma, who was out touring for donations for a new SBC worship hall.

Who needs to know? The woman looked up at him, though he couldn't quite see her face. The light shone on her ruined feet, her scarred legs, each bone showing sharp through her skin, translucent and fragile as onionskin.

Nobody, he said. I mean, I don't care, I just don't want you to—

Okay, then, the woman said, standing up. Christopher heard the crack of her ankles and knees. Go about your business, she said. Get on. She waved him away. Get out of here. Get on home. She had to keep her hands down to keep them from shaking. What was he doing out here with all that light, shining it into the house? Was he with the Sheriff's? Was he one of Glenn's friends, here to keep tabs on her, rat her out?

You know Glenn? She asked as he bent over to retrieve his lamp. You know Glenn?

The woman's hands shook by her sides. When he stood up, the light flashed across her stomach, her chest, her face. She was missing a front tooth. Her mouth flaked with dry skin, cracked and bleeding at the sides. Her cheeks were hollow and her eyes, a light blue, seemed huge, like the eyes of a cartoon character.

I don't know any Glenn, he said. I don't think I do, at least.

The woman nodded. I bet you don't, she said, shaking her head. Her body shook: she was shivering in July.

Why don't you come to my house, he said, instead of that trailer?

A moment of kindness, he thought, I can deliver some kindness. He had rarely had the opportunity to do so in the past, not like this. This woman might die. He imagined himself feeding her soup, sitting up with her as she wretched and shivered the crank away. She'd fill out. She might be beautiful when it was all over with. She might be grateful to him.

We can call your family, he said, have them come get you. We can take you somewhere safe.

Fuck, she thought. Fuck you, Glenn. Somewhere safe and clean like the hospital. Somewhere safe and clean like the jail. Clean had never helped her.

You just go on now, she said. Her voice rose shrill and cracked on now. Her bony hands fidgeted violently at her sides. Christopher nodded, holding his hands up.

Ok, he said. Ok. No problem. He turned and adjusted the headlamp so it shone straight forward across the path of broken leaves and mud that led out into the road.

He was going to go, she wanted him to go, but he couldn't. There were few times in Christopher's life when he had had the opportunity to do something courageous. It would be heroic to help this woman who was so hungry and fucked up she was hardly a person anymore. He'd take her to the house, have her call someone, give her food. He turned, forgetting about the light on his head.

Look, he said, why don't you come back—

She leapt upon him from somewhere below the light, as quick as an animal. She had something hard and sharp—a rock, a broken bottle, something that both cut and bludgeoned the thin skin around his throat: he could feel the blood. He had time to wonder what it was, to try to swat her away, but that was all, before she hit the artery or vein, he could never remember which it was that beat in the throat, that squirted blood into her face. He clutched his throat: she had jumped up and away and he could not see her. He heard, vaguely, leaves shuffling and then nothing. It had happened so quickly. He had the thought *she'll be in trouble when somebody finds out* and wished that he had learned her name so he could tell who had done this. *But I won't be able to say anything when they find me.*

He had a few minutes to fully register this fact before his vision went dim.

He would not be able to be brave. He wouldn't get to help the girl. He tried to shout; there were houses nearby, nestled in the trees. He could not make sounds come from his mouth, and the attempt filled his throat with blood. He tried to breathe through is nose, his hands beating against the ground until his hands grew tired and heavy and it was easier to let them fall than to hold them up.

12

I think I found it, Jonathan shouted, motioning Emily over. 1965. Right at the end of the article. I see your mother's name. He sat up in his chair and squinted at the screen. Emily hung over Jonathan's shoulder, squinting at the worn type.

COLLINS GIRL MISSING:
Family Searches For Answers

Constance Collins, thirteen, the youngest daughter of Edward and Mercy Collins, went missing somewhere between Heartshorne Middle School and her home on August, 23rd, says Sheriff Morgan Deeds. "We are searching the area and ask for the cooperation of anyone who has seen or heard any sign of this young woman."

Edward Collins, the father of the missing girl, told *The Heartshorne Star* that he believes the girl is safe and well and that somebody in the Heartshorne community has more information. "I think she's somewhere here in town. Somebody better step forward and say something."

Constance, called "Connie" by her family, was last seen leaving Heartshorne Junior High School. She had in her possession a few school textbooks and was wearing a yellow sweater, black skirt, and black shoes.

Sheriff Deeds asks that any able-bodied men volunteer for the search party on Sunday, 4:00 PM.

At the top of the page was a school photograph of her mother that Emily had never seen before. In this photo, Connie's hair was slicked back into a complicated updo. She wore a pleated skirt that reached down past her knees and a white, button-up shirt, tucked in. She had a woman's figure, her breasts and hips prominent, and stood up straight, smiling directly into the camera.

Jesus Christ, Emily said. She ran away. Or was kidnapped. Does it say? Does it say what happened?

I don't know, he said. That's the end of the article. Let's look at the next day. They skimmed the headlines for three days, passed advertisements for overalls and shoes, wigs, and Roys Cardinal grocery store, which had a sale: hamburger for five cents a pound.

Look. Jonathan hovered his finger above a headline: *Local Girl Found Safe.*

Constance Collins, thirteen, was found safe wandering the streets of Heartshorne after a three-day-search.

Emily laughed in surprise. The streets? She said. What streets?

Constance has been hospitalized for dehydration and minor cuts and bruises. She claims to have no memory of her wherabouts for three days, and there has been little luck in gathering evidence about her location during this time period. "We are still on the case, but we have no leads yet," said Sheriff Deeds. "We still hope to hear from somebody who can give us the information we need."

Emily stood up straight. She pushed her hair away from her face and sighed. Wow, she said.

Fuck, Jonathan said in return, looking up at her, pointing at her mother's photograph. There's your Tower.

He took her to dinner afterward, though she protested that she had taken too much of his time already. He brought her to a restaurant with cloth napkins and candles burning at each table, the tea candle floating in blue oil in a small crystal glass.

Oh Jesus, she said. I'm not dressed for this. She wore a brown t-shirt and jeans. She'd been in a small room for hours and smelled of dust and old books and lemon furniture polish.

I'm not either, he said. So at least we'll both be badly dressed. She ordered a glass of wine, red, the only kind she drank, though it gave her headaches some mornings. She could never tell when she'd wake with one, but the she knew when the headaches were wine-induced: they were dusty, pulsing headaches, like the throbbing of a dry socket. Still, she loved the taste—how wine could smell of dirt and tobacco and plum and taste like the dark or something you might remember vaguely, some taste from your childhood that had surprised you and made you realize there was more to taste than just sweet and salty and sour. The waiter brought her a glass, filled to the brim. It smelled like grape juice gone wrong. She sipped it anyway, trying not to taste as it went down.

It's probably not good, Jonathan said, glancing up at her. He was examining the laminated menu, sticky with fingerprints and the steam and grease of other people's meals. The habit of eating with other people, people you didn't know, eating food prepared by somebody you had never met, seemed suddenly a strange gesture of trust to Emily. Who knew who any of these people were? And other people had recently sat in the same seats, licked the same forks and knives, scraped the same plates. What a strange custom, she thought. She was in a certain mood, one in which she saw herself from a distance, the entire scene from a distance, and fully felt the overwhelming strangeness of everyday human life, as an alien might.

It's strange we eat with people we don't know, she said out loud. She took another sip and winced at the bitter taste.

I actually know some of these people, Jonathan said, by sight, anyway. He responded as though she hadn't said something even slightly strange, and she liked him for it.

My high school science teacher is back there in a booth, Jonathan said, his beard full of soup, his wife across from him wearing the same blue make-up she did at basketball games and year-end assemblies ten years ago.

But I don't know them, she said. I don't know anyone here, except you. She sipped again.

And the people at the church, she said. I know them. She imagined Colleen, shaking her dry hands, her knowledge of Emily's family longer and so much deeper than Emily's own. The waiter came to take their order. He was older than most waiters she'd seen in Heartshorne, not the usual high-schooler or career waitress, women who all looked tired, haggard, but full of sourceless energy, zipping from table to kitchen to table. The waiter had memorized the specials and did not write down what they asked for. His smooth, dark hair did not move when he spoke or bent to remove the menus from their hands. He was a perfect servant.

It feels wrong to be here now, she said, swirling the wine in her cup, trying to extract something besides the smell of fruit and alcohol. She felt irritable with Jonathan for taking her here and irritable with herself for being so ungrateful.

Why? Jonathan asked, looking at her, smiling slightly. He

looked nervous, she thought. Afraid she might say something stupid or crazy.

I'm not drunk, she said, pushing the glass away. If that's what you think.

I didn't say you were.

But you think I am. She wanted to cry. And then she was crying: not sobbing, but leaking uncontrollably, her body working against her again.

I'm sorry, she said, spilling the heavy silverware from the folded napkin. It was made of slippery polyester and didn't soak up her tears: they slid along the surface, shaming her with their wetness. She was crying in a restaurant on what was technically her first date, a date that had taken place largely in the periodical room of the library. She could not make herself stop.

Jonathan leaned across the table. Are you upset about your mother? He asked. About what we learned today?

I saw that girl who died, she blurted out. The one who died last weekend in that accident in Heartshorne. She was on the road, twisted back, her face down. I didn't see her face. But I saw her body.

She released it all now, not caring if the people around them heard. They craned their necks, staring at her, but eventually turned back around, their manners winning out over their curiosity.

She allowed him to scoot his seat next to hers and take one of her hands, though she saved the other for her napkin. Crying was bad, but public crying was even worse. She allowed the idea of another date to leave her head immediately. She imagined going home and never seeing him again. And then, with this eventuality in mind, once she had accepted the inevitability of it, she could speak.

I don't know how to understand what I saw, she told him. I keep thinking about her. I see her turning on the ground, her face turned to me, ground away by the pavement. I can't make it stop.

He picked up her hand and held it against his chest, a curious gesture that surprised her so that she pulled away slightly out of instinct. He did not let go.

I'm sorry you had to see that, He said. You can talk about it as much as you need to.

And my mother, too, Emily said. She couldn't make herself stop talking. It's not just the girl. My mother never told me anything about this. Never said she'd gone missing as a teenager. I never had a clue. Why would she keep something so big from me?

Emily touched the folder she had placed on the table by her plate: thirty pages of articles about her mother's dissapearance and the six months after her return. The last article said nothing except that the case was still a mystery: Constance Collins claimed that she remembered nothing about that weekend, and nobody had come forward to provide further information.

Why wouldn't she tell me? Why didn't she want me to know?

Maybe she really remembered nothing, he said. Maybe there wasn't anything to tell.

If she didn't remember anything she would have told me this funny thing happened and she didn't remember any of it. That would be something worth telling. I'm sure she remembered.

I'm sure she never forgot. Maybe that's why she hated it here. Something happened to her, and she never wanted me to know. But why?

The Tower, Jonathan said. It's a Tower, she can't just go telling everybody. Maybe she was trying to protect you. It must have been very heavy for her to carry.

Emily nodded, but said nothing. She could not contemplate her mother's sadness right now. It was enough to hold her own.

I get them both mixed up in my head, she said. The girl's death. My mother's disappearance. And then her death, which I didn't see in person at all: I only saw her barely alive and then, later, I saw her coffin lowered into the ground, a closed-coffin funeral. I didn't ask to see her before the funeral. She wouldn't have wanted me to. I respected her privacy, even then.

I'm sorry to burden you with this, she said. You are very kind to listen.

It's okay, he said, waving away her apology. I'd want somebody to listen to me if I had just learned something like this. How about this, he said. He took her free hand in two of his. He pressed her hand hard between them. We finish our food here and then you come over to my house for drinks.

Emily wiped underneath her eyes with the napkin. How about you come to mine, she said. I need to have somebody else in the house, she said, surprising herself. It's just been me. And Levi, the pastor. And Fran, of course. That's the problem.

He nodded. Of course. I'd be happy. We'll pick up some better wine on the way.

He released her hand and Emily ate her food without tasting it. Her tears had dried and now her cheeks were hot—she had asked him over to her house. She imagined the tangles of socks and underwear in the living room, where she often dressed and undressed while listening to the news on her tiny radio because its sound didn't reach upstairs. There was probably ample evidence of her unhealthy habits: empty bottles with dried bits of red wine caked in the bottom, empty packets of instant breakfast, an ashtray with a few smashed butts.

She tried to concentrate on her food, though the bland pasta sauce couldn't hold her attention. She saw her mother as she was in her junior high school picture, poised and cone-breasted, her hair stiff. Her mother had wandered away in the dark and had come back three days later with bruises and scratches on her arms and legs and her face, had come back close-mouthed and angry until the day she'd died. Emily had not seen the exact moment of that death—she'd been called home during the night, her mother had died sometime between nurse checks, hours before dawn.

Before her death, after the first round of chemotherapy hadn't worked, after she'd lost her hair and could hardly eat, her stomach rejected everything she gave it, she had told Emily that she wished they would just stop trying to save her.

Why don't they just let me die? she'd asked, her bald head covered with a scarf in cheerful cherry print, a scarf that had seemed ridiculous and even offensive to Emily at the time. Who had given it to her? A nurse? A nurse who didn't know that her mother hated cherries and had always plucked them from sundaes before she ate them? They taste too much like candy, too sweet, too fake, she'd said. She'd seemed proud of the scarf, though, and never said anything about where she'd gotten it.

But when the doctors had suggested radiation, Connie had agreed.

You can tell them to stop at any time, Emily had told her. You can tell them to stop and we'll stop.

You tell them to stop, Connie had said, turning her eyes, the most live, liquid part of her, those globes that stood out from her face, big as mirrors.

I can't do that.

It was harder than Connie had imagined to just give up and let herself die, even if she wanted to.

I'll see you next Christmas, Emily would say each time she left for home again after the holidays.

If I'm even alive then, Connie would invariably answer. Emily had never believed this. Her mother had seemed incapable of dying.

Connie was buried in a plot that she'd chosen, a small place at the back of a graveyard in the Maine town where she'd lived the last seven years of her life. The graveyard was curiously hilly, so old that some headstones were made of thin slate, the names and images carved in by hand. Some tipped sideways, falling down the hill. Her mother was buried on a flat, grassy spot, surrounded by gravestones decorated with plastic American flags. Emily remembered being confused by this burst of patriotism until she realized that it was memorial day. Even the long dead in the graveyard, those dead from the Revolutionary war or Civil War, had flags. Somebody had remembered them.

•

She thought of her mother as she sat in the passenger seat. Jonathan drove her home: she had drunk another glass of wine at the restaurant and her head swam. She imagined her mother on the side of the road as they passed Jonathan's shop and grew closer to Heartshorne, her mother with her thumb out, her hair out of those meticulous configurations of pins and barrettes. The trees gathered close. They thickened as the sun fell. It would be easy to get lost here, easy to be knocked on the head and forget where you'd been or what you had done or what someone else had done to you. Maybe it wasn't so unlikely that she didn't remember.

Emily watched Jonathan drive, watched the lights from approaching cars stripe across his face. She hadn't learned anything new about him today. It had been all about her, her Tower.

I'm sorry this has all been about me, she said. I'm sorry I made you sit in a library and look through microfilm. I want to ask you something about yourself, ok?

Shoot.

What's your favorite book?

You'll laugh. *The Hobbit*. And my better answer is *Catch-22*. I haven't read much since I was a teenager, though. Not much time anymore. I mostly read graphic novels now.

What's your favorite album?

The Velvet Underground and Nico.

Favorite comic book character?

Batman. He didn't have any superpowers. He just made a kickass suit. That's talent, not luck.

He had money, too, she said. Don't forget that.

Yeah, he said, but all the money in the world can't make you a superhero. Otherwise, Paris Hilton would be one. Johnny Depp would be one. It takes smarts.

True. Thanks, she said. I'll have more questions, eventually, but for now, that's good enough.

That's all you need to know? Those are the most important questions you can think to ask?

She shrugged. They're the first ones that came to mind.

Hmm, he said. I'm not sure what that says about you.

It was easy to talk to him. She was sad that he'd probably never come back, but she pushed that to the back of her mind. She would enjoy now. That's all she had anyway.

I have a theory about superheroes, by the way, she said. People who love Superman idealize the world too much, they are too innocent. People who love Spiderman are eccentric but basically normal. People who like Batman are the best, though: they understand gray areas and can take the darkness, but they still try to do what's right.

I like that theory, he said. Who's your favorite?

She shook her head. I don't like any of them, she said. Superheroes are like cheating.

When she brought him inside, she found the house cleaner

than she had thought; no stray clothes on the floor or bottles on the counter. Her cigarettes were in the kitchen drawer, the ashtray cleaned out and only a faint smell of ashes lingered by the kitchen trash.

This is all mine, she said, holding out her arms to indicate bounty, ironically. My family inheritance. Everything I have left under the Collins name.

Jonathan walked through the house, touching the walls. He found the penciled notches in the hallway. Look, he said. Somebody measured a child here.

Emily shook her head. Frannie didn't have children.

It could have been her neices, nephews. Maybe your mother. He ran his finger up and down the marks. It's beautiful—I wish everybody did this, kept a record like this of somebody growing.

The wine made her clumsy, so when she reached out to touch his back she caught his elbow instead. She held it.

I like listening to you talk, she said. Because you only talk when you have something to say.

13

Lillian put the children to bed, pulled the blankets up to their shoulders, and kissed them. She stood outside the door until she heard them snoring, heard them lay still, not restless and kicking as they were on nights when they wouldn't go to bed and whined to have drinks of water or to stay up late and walked in, crying, red-cheeked, when she'd sat up late smoking cigarettes and listening to the radio. But they were good that night, tired out from playing in the woods all day. She'd helped them build a playhouse with old sheets and furniture—had cleared out a circle, raked up the leaves, scared away the snakes—and they had played there all afternoon, pretending to have a house of their own.

It was funny that kids played house like adults. They must think it's fun, paying bills and making dinner and cleaning, Lillian thought. Did it seem fun? Shelly had sounded just like an angry wife when she'd called Dennis in for make-believe dinner. Get over here, she'd said, before it I throw the whole thing out into the woods.

Where had she learned that? Lillian hadn't lived with a man for years. It wasn't worth the trouble to let them move in, not until she found one worth sharing space with. But she was beginning to grow used to having her own space now, used to the way that she could leave her clothes out and take up the whole bed without anyone else there to pull the blankets off or kick her toward the edge. Maybe she'd never live with another man again. The thought both saddened and relieved her.

When she heard their snores she went to the bedroom, slipped out of her pajamas, and put on her skirt and her sandals with straps that wrapped around her ankles. If the kids knew she was leaving, they'd whine and cry, they'd make it impossible for her to go anywhere. She did not feel guilty for fooling them. Parents were allowed to fool their children. It was one of the benefits of parenthood. She took the bottle of Aftershock from the fridge and put it in her purse. She wanted the small purse with the snap-top, the one covered in beads that could fit right into her hand, but she had to take the big purse covered in buckles—it was the only one that could fit the bulky, square bottle. Better she brought her own drink—otherwise she'd be stuck drinking Old English or that rose wine that came in jugs and tasted like old cough syrup. She put the cell phone in her pocket—she'd set it to ring at one so she'd be on her way out by then in case the kids woke up and were scared to find her gone. She never wanted them to wake without her in the house.

When she was five years old, Lillian had woken up in the middle of night with one of those sudden, acute fevers that children get, sicknesses that last for days and leave them limp and damp. She woke and cried from the confusion of being both suffocatingly hot and chilled. She'd crawled down from her bed, the house dark and silent around her, not even the dogs barking, and pushed open the bedroom door to her parent's room to find an empty bed, the blankets twisted, the closet thrown open and her mother's clothes crumpled on the floor.

She'd seen this before on television—a messy room ("ransacked", the man on *America's Most Wanted* always said), the drawers emptied and furniture overturned. Next, she'd find bodies somewhere, she knew from those shows, people dead or dying from gunshots. Her parents loved true crime TV, each case re-told in slow motion, the action drained of color to indicate a fictional account of real events.

So her parents were dead, she had reasoned, and the certainty paralyzed her. She had lain down on the floor at the base of her parent's bed and curled into a ball with her arms around her knees and her bare feet tucked under the hem of her nightgown. Her parents had found her there an hour later, returned from a party, her mother in glittery eyeshadow and her sandals with straps that bit into the skin of her feet. When Lillian saw them, she began to weep with relief, crying so hard that she threw up on the carpet.

Lillian didn't want the children to ever have to imagine what they'd do if she was gone, if she were dead.

But they were asleep, fast asleep, and when they were tired and snoring, almost nothing could wake them. Lillian took the Aftershock from her purse and swallowed a mouthful. It tasted like sugar on fire.

The party was at Keith's, just across the lake. He lived in the woods, hadn't even bothered to clear the trees around his trailer so he'd have a yard.The trees rushed up to the house, brushed against the windows when the wind blew. But there was a clear, wide path from the lake to his house, right through the woods, and she wasn't worried about getting lost. She'd grown up here. The moon was full tonight and the lake reflected the moon back. She'd made the trek before, sometimes several times a week, back when they'd been seeing each other. It had been a short, mostly sweet time, though she'd never had any intention of making the relationship permanent. He rarely had a job and spent most of his money on weed and pirated DVD's from Rod's Swap Shop. Still, he was affectionate and had a kind of sloppy, catholic kindness that she'd needed at the time. That's why she still went to his parties, still hugged him when they met at the grocery store, and hoped

142

LETITIA TRENT

that someday his brain would catch up with his age and make him worthy of trying again.

Lillian's heels stuck in the mud as she skirted close to the lake, near where the ledge above the water sloped down into a small, rocky beach. It was hot out, almost as hot as it had been during the day—the weather reporter had said highs up to 99. Lillian tried to stay inside as much as possible during the daytime in July and August, when the heat was sometimes so strong it could make her sick just to be in it. She had air conditioners thrumming in each room of the trailer, keeping the indoors so cold her fingers seized up—but that was better than the alternative. Once, she'd seen some woman on one of those morning shows talk about how air conditioning was one of the biggest contributors to global warming, energy usage, oil usage—pretty much everything bad in the world. Below her name on the screen, it said "Director of Vermont Environmental Solutions." Lillian had turned the television off then. A woman from Vermont telling her about the evils of air conditioning was like a eunuch giving sex tips.

Though the sun was gone, it had left its heat behind, sticky and heavy in the air. Being near the lake didn't help. It held the warmth and beamed it back out, damp and sticky like the spray from a humidifier.

She wiped her palms on her skirt. She felt sticky everywhere, in the crooks of her elbows, her armpits, the backs of her knees, the strip of underwear elastic that branded her skin. She stopped and took another sip of Aftershock.

The moon streaked the surface of the water with light. Across the water, a line of trees blocked the horizon. They bloomed crazily and dropped their green leaves into muck below. The opposite bank angled in close to her bank, creating the shortest point across the lake, a shallow, muddy corridor of water with a footbridge across it. That was the way to Keith's house.

Lillian stopped and watched the moon on the water, the ripples of light that moved sluggishly with the small tides. How did a lake have ripples and tides? Wasn't it just standing water, a big pond? She continued to sip the Aftershock. The light on the water moved in zig-zag patterns. The air smelled different here, different than she'd remembered: not quite sweet, but something like sweetness. Lillian dug at the bug bites on her ankles and closed her eyes, breathing in deep: it smelled like grass, torn petals, a little bit like bad weed, and sweat.

Lillian touched her throat as something trickled down it and into the gap between her breasts—sweat. She was hardly halfway there, and already she was dripping, covered in bug bites, half drunk, and exhausted.

The walk to Keith's seemed, now, after a quarter of a bottle of aftershock, after the heat and the bug-bites, to be more trouble than it had been worth. Lillian sat down amongst the dry rocks on the shore. She'd sit out here and drink a while, calm her nerves, and then go home and put on the radio. The classic country station took requests on Friday nights. She'd call in and ask for Dolly Parton's *Coat of Many Colors*. She'd probably be in bed before midnight.

She had only wanted to go out in hopes that somebody new

would be there, somebody she hadn't met before or slept with before or smoked weed with before, somebody, man or woman, who might have something new to say. But there probably wouldn't be anyone new. Maybe one of Keith's many cousins from the next county over, each with worse teeth than the next. Nobody like the person she hoped for. Even hoping seemed like more effort than it was worth.

There was nothing new in Heartshorne. Everything ran on a loop. Her mother had raised her alone (most of the time—her father was there, but in and out) in a little house near Echo Lake (the other side) and now she raised her own children alone in a trailer near Echo Lake. Shelly and Dustin would work their way through Heartshorne Elementary and Heartshorne High School, doing average, as she had, and they'd be spit out into her life again, fifteen years later. The only difference would be technology: maybe they'd have fucking hover cars or flying shoes or something that wouldn't change much of anything except the speed at which they moved toward the same life as always.

She threw a rock out into the water and it rippled out and out, the light moving with it. She didn't like these moods. They were pointless, what her mother called "dwelling" or "moping."

It was beautiful just to look at the water. A greenish mist rose from it, carrying that peculiar smell. Strange she hadn't noticed it much before. She'd heard stories about Echo Lake's special mist, particularly during her childhood, when her mother hadn't let her swim outside in the dark.

God knows what's out there, she'd said.

Lillian's hearing sharpened in the dark and she thought she heard the keening cry of something caught in teeth or a trap—a rabbit, maybe, or a squirrel treed by a cat. She'd seen that once, a cat waiting, still, its tail twitching, as a squirrel stood on a tree branch screaming down at it. The cat had only stared at the squirrel's dramatics, neither interested nor surprised, merely waiting for the squirrel to tire itself out and try to come down again.

The warmth of the cinnamon liquor seeped through her body. She breathed in deeply, the smell of the lake seeming sweeter as she drank, sweeter as she breathed it in. A fog rolled up from the surface. Her head buzzed slightly, a small ache that wasn't altogether unpleasant, like the buzz of an electrical current.

Lillian undid the buckles of her shoes and slipped them off. They seemed silly, those thin-soled things, the heel stabbing into the ground each time she walked, the strips of leather too thin to really protect her from falling or losing the shoes from her feet. All of her clothes seemed silly, come to think of it—these swaths of fabric covering up body parts that everyone had. And it was so hot!

She unbuttoned her blouse and threw it on the water. The water took it away slowly and the moon illuminated its wrinkles. Her skirt was made of denser stuff and didn't reflect light. It ate the moonlight and eventually sank.

Lillian unpeeled her underclothes and lay down on the rocks. They bit into her back, but she didn't mind the feeling. She closed her eyes and listened to the sounds from the woods behind her and across the water, the bugs pulsing and unseen animals picking their way through the burnt grasses and leaves that were unfortunate enough to fall from the trees.

But she was still too hot. Her skin itched.

The Aftershock bottle lay on its side, the sticky red liquid dripping out. She'd left it opened. At the bottom, the rock-candy gathered in crystals.

Lillian smashed the bottle against a large, flat rock until it cracked. A sliver of glass flew out and knicked her stomach (she felt the blood, the slight itch of the glass). Now, the candy was exposed, glittering. She reached in, trying to avoid the glass, and picked out a marble-sized piece of candy. As she sucked on the candy, cracking it between her teeth, she noticed a long, slick black trail of liquid dripping from her fingers, into the well of her palm.

She had cut her wrist on the glass. The wound was wide and blood spilled from it, as if she had slid the bottom of a milk jug with a razor. She could barely feel it. She could only feel the heat and tickle of the blood.

It was beautiful, though. The moon was directly above her like an enormous flashlight. The blood reminded her of the moon on the water, of her shirt illuminated in the light, of how beautiful it had been to allow the current to take her clothes away. She took a shard of glass from between the rocks and moved tip of the arrow-shaped glass along the surface of her opposite inner arm, along the white skin. A thin black line emerged and then erupted, spilling its own widening lines down her arm. She began to feel light, closer to the moon than to the dirt or the water, that great breathing thing that had carried her clothes out into itself. As if it had heard her, a gust of air pushed the fog from where it hung over the water and into her face. She breathed it in, tasiting salt and rust and muck.

Her arm was a collection of thinning black lines. She held it up, trying not to smudge. She took the triangle of glass in her free hand (it shook now—she'd have to lie down soon, to sleep it off) and slid it from her inner thigh all the way down to the knee. That swipe bled too quickly to be worth much, at least aesthetically. It made a sheet of blood, no intricate design.

She could barely hold her head up. She'd have to work quickly. She stood up and tilted her head back. The sky was lit, the moon huge and suspended directly above her, big as a clean Christmas plate. The glass slid smoothly across her skin and she felt a tingle and sting when her skin broke. It hurt at the endges of the cut and she let her chin snap back down so she could watch the lines collect and run down her chest, skirt around her breasts, and drip down her stomach.

She was tired. She pitched the shard of glass into the water and lowered herself down to her knees and lay face down on the ground. Her legs and arms ached now where she had cut them. She was almost asleep when she heard the shrill song coming from her tangle of shoes and underwear. It was her phone. She had forgotten all about the children for a while, but she remembered them now.

Lillian tried to push herself up by her arms, her palms dipping deep into the dirt, but her whole body was leaden, so tired, and it would not move.

She couldn't remember how she had gotten here. She was wet—had she gone swimming in the lake? She hoped not. It was notoriously dirty and children cut their feet on the bottom, which was filled with beer bottles and car parts.

She tried to open her mouth, but no sound came out. Her throat felt hot and throbbing and she wanted to touch it but her hands wouldn't listen.

She closed her eyes and hoped that before the children woke, somebody would find her and help her to her own bed. She hoped that her absence wouldn't make them afraid as she had been, curled at the bottom of her parent's bed, holding herself tight and certain that she was the only one left, that she was alone and that their stories and songs soothing her to sleep had meant nothing at all.

14

Emily slept throught the night without visits from her mother or dreams of travel. Jonathan didn't pull away the covers or crowd her. He slept in a self-contained ball, warm and complete and turned away from her. Not unfriendly, but enough for himself, needing no heat from her. When they woke, almost at the same time, he touched her hair and said he was hungry and that he was sorry that he had to leave so soon.

I have to open the shop on time, he said. Most of our customers are early-morning people. They ate cereal in her kitchen. It was the first time that somebody else had eaten with her in the new house, the first time somebody had spent the night.

She asked him if she had snored, if the house had kept him awake (as if the house itself were particularly loud or difficult to sleep in).

Emily watched his face for signs of lying as he said no, that he'd slept well. She felt panic, which tasted like tin and felt like buzzing in her teeth, as he prepared to leave. He found his clothes and kissed her goodbye. I had a very, very, good time, he said, pressing his forehead against hers. I'll give you a call tonight, okay? He said. She nodded and waved on the front step as he left, feeling silly for doing something so cliche, something that probably made him laugh as he viewed her in his rearview mirror.

When she stepped back inside the house, she got on her knees, pushed aside two days of mail collected from the mail slot, and lowered herself to floor. She began to cry in ugly waves.

Her body surprised her. She was afraid—her stomach hurt, her eyes ached from behind, as they did when she was particularly tired. But what was she afraid of? That he wouldn't come back and she'd be left in this house like Frannie until she died of old age, or was killed? That somebody would find her dead after a week, maybe, her throat cut and one bowl of instant soup cooling and thickening on the kitchen table, and that nobody would really care?

He was kind. He said he'd had a good time. Why do I expect it to fail?

She hardly knew him. He knew so much about her. It made

her nervous to be at a disadvantage. And she was letting him too close, too quickly. It was a bad idea, all of it.

When she was done crying, she rose and wiped her face clean. At least she knew exactly why she was upset. So often, in the past, she hadn't. She would cry for hours and Eric would come to her asking if he could help, asking if it was his fault, and she honestly could not answer. But knowing helped: she knew what to do. She put on a pot of tea. She went to the bedroom as it warmed and made her bed, smoothing away the imprint of Jonathan. It was only the trace of his body that made her act like this, the inevitable feeling of connection and fear of that connection being severed that came from sharing certain parts of one's body with others. She'd learned this in college, in biology class, and so the knowledge had stuck with her as fact, as yet another sad example of how little humans really could control who they loved, for how long, or why.

If he didn't come back, she would be fine. She ran downstairs when the kettle screamed and made herself a cup of tea.

Emily fished the folder full of photocopied articles about her mother's disappearance from her bag. She decided that she wouldn't think of him, that if he didn't decide to come back or call again, she would go back to her work of finding out about her family. Maybe it would even be easier without him. She wouldn't be so distracted. She wouldn't have to clean or hide the wine bottles. She'd have time to put herself together properly before she met somebody, a real somebody who would not sleep over and then leave quickly, as if to get away before anyone was awake to see him. She wouldn't be suprised if he didn't call or if he called with one of those messages full of throat clearing and apology, something about her neediness and her Tower and how he just wasn't ready. Though, he probably wouldn't have to resort to that kind of behavior. There was something cool in his self-possession. He would be able to say, simply, that it just wasn't going to work out. She had been such a burden to him already, all of the microfilm spools and the photocopying in a dusty room, and she had cried last night at dinner—actually cried so much her face turned red, her eyes swelled, and her stomach felt empty thought it was full of cheap wine.

She shook her head and spread out the newspaper clippings before her. They were scant, but they at least gave her an area of investigation, a particular place to look. It was nearby, where Connie had been finally found, within sight of Rod's Swap Shop, not far from where Echo Lake ended. She'd gone missing outside of the school. It was down a road that Emily hadn't visited yet that led to one of the few scenic outlooks in Oklahoma, one of the only places where you could stand above anyplace else and see swaths of green below. She hadn't seen the mountains yet, though they mounded gently on the horizon when she drove from Keno. The articles mentioned the people who had seen Connie last (she imagined her mother as *Connie* now, even in her thoughts, she was so far from being her mother yet at this age): Mrs. Hanson, the English teacher, and a few names of people who were surely so old that they were dead by now. No Colleens. Still, she'd have to ask Colleen. She'd have to figure out why her family had been wild.

She washed the used cups and cleaned the kitchen until there was nothing left to clean. Even the dirt that collected between the metal sink and the countertop had been bleached away. She'd have to start now. Not with Colleen, Emily wasn't ready for somebody so unfriendly yet, but somebody she knew. She'd talk to Levi. He had to know more, have some memory of this event that, if the papers told any truth, had been an enormous shock to the community. But first, she had to go to the high school.

•

Heartshorne High School was made of stone and mortar, the rocks varying between black, brown, and the orange clay of the dirt roads Emily had crossed to reach it. A wide, stone staircase led up to the glass doors at the entrance. It was a Sunday, no school, though there were a few cars in the school's gravel driveway.

Her mother had walked here almost every morning, had run down these steps to get home. Emily touched the metal plaque at the entrance of the school. It had been built in 1910, just five years after the town was established. She walked up the steps and when she reached the top, turned and leaned her back against the glass. Her mother had stood in this spot the day she had disappeared. She had come down the steps. Emily stepped down each deliberately, imagining herself as her mother forty years before. She tried to imagine herself in white stockings, a skirt made of heavy polyester, a blouse buttoned up to her chin, a bra full of wires and cones and fasteners. Her mother had worn her hair curled, though her hair, like Emily's, was aggressively straight and flat. Connie had talked about sleeping in curlers and how sick hairspray made her, how she woke each morning with a headache and hair that smelled clean and poisonous and moved like a collection of soft springs. Emily imaged her hair bouncing, the smell of hairspray faint, her clothes buttoned and tucked and made of heavy fabrics. Even in her later years, her mother hated how women *let themselves go*, how they wore sweatpants outdoors and couldn't even be bothered to put on lipstick even when they *looked like death*. Emily imagined herself in her mother's body, a small, constricted body, hot under her clothes but used to being so. She imagined that peculiar smell of sweat on polyester, reminiscent of burning rubber.

She walked down the steps, one-by-one, imagining her mother's tight shoes (she bought size seven shoes as an adult, though they pinched her feet, a strange and painful sort of vanity) on her own feet. Her mother had been thirteen. She imagined Connie's face, the slightly receded chin, the fuller mouth than her own, the broader but straighter nose, the blonder hair. She imagined Connie's face like a mask over her own face. She was going home from school on that afternoon, but how did she get off course? Maybe she never intended to go home. Maybe she had a secret boyfriend, somebody she was going to meet. Maybe she was going with a girlfriend to do something forbidden: drink, smoke weed. Colleen had said that *those Collins kids were wild*.

Emily opened her eyes. The day had turned hot. She peeled off her long-sleeved shirt. The sun was almost directly overhead.

By the road, the school's electronic sign played the same message in neon dots over and over again: *We will miss you, Jenny.* Jenny, the girl in the accident. Like Connie, Jenny had been somewhere she shouldn't have been, but she hadn't returned. In the last few days, the newspaper had reported that Mr. Rodriguez, Jenny's high school history teacher, had been having an *illicit sexual relationship* with the girl for several months. In questioning, he claimed that he could remember nothing about the accident.

The sign flashed her name again and Emily wondered if this same sign, with black letters that the janitor had to change every morning instead of a digital screen, had once said her mother's name.

PART TWO

room. She smelled of bathroom soap now, sweet and cheap, but it was better than sweat.

Billy hadn't known that she existed before this year. He ran in different circles. She'd known vaguely that he was a church kid, that his family worked in oil and that he lived in a beautiful, two-story ranch house just before the lake, but all that was from rumor. He was popular—he went to parties, smoked cigarettes behind the bus barn, and did things that normal kids did, but he did them in a way that made him seem slightly outside of them, as though he was only passing through. She'd never heard a story about Billy getting in trouble for smoking or Billy getting so drunk he passed out in the woods. He was there, but he wasn't quite there.

Connie, too, had a strange kind of popularity. She was poor and everybody knew it. Her father worked at the gas station and her mother stayed home, usually drunk or passed out from taking her pills at noon so she wouldn't get *nervous* after the children came home. When she was nervous, she shouted and her body tightened and twisted until she released her nerves in fury of shouting and crying. Still, Connie managed to make herself more than the daughter of a couple of trashy drunks. She wasn't beautiful, but she was sharp and pretty and dressed well and didn't take bullshit. When somebody as much as hinted at her mother's problems or something unkind about her brothers and sisters, she didn't let it go: she'd go straight to the person, whoever it was, and tell them exactly what she'd do if she heard anything like that again. She had learned soon that this was enough and she hardly

PART TWO

1

Heartshorne, 1965

Connie waved the cigarette smoke away from her face and toward the screened windows in the girl's bathroom—everyone else was gone, pretty much, and so she could have a smoke in peace without being caught outside by the elementary school teachers who beat chalk from their erasers and gossiped together like teenagers in the hour after school had ended.

She had stayed behind to finish her homework, which she hadn't completed for three days in a row. She'd finished it in five minutes and spent the last twenty minutes of detention writing her name next to Billy Sisco's name on a full sheet of notebook paper.

When Mr. Colchester let her out, his bow-tie as bright and his comb-over as stiff as it had been that morning, despite the heat. Connie went to the girl's restroom again to smoke another cigarette. She wiped the dampness from her throat and underarms with the rough, brown paper towels in the girl's room. She smelled of bathroom soap now, sweet and cheap, but it was better than sweat.

Billy hadn't known that she existed before this year. He ran in different circles. She'd known vaguely that he was a church kid, that his family worked in oil and that he lived in a beautiful, two-story ranch house just before the lake, but all that was from rumor. He was popular—he went to parties, smoked cigarettes behind the bus barn, and did things that normal kids did, but he did them in a way that made him seem slightly outside of them, as though he was only passing through. She'd never heard a story about Billy getting in trouble for smoking or Billy getting so drunk he passed out in the woods. He was there, but he wasn't quite there.

Connie, too, had a strange kind of popularity. She was poor and everybody knew it. Her father worked at the gas station and her mother stayed home, usually drunk or passed out from taking her pills at noon so she wouldn't get *nervous* after the children came home. When she was nervous, she shouted and her body tightened and twisted until she released her nerves in fury of shouting and crying. Still, Connie managed to make herself more than the daughter of a couple of trashy drunks. She wasn't beautiful, but she was sharp and pretty and dressed well and didn't take bullshit. When somebody as much as hinted at her mother's problems or something unkind about her brothers and sisters, she didn't let it go: she'd go straight to the person, whoever it was, and tell them exactly what she'd do if she heard anything like that again. She had learned soon that this was enough and she hardly ever had to follow through. People respected her. And when she reached eighth grade, she began to see the weak, the poor, the cringing, much in the way that other kids did: they asked for it by not standing up. If only they'd stop stooping, stop flinching, stop their sniffling, they'd be fine. She didn't think of herself as one of them, although she lived in a shack with a dozen brothers and sisters, skinny dogs wandering the yards, cats underfoot, and her knuckles bruised from scrubbing sheets on the wash board.

On the third day of school, after her first detention (this time for chewing gum in chorus and being caught trying to hide it under her chair), she had emerged from the front doors to find it drizzling, the sky roiling and gray. It would downpour.

She hadn't brought a jacket, not even a sweater; the morning sky had been clear. She placed her science book on her head to keep her hair and face from getting wet and started walking.

Hey, I can take you home, a voice called out. A car slowed and stopped when she stopped. The window rolled down. It was Billy in his El Camino.

That's ok, she said. She thought maybe he was picking on her, that she'd move toward the door handle and he'd peel away, splashing mud into her face.

The clouds released then, soaking the paper bag her book was covered in.

C'mon, he said. You can't walk that far in this rain.

She got in and shut the door behind her.

He started taking her home everyday. He took her to Sonic sometimes and bought her a hamburger and soda. He told her about his parents, his father who was a church deacon and his mother who worked as church secretary and led women's Bible classes. She told him about her mother's nerves and how her father came home with a twelve-pack of beer every night and usually finished it before he fell asleep, his snoring thick through his troubled breathing.

They became friends. She wanted to touch his hand sometimes when it rested on the dashboard. She caught him staring at her as they drove. Sometimes he crept from the road, the car's wheels spinning in the gravel, and she looked at him, sharply, only to find him looking at her, too.

At school, they didn't let on that they were anything more than friends, though people asked and teased, as people did. They'd seen him take her home.

He just takes me because it's on the way, she said. Because he's a gentleman, not like the rest of you assholes.

Connie liked it secret.They didn't have to sit together at lunch or hold hands or do any of the things that couples did in school. It was almost more real that way, more adult.

After a few weeks, they hadn't even kissed yet, though they had an understanding. They had told each other too much to be just friends. She didn't know what they were to each other, exactly, and she liked that, too. She watched him at lunch, his mouth moving as he spoke to other people who had no idea the things she knew about him, like that he had dedicated his life to Jesus at twelve during a tent revival in Keno and had cried the first night after he got drunk at a party, feeling that he had disappointed Jesus, but he'd done it again anyway, and still did, over and over again.

He told her that his mother was beginning to be suspicous.

She likes me to be around girls from church, he said as he drove her home on a drizzly day, much like their first drive home, if I'm going to be around girls at all. She says she's heard I've been taking you out.

Taking me out, she repeated. Connie hadn't thought of it that way.

I'd go to church, Connie said, but Mom and Dad don't and they like me home on Sundays for laundry, she said.

Truthfully, her parents had called the Baptist pastor Jenkins a leach on society. Her mother called herself a Pentecostal but kept nothing of the religion except a belief in faith healing and a love of dancing.

It doesn't matter what she thinks, he said. I'll be with whoever I want.

Connie's stomach flared. *I'll be with whoever I want.* So they were together. Like a couple, the real thing. She tried not to blush as she sipped on the soda.

Connie had never heard him say anything unkind about his mother. She was a saint, knew the Bible backwards and forwards, prayed every night for the safety of her children and the salvation of every person in Claymorecounty, and then every person in the world.

She really means it, he'd say. She really wants every single person saved.

He gripped the steering wheel and grimaced. She's a wonderful person, he said. But she just doesn't understand sometimes.

•

The day she disappeared, Connie took the path behind the high school. It went straight through the woods, skirted the wire fence of a pasture where cows stared dully but rarely ever moved. Once she cleared the pasture, she'd be at the back of the general store, where she was supposed to meet with Billy. They were meeting secretly now, no more car rides out in the open, just until he figured out what to tell his mother. They had kissed in the car at Sonic and he said that he didn't care who knew. They were a couple now, and he loved her, and when he turned nineteen, he'd file for an Indian house and take care of her. Her stomach had been so nervous and sick then that she couldn't finish her burger and when he dropped her off at home, she had spent the afternoon in a fog so thick that her mother had to ask her three times if she wanted dinner: she'd just been lying on her bed, staring up at the ceiling fan. She couldn't sleep that night, either, imagining herself in her own house, cooking food she liked, picking the colors of curtains and sheets and towels and watching whatever she wanted on television.

She had almost reached the edge of the woods, where the trees thinned out and became pasture, when she saw them: a group of men gathered around something on the ground. The object was metal and the sun through the leaves speckled it with light.

One knelt down by the metal object with a butcher knife (she saw its broad flashing), trying to pry it open. The other three stood around him, smoking, talking low. She didn't recognize them from behind: they wore plain and plaid button-ups and jeans. Each wore boots, not the fancy kind that cowboys wore but the kind of work boots with steel inside the toe to keep men from getting their feet broken if concrete or rerod fell on them.

It was a cash register, she saw, as she stepped closer, though it was misshapen now from their attempts to beat it open. She saw the man kneeling down on the ground more clearly than the others—his face was partially-hidden by his greased hair, which hung over his eyebrows, but she recognized him anyway. It was a man she'd seen before hitchhiking on the side of the road, holding his dirty thumb out on the roadway from Heartshorne to Keno, walking backwards along the roadway.

Blackshaw, her father had said, passing without even as much as slowing down the car. Her parents knew him. Her mother said she remembered James Blackshaw from school—he was about five years younger than her, but he was wild enough that even the adults knew his name. He got kicked out junior year. He got a girl pregnant—ruined her life and left her alone. Nobody would touch her after that.

Connie didn't know much else about him. She'd seen him in the general store from time to time, looking over the canned beans or asking for the cheapest pack of cigarettes.

Her mind didn't put together what she was seeing—a closed cash register, men bending over it to pry the drawer open—until it was too late to turn around. She had come to close and they'd heard the dried leaves crackle under her hard-soled mary-janes.

I can't believe he didn't give you a key, James said. Seems like they don't trust you to begin with.

One of the men shrugged. I don't know how all that works. I just stock.

Hey! One of the men had sighted her. James looked up, the knife still in his hand.

She could have run back to the school in five minutes. She could have run back shouting the entire time, and they might have let her run, hoping that she wouldn't talk out of fear or a desire not to be a tattletale. Children in Heartshorne were taught young, and with great emphasis, not to be tattles. The worst violation, even worse than lying, was to tell what wasn't supposed to be told.

But she didn't turn around and run. Men made her fearful; men older than her but younger than her father, in particular, made her blush, made her feel as though she could do nothing but exactly what they said. She wanted them to look at her but was afraid when they looked too closely or carefully, afraid when they smiled and afraid when they didn't smile.

She stepped forward. She would be good and wouldn't make them upset.

I'm sorry, she said. I'm just trying to get over to the general store.

2

Emily bought a *Heartshorne Star* from Rod's Swap Shop. On the front page, Jenny's face in her senior photo was placed next to another school photo, this time of an adult man—he was a teacher at Heartshorne High School, the science teacher and girl's softball coach, and the man who had been driving the car in the accident, Mr. Rodriguez. The article said that in custody, he had admitted to a sexual relationship with the girl, one which had been going on for almost a year by the time of the accident.

I loved her, he had told the police. I was going to marry her when she turned eighteen.

They had spent the afternoon at the lake, swimming and picnicking. The accident occurred on the way home, on an otherwise safe and deserted stretch of road, the speed limit 40 miles per hour.

The accident was deemed suspicious by the Keno authorities. There was no apparent cause of the car going off the road and Rodriguez's blood was free of alcohol or other intoxicants.

Emily brought her newspaper home and lay it on a stack of papers, each from the last few days with a picture of Jenny's face in black and gray somewhere on the front page, though each said mostly the same thing: her family was asking for answers and that Rodriguez claimed that he couldn't remember the accident or the reason for it. She read each article greedily upon getting the newspapers in her hands and then couldn't look at them again.

Emily remembered Rodriguez, the cut on his forehead that

bloomed and spilled as he told her that he didn't know what had happened, that he was afraid he had hurt the girl and that he had not meant to.

Emily touched her own forehead, which ached with a vague, dry pain that had hidden under the surface of her activities all day, too slight to urge her to make the effort to do anything about it. Now, at the end of the day, it crept up to the surface. She pressed the her left thumb and forefinger in the soft spot between her right thumb and fingers, an old trick she had learned to ease her headaches. She didn't know if it worked, but at least it distracted her mind until the ibuprofen kicked in.

Her hands felt rubbery and weak and her fingers collapsed around the objects they touched. She hadn't eaten since breakfast. She took a plastic-covered package of saltines from the cabinet and sat down. She took out the folder full of her mother's articles and examined them—not the articles themselves, she had already read them, but the neat columns of text around them.

Most of the articles accompanying the one about her mother's disappearance were about petty crimes and small tragedies— cars crashing into trees, floods, thefts, the deaths or escapes of farm animals. Emily turned back to the very first article, the one published the day after her mother had first gone missing. In the column next to the notice about her mother's disappearance, an article about the new Keno Police Chief featured a barely visible photograph of a man with black hair, black eyes, and cheekbones that slashed along the sides of the otherwise featureless face. At the bottom of the page, there was only a small column—a robbery from the general store, a stolen cash register that had been discovered missing only that morning. There was no sign of forced entry, though no employees had seen anything suspicious and all had posession of their keys.

The General Store had been on Highway 2, at the junction between the highway and Echo Lake Road.

Emily knew exactly where that was. It was Rod's Swap Shop, around where her mother had been discovered when she finally came home, malnourished and covered in cuts and otherwise fine, though she couldn't (or wouldn't) remember anything about where she had been.

The General Store had been owned by the Richardsons. Their sons helped out and they hired no outsiders, preferring to keep the business in the family.

Richardson, Levi Richardson. It was a common name, but maybe they were related. Was he old enough to have been alive then, maybe even a child, old enough to have memories of this missing girl?

Emily closed the folder and ate saltines until her mouth was so dry she swallowed hard to get the ball of crackers down.

She planned what she would say to Levi when she went to him. She's ask him if he remembered Connie's disappearance. She'd tell him that she needed his help.

She went to the kitchen sink and turned the tap on and bent down to drink directly from the stream of water as she did sometimes when she stumbled into the bathroom at night from a sharp, sticky feeling of thirst, too tired to go down to the kitchen and get a cup, her hair darkening in the metal basin though she tried to hold it back and out of the water.

3

I'm sorry to bother ya'll, Connie said, crossing her arms across her chest. I'm just on my way through. The man who had turned faced her and smiled, though the others looked down at their shoes. One said *fuck* as he exhaled smoke and threw down his cigarette to crush under his feet. She recognized one of the standing men: he worked at the General Store. He was just out of high school, a Richardson, John Richardson. His family owned most everything there was to own in town: the gas station, the general store, and a cafe between Heartshorne and Keno that served breakfast all of the time, their eggs salty and tasting of butter and bacon even when nobody at the table had ordered bacon. They just looked at her. Connie stepped forward, holding her books close to her body.

I'm sorry, she said again, I'm just trying to get by. She walked forward, hoping that they would part their tight circle in the middle of the path let her go. She wouldn't say anything: she wasn't a snitch, and if a Richardson was out here, maybe it wasn't something funny after all. Maybe they were just fixing the stuck cash register.

Hey, hey, wait. James stood, letting the cash register fall to the ground and the coins inside clatter.

She stopped before him. He pushed his black hair out of his face. He was gaunt and leaned to the left, his posture unsteady. He was tall and seemed to slouch to make up for it. He had the posture of an animal that ran quickly, its belly against the ground.

It felt wrong, everything about him.

I don't think you can go, he told her.

I won't tell, she said, stepping backward. I just want to get to the—

Won't tell what? James hooked his fingers in his pockets and slouched backward, rocking on his heels. You think we done something wrong?

Connie looked to the other men, looking for one who would meet her eye, that would step forward and say *cool it James, she's just a kid*, like something from a movie, like how the boy on a motorcycle in a movie could break windows and smoke cigarettes but still wouldn't hurt a girl; those boys were always good underneath their leather and their slang and their hair oil. But nobody looked at her. They looked at the ground or at James as he rocked and smiled slightly and waited for her to respond.

I don't know what's going on, but I'm not gonna tell and I want to go, she said. Her anger was rising. She wondered if she could run faster than them. If she threw her books and ran back she might run into somebody at the school. There were a few scattered houses just past the school, too. She calculated in her head how long it would take: not long. She could scream the whole way.

We can let her go, Jimmy. She won't say nothing. A man with the scars of old acne under each cheekbone and blonde, greasy hair spoke up.

She wished he hadn't. He wasn't in charge and hung towards the back, smoking nervously.

James shook his head. I can't risk it.

Then what are we supposed to do with her? Another asked.

She didn't hear the response because she had thrown down her books and started to run back toward the school.

4

Levi invited Emily inside his manufactured home. It had the appearance of stability, the same beiges and whites of any middle-class home, but when she leaned against a wall, she could feel it give beneath her shoulder.

Would you like some tea?

Emily took the tea, not sweet, as she'd expected, but acidic and bitter with lemon.

I'd hoped to see you at church. Levi sat across the kitchen table from her. In the middle of the table, a napkin holder burst with square paper napkins, each with the same autumn print she'd seen at the church dinner. His kitchen was immaculate. A list of groceries was pinned to the refrigerator with a magnet that said *Heartshorne Free Will Baptist: Welcome to the Family!*

Do you need the church bus to come out there to pick you up on Sundays? He asked. He looked up from his glass, excited. Sometimes people don't go because of transportation issues, he said, but the church family can always help.

He seemed so hopeful that she would say yes, that her lack of attendence had just been a matter of the church van not going quite far enough down the road.

No, she said, that's fine. I'm not really—I'm not really a Christian, I suppose. He sat up straight and nodded, interested now, animated with purpose. She could feel where the conversation would go next if she didn't take control of it.

But I am not, not anti-Christian, she said, and I understand why you would want to be. Want to be a Christian, I mean. She paused, not sure what to say next. He readied to speak, but she cut him off.

I'm sorry, Levi, I know this is important to you, but I actually came here to ask something specific, not about religion. She breathed in deeply. I need to ask you about my family.

When not in church, he seemed smaller, older, his skin thinner and more delicate. He seemed vulnerable in this gleaming, plastic house. He sipped his tea and nodded. He sank back in his seat, the energy leaving his face.

Okay, he said. Shoot.

My mother grew up here, Frannie's neice. Her name was Connie, Connie Collins. Levi nodded.

I recently learned that she disappeared for two days in the mid-sixties, right after school one day, and was found again stumbling along highway two, near where Rod's Swap Shop is right now. She wouldn't say where she'd been—she couldn't remember. But I never knew about it. She never told me anything. Which makes me think this has something to do with our whole family leaving town soon after.

Except Frannie, he said. Frannie stayed.

Yes.

He nodded. I was small when it happened, five, six. It wasn't something I knew about personally, but I do remember. I assumed you already knew.

Emily shook her head. I was told nothing. So, the general store was called Richardsons, the place where she was found by. Was that your family's business?

He nodded. Cousins, though. We didn't have much to do with them. They were Pentecostals, he told her, as way of explanation.

Your mother really never told you anything about this? He asked. He looked at her, his eyes assuming a look his parishioners must have known well—a moist, focused concern.

She shook her head. I only know that my family left sometime in the sixties. I know they scattered, but we didn't keep in touch. My mother didn't keep up with her sisters and brothers, her parents, anyone. Emily laughed. Honestly, don't take this personally, but the only things she had to say about Heartshorne was that it was a pit—a place you get sucked down into and can never escape. She hated it.

I can understand that, he said. Some people find life here too quiet—they want bigger things. Maybe she was one of those people.

Emily looked down into her tea. Her mother had always wanted something bigger, but she had never gotten it. Probably because she was never sure what she wanted, only what she did not want.

I don't feel the same way she does, Emily said. I like it here, even if I don't quite know how to live here yet.

Levi nodded. I bet it's hard, not knowing anyone. Not having any family.

Emily nodded. That's what I'm here to talk about, she said. I just want somebody to tell me the truth, she said. What happened with my mother, as far as you know? What did you hear? Anything is more than what I have right now.

He sighed and leaned away from the table. I was so young, he said, that nothing I knew came firsthand. I'd hear my mother on the telephone with her sister, or the things my father said after going out on his visits to parishioners. It was big news then, the biggest we'd had in a while. Your mother was a regular, decent girl—that's why everyone was surprised when she didn't come home. There wasn't a boy, not as far as anyone knew. She was just gone.

I think that's what scared everyone most, he said. And when she came back, she wouldn't say a thing. Levi stood up abruptly, interrupting himself. He walked over to the kitchen and and brought out a dishtowel. He wiped the rings of condensation from their glasses and then wiped the sweat from the bottoms of sides.

I'm sorry, he said, folding the towel on the table by his glass. I like to keep things neat. He smiled. I don't really believe that cleanliness is next to Godliness, but I do try to keep my spaces in order. He shrugged.

Emily got the feeling that people didn't always react well to his neatness.

So, anyway, he said, taking his seat again, your mother, she was a good girl. And when she came back, everyone was happy, it seemed to me, though nobody knew what had happened. I don't remember much until a week or two later, when the boy went missing. Then talk started again.

Emily sat up straight. Missing? Like my mother? She hadn't read about anyone else missing. Levi shook his head. He wasn't a boy, really—more like a young man. In his twenties. I remember my Mother on the phone, saying that it had something to do with that Collins girl, that it was payback. My Father wouldn't talk about it. He called it gossip and said *it's a tragedy, whatever happened, when young people go astray*. I remember that specifically.

I remember the day we heard about your mother, he said. My father had come home from visiting a widow, a woman with her teeth missing and a foot swollen from diabetes, too sick to make it to church. Back in those days, older women without family needed somebody to take care of them or they'd end up with twenty cats and nothing to eat. That's what the church did. He came back from the visit full of gossip that he'd heard from her, not to dispense, mind you, but to teach us something. He wouldn't tell us the details, but he said that the Collins girl was missing and there were rumors of her running off with some boy. He said that nobody but God knew what had really happened to the Collins girl, that gossip was malicious. My mother nodded along with him and then went and told her friends the very next day.

And then, soon after, after your mother came back safe, the Collinses left, soon after the man went missing. I know it got bad enough around town—apparently they had a falling out with somebody, or people just didn't like the fact that Connie wouldn't tell— that my father visited them to see if he could mend the rift. They wouldn't speak to him. They were packing their things to leave when he visited. Connie, your mother, she wouldn't speak. She didn't talk at all to strangers for a while, that's what my father told us.

So they left then, after a man disappeared?

Levi nodded. The boy died—it was probably in the paper, if you want to look it up. They left soon after that. All but Frannie, who had a job at the diner and was engaged to a man here in town, though nothing ever came of it. She never married.

The kitchen clock, a red cat, the plastic tail hanging down and ticking the seconds, suddenly sounded the hour.

I'm sorry to keep you for so long, Emily said.

It's nothing. Levi shrugged. I'm not that busy today. I don't have quite so many widows as my father did. Everybody lives much longer, now, and fewer people want the church to visit them at home. They think I'm there to sell them something.

If you don't mind, I have one more question, Emily said. I don't understand about the man who died, or disappeared. What did it have to do with my mother?

Levi leaned forward again, fixing her with those practiced, pastor eyes. I'm going to be honest with you, Emily. People believed then that your family killed that man. And that he deserved it, for some reason, and that it had something to do with your mother's disappearance. There were never any official charges against anyone regarding your mother, but it didn't matter what happened officially—everybody seemed to know something I didn't. My parents were quiet and hushed when the subject came up, afraid to give us bad dreams or fuel for telling tales, I guess. And that's why your family had to leave. They were driven out, I guess you could say. Not literally, but by all of the rumors, the whispering, the way people looked at them. It was probably impossible for them to go back to normal life after that, despite their guilt or lack of it. Things like this happen, and they're kept quiet, but for some reason, your family couldn't keep it quiet.

Emily wrapped her hand around the glass of iced tea and took a sip to occupy her mouth and hands as she tried to understand what Levi was telling her. He offered her another glass and she shook her head.

I have to leave soon, thank you. She downed the rest of the glass despite the bitterness. I appreciate your help, she said. She looked at Pastor Levi, his kind eyes, his tired face, his spotless home.

Could I ask one more favor?

Anything.

Could tell me how to get to Colleen's house?

5

James chased the girl through the woods, toward the high school. Running toward that school made his stomach recoil and he fell back a step at the thought of it. The girl was young, and long-legged, and she'd outrun him if he didn't go faster.

He had hated it at Heartshorne High School—fucking spinster teachers and bastards with their paddles they hit you with and offered you right after to write your name on, like it was really a prize to let them hit you. He'd written his name large across the width of the paddle and dug his name in deeper each time he was sent to the principal's office, where he was offered a paddling or detention. He always chose the paddle instead of detention, and each time he had to bend over the desk and let that fat fuck Principal Knight hit him square in the ass he thought *they will all pay*. All he could remember of those punishments was the anger it created in him, the feeling that he had to go out and punch something, hard, until his knuckles split and the person or thing he was beating broke, too. But they didn't pay—soon after he dropped out in eleventh grade, he was arrested and spent for his 4-year jail stint for burglary. James didn't know what had happened to Knight after he'd left school. He probably had a cushy retirement to Keno. Probably thought that he had touched the lives of many children in a positive way and woke up proud of himself every morning for what he'd accomplished.

School and jail, the two places he'd hated the most and spent more time in than anywhere else so far in his adult life. They were both pretty much the same, and he wasn't going back to either of them. But he needed the girl to be sure of that. He pushed harder and reached her, snagging her hair as it flew behind her, a hunk of it escaped from her stiff hairdo. She screamed and he pulled her close, covering her mouth with his hand. She didn't bite, as he feared she would, and she seemed to go limp. She knew when she was caught, at least.

Shhh, he said, shut up. I'm not going to hurt you. Not if you do what I say and shut the fuck up.

6

Emily came home from her visit with Levi and almost immediately fell asleep. Too tired to make it even to her bedroom, she pressed her body into the seam of the couch, her knees drawn up against her stomach, her arms over her eyes to keep out the sunlight the miniblinds.

Before that first dream of driving with her mother, she hadn't remembered much of her dreams. She had become too used to sleep uninteruppted by anxiety, sleep that was just sleep—a complete shut-down of the body with pleasant or puzzling or harmless images flitting through only to be forgotten upon waking. She had attributed it to peace of mind, but she wondered now if it were simply another symptom of her growing boredom; even her unconscious had been too numb to make up something interesting.

Now, she could feel herself entering the dream and could also feel her bare knee pressed against a hard plank of wood that made the couch backing. She tried to wake herself, but it didn't work. She could feel both the low sun slanting on her shoulder and the cool air on her face; she was in the car again with her mother.

She was herself, not a child, but an adult, all of the small scars and wrinkles in her hands, the subtle feeling of bra straps sinking into her skin.

Thank god I'm old enough to fight her, she thought, and felt upset with herself for being so petty. Here her mother was, alive again, and she was already gathering her weapons.

Emily said nothing. She didn't even look over at the passenger seat where she knew that her mother was seated (she knew as you know things in dreams—with absolute certainty and the ability to hold impossibilities in your head).

Look at her, her mind said, the mind that was curled on the couch asleep, vaguely feeling the world outside that pressed against her body. The mind in her dream, though, looked out at the road before them, a wide, featureless highways, the same boxy gas stations and convenience stores passing by over and over again. They could be anywhere.

You shouldn't be mad at me, Connie said.

Emily turned to look at her mother, who was now the age she'd been at her death: fifties, her hair in patches from the chemotherapy, cheeks sunken, her mouth cracked and dry. She held a cigarette in one hand and had the other on the steering wheel.

What?

You shouldn't be mad at me. It's your pickle.

Emily imagined an actual pickle, a sour, green thing suspended in vinegar.

It is your fault, the way you feel right now, Connie said. You're not taking responsibility.

You always say things like that, Emily said. You always put it back on me.

Her mother took her hand from the wheel and wagged it at

Emily. Avoid words like *never*, like *always*. Don't you remember all those books you read about communication? You tried to get me to read them. Maybe I did read them. It's not liked you'd know the difference anyway. You thought the worst of me. She turned back to the road, which was so straight that she scarcely had to steer.

You assume so much about me, Connie says, about why I did what I did. She threw the cigarette out the window and closed it, making the air still and filling the car with the smell of mint, a smell that Emily associated with her hospital room and the candies that filled a bowl by her bed, god only knows why: a gift from somebody, probably, since Connie couldn't eat through her mouth by then, just through a tube. The candies had staled and filled the room with their aggressive perfume.

I can only assume, Emily said. You don't tell me anything.

Connie shrugged.

It's strange how like our real conversations these dreams are, the waking Emily thought as her sleeping self started to feel that familiar irritation rise up from her stomach, one she hadn't felt since her mother died.

Her mother took her hands from the wheel, turned, and took the dream Emily's shoulders and shook her, hard, until the waking Emily was gone and couldn't comment anymore.

Listen, she said, her teeth yellow, her breath sickly, her hands bony and dry, catching the fabric of Emily's shirt. If you want to know, just ask.

Ask who?

Ask everyone who might know. Just ask. Stir the pot. Make the graves come up. Drag the bones out of the trash. Do what you need to. Stop blaming me and do something.

The car continued to travel down the straight road, though Connie no longer had her hands on the wheel. She started another cigarette and leaned the seat back, napping. Emily turned on the radio, looking for a classic country station. She wanted to hear Patsy Cline's *Crazy Arms*, but all she could find was Willie Nelson singing about the things he should have said and done and Hank Williams crying that he hadn't had any kissing or loving or hugging for a long, long time.

Emily woke feeling dirty, her face sticky from the press of her arms against her cheek, her hair matted against her head, her whole body hot in the sunlight and the itchy polyester of the couch.

She tried not to think of how her mother had been in those last months. Emily had not visited as frequently as she would've liked, not until the end, but still, she had too many memories of Connie's decline, of her scalp showing through the thin hair and her anger at her body and her final inability to even be angry anymore, which had frightened Emily more than anything: anger was the current that ran through her mother's personality. Anger made Connie go right back into the elementary school when Emily was in fifth grade and had come home with a bruised eye and demand that the teachers find out who had done this to her little girl. Anger made her lock a sixteen-year-old Emily outside during a January winter when she had broken curfew. Anger made her move from town to town, job to job, unsatisfied with herself and the people who she said stood in the way of her happiness.

When the anger was gone, there didn't seem to be anything left. She asked for the television turned on and her pills and her juice and she could hardly keep her eyes open when Emily was in the room and instead dozed fitfully.

She had not died like people on television or in movies, people who suddenly became oracles or started to live their lives to the fullest just as life was being permanently taken from them. She didn't exhort Emily to do something that would make her happy. She didn't make proclamations of her love. She died as bitterly as she had lived in her last years, seeing this as nothing but more bad luck.

Maybe, in those last moments, when only the nurse was there, she'd made a reversal, had wished to give some message to her only daughter. But it was too late, by then. She hadn't earned a loving daughter to sit by her side and so the moment had been lost, if it had existed at all.

So, Emily didn't think of that time if she could help it. There wasn't much of a reason, there were so few reminders: no family, few pictures. For years, she'd practiced forgetting. She'd made her mother's death a numb space in her head: she imagined it as a spot on her brain that she could press her fingers and nails into and get no reaction at all.

The dream had brought it back—how slow her illness seemed (and how often Emily had wished it could finally be over), and then how quick it seemed when she was finally gone, having dreamed her way into a coma during the night and then dead the next, slipping out of the world as tracelessly as she had left towns and rental houses and post office boxes and people who had disappointed her.

•

Emily let her shower water heat up until it was almost unbearable and stepped under the spray until she couldn't stand it and let the cold back in. She scrubbed her hair hard with the pads of her fingers as her mother had when she was a child and had gotten sticky and dirty from playing outside all day in the summer. She stood under the shower for fifteen minutes, washing the sweat from her hair and skin, letting the thoughts of her mother go.

She rubbed away a circle of fog from the mirror. She saw her own face, red and puffy, bearing the same creases from nose to mouth, the same slightly dented chin, the same hair that naturally split in a perfectly middle part, as her mother's had.

When her mother was thirty, she'd had a six-year-old daughter. She had been alone in West Virginia, learning how to cut hair during the day and waiting tables at night after Emily went to sleep. By all accounts, Connie had, at the very least, a real life: a child, a job, and, always, the thought that soon, when she got the money or time or found exactly the right thing, she would finally be who she was supposed to be.

I don't have that, Emily thought. I'm not real. Emily had nothing to anchor her in any place, nobody to be responsible for, no reason for waking up and nowhere to go when she did wake up. Connie at least had that. She had something to care for aside from herself. She couldn't just drift. She had to establish herself quickly, find a place to live, shoes, a place for her child to go to school. And she always had.

This is going to be our year, Connie would say, just after they moved in to a new home or she started a new project, forgetting that each time she'd said this before, she'd been wrong.

Maybe, Emily thought, she would have been suited to my life better than I am. She wanted to be untethered. She would have used her time for something useful—she could have perfected something, become an expert, like she always wanted to be. She could easily imagine her mother as an artist, a scientist, a writer—somebody who did something solitary for hours at a time, enjoying every precious moment of absolute silence.

Emily thought of all of the projects she had dropped when they became too difficult, all of the books she'd quit reading halfway through. Connie, though, would have flourished with the time and solitude that Emily had squandered, most nights watching reality television on the small screen of her laptop.

Emily imagined her mother as a thirteen-year-old, so frightened of something that she could not, or would not, tell where she had been or what had happened to her for three days. This seemed like her, the more Emily thought of it. She was not the kind of person to tell, to let other people in. She prided herself in being able to take care of her own business. Maybe she had always been like that, always with a spine so stiff that it made it almost impossible for her to bend.

Emily tried to remember herself as a child. She remembered eating ice cream on various front steps, the feeling of being pushed from behind on a swing, the feeling of her stomach sinking when the bus pulled up, full of kids she didn't know that she'd have to figure out exactly how to sit with. Had she always been this shapeless, spineless thing?

Emily looked at herself, at her no-longer-young face, never beautiful. What else did she have to do with this squandered life? She would agree to dig up the graves, as her mother had told her. She would stir things up. She would not leave.

7

Connie didn't speak or kick or scream. She knew it was pointless, all for show, and that it might get her hurt worse than she might already be hurt. She let James lead her back to the group of men who still stood around the still-unopened cash register, most of them now smoking cigarettes. They were afraid. When James came back, they looked from her to James then back down at the ground. They wanted to speak, she could tell, but something had terrified them. Could it possibly be James, this wiry, skinny boy? He held her tightly and she could feel the bruises forming on her arms. Shit, one said, throwing his cigarette down and crushing it under his heel. What are we gonna do with her, Jimmy?

James' voice was close to her ear. She felt his breath, which was smoky and smelled of liquor.

You let me worry about that. He jerked his head down toward the dented cash register. I'll take the register and I'll take the girl. You all didn't see anything, okay? John, you left as usual, locked up tight. You didn't notice anything strange.

John nodded.

The rest of you were somewhere else—fishing, like you told your mothers or your girlfriends or whoever you explain yourselves to.

And her? The one who had asked first, the one who would meet her eyes, he pointed to her without looking in her direction. What are you going to do with her?

James pressed her arm hard, pulling her towards him.

She won't be hurt, he said, though that's not what had been asked, Connie noticed, and she knew that he had it in his power to hurt her. Nobody knew where she was—she was supposed to be at school, doing an after-school activity for the yearbook, that's what she'd told her parents. Only Billy knew she was supposed to be somewhere else. He was waiting for her and probably thought she was just late, dawdling. And soon he would leave, thinking she had chickened out and didn't really care for him. He probably wouldn't tell, if asked, where he'd been and where she would be, out of embarrassment.

It was supposed to be their first official date.

She won't be hurt if she does what I say, James said, pressing his fingerpads into the sore spots on her arm again.

8

Emily unfolded the newspaper and saw Rodriguez on the front page, his school picture featuring a smiling, shaven, professional man, hairline slightly receding, looking nothing like the man that would later be found with a dead teenager thrown from his car.

Local Man's Death Ends Tragic Story

Charles Rodriguez, 39, a former teacher at Heartshorne High School and suspect in the death of Jenny Willis, was found dead on the shore of Lake Echo. The cause of death was drowning.

Emily skimmed the article. He'd left a suicide note in his house saying he was sorry, admitting that he had killed the girl because she refused to sleep with him anymore, that he had given in to the devil and knew that he was completely responsible for her death and his own.

Emily set the paper down and looked out the small kitchen window that pointed out into the woods that stretched all the way to the lake. She squinted, the green gathering into a mass in her eyesight, and then opened her eyes, letting the leaves and trees separate out again into individual trunks. It seemed so strange that something as serious as a person dying could have happened so close by. She wondered if he had passed her house on his way, if he had seen the light from her windows through the woods.

Jonathan had called the night before and left a message while

Emily outside in the backyard, drinking cheap wine in the dark. She had heard, faintly, the telephone ringing in the house, but there was nobody she had wanted to speak to that night, especially not Jonathan. After a few glasses of wine, she wasn't good on the phone. She took every silence as an affront when she was drunk. Instead of answering the phone, she had sat in the dark, staring into the inky forest until she could no longer tell the leaves from the gaps between them.

She listened to the message that morning, after folding the paper and pouring out the cold coffee into the drain.

I want to speak with you again, he said. I had a good time. I'd like to do it again. Like I said, it's my treat.

By the time she listened to the message, she'd already decided not to call back right away. She was too tired to make herself sound as happy and untroubled as she wanted to sound.

Her thoughts were filled with Mr. Rodriguez and his supposed suicide.

She could almost see the scene, not as the paper told it, but as it had really happened, based on what she knew now about how things worked around here. Maybe he, like James Blackshaw, had been killed. Somebody might have drove up to his house at night and knocked lightly on the door, as any neighbor would. When he came to the door, somebody had covered his mouth with their hand and drug him to the truck. Or maybe they'd done it right there in the house—filled a bathtub with water and held his head under him under until he wasn't kicking anymore. Then, maybe they'd thrown his body in the back of the truck and drove to Echo

Lake, to one of the little enclaves you had to park and go through a small trail to get to, a place where teenagers went to skinny-dip and smoke pot.

She closed her eyes. She wouldn't think of that now. She wouldn't let herself make a story out of it, as her mind liked to do.

She would make things right tomorrow. Tomorrow, she would look for a job. She would call Jonathan back and explain that she hadn't called because she'd been afraid, that she wasn't used to another body in the bed and in the house, wasn't used to having more than one bowl and cup of coffee out at the same time, and however he took that, it would be okay.

And she would talk to Colleen.

The Collinses were always wild, she'd said.

Emily would find out how wild.

9

Men who worked on the county roads and at the logging camps, who had to leave home before the sun came more than a sliver over the horizon, gathered in groups in the early morning to drink coffee at the card tables and fold-up chairs in the back of Jimmy's store. They spoke about Rodriguez's death. They agreed that it wasn't much of a loss.

He had it coming, one said. His wife can hold her head up now. That little girl's family can rest.

I hear the note misspelled words everywhere, one said. You

191

think the geniuses up in Keno will notice something funny about a teacher hardly able to spell? He didn't even spell his own fucking name right, I heard. Some of the men laughed, men drinking weak coffee, the first coffee from the pot at Jimmy's Store and therefore always the worst. The girl who worked there, seventeen and liable to run home at any time to see her baby, her breasts hurting and needing to release their milk, couldn't make a decent cup of coffee to save her life.

The geniuses up at Keno probably will never see that note, one said, and a few nodded, though some simply kept their mouths shut or chose that moment to walk out and get some air before they headed out to work.

At the school, kids passed notes about what they had heard from their parents.

Daddy said he had it coming.

They shut the door and told me to go to bed but I stood at the crack and listened through the door. They talked about holding him down while he kicked and how he kicked one right in the teeth and his tooth is all bloodied and empty.

And life went by as usual. The general store sold lighters and flour and the bait shop sold nightcrawlers in buckets and Tony Soltz sold weed after school in the driveway of his parent's house. Rodriguez's wife went to the funeral along with a handful of close relatives and almost immediately put her house up for sale, packed up, and left.

And the lake breathed and heaved against its shores, gently pushing its edges outward.

Jonathan, she said, and she was almost embarrased at how relieved she sounded, how relieved her body felt after she said his name—she felt as though she had lost a weight from her stomach, a weight that she hadn't known was there until she felt it lifting.

Emily pulled the telephone down to the floor and sat with the cradle in her lap like a cat.

I'm sorry I didn't call sooner, she said. It was too much for a while there. My mother, what happened with her, and then you were so kind. I thought maybe you'd start to hate me for being so fucked up right from the beginning. Usually it takes a little time before I let somebody see all of that.

She heard him breathing. He was probably in his apartment or at the shop, closing it up, counting the register before putting the money in a soft brown bag to deposit in the bank.

Are you still there? She asked.

Yes. He cleared his throat and the sound made her think of the fine line of his throat when he swallowed or leaned back.

You aren't fucked up at all, he said. You'd be surprised how fucked up I can be, too.

He cleared his throat. But listen, I can't spend all my time telling you how much you don't annoy me. That gets tiresome, you know?

I know, she said. And I'm sorry.

He laughed. You did it again.

I'm trying, she said.

How about we get you out of the house? He said. I'll take you somewhere with wine worth drinking.

She pulled the phone away from her ear to wipe under her eyes. She wasn't sad now. Crying was such a stupid habit, this leaking at any upheaval of happiness or sadness or anger.

I'll take you to a place where we can sit on a patio and watch the sun fall down over some body of water—a lake, it would have to be, but not Echo lake, we'll get you away from it.

She laughed. That sounds perfect, she said. I would love to. But can we do one thing first?

She tried to see him holding the telephone, the exact placement of his hands around the receiver, the way his body leaned into whatever he was doing. She had read, and imagined it was true, that you began to hate the things about a person that you had first loved, those things that marked them as separate and not you and therefore something worth being near. Maybe she would someday hate his point-perfect attention, the way he leaned into her words and her movements toward him. But she didn't hate it yet and tried, for once, not to anticipate everything falling apart.

I'd like you to give me another Tarot reading.

11

James brought Connie to his trailer-house out by Echo Lake. They took the back way, skirting the forest behind the general store until the reached the dark, pine-heavy area at the west end of the lake. His trailer was there in those gnat and mosquito-infested woods. Connie felt them flying around her face, catching in her nose and one in her mouth, a tiny, struggling thing.

Connie didn't struggle, afraid that if she ran again, he would catch her and hurt her. Going with him, his hand around her elbow, she wasn't as afraid as she should be. Her skin was tender where he had held it and where he pulled her, but she wasn't afraid. She didn't believe that he would hurt her, not now. There were too many witnesses who knew where he was going, for one thing, and if he wanted to hurt her, he could have done it already?

She watched the back of his head, the precise place where his haircut came to a point at the back of his neck—it must have been freshly cut, as little pinpricks of black hair pepper below the hairline. She could smell him—cigarettes and hair oil and sweat and dirt.

She wondered what he was planning to do to her.

His trailer was filthy—not just messy, as the inside of her family's house often was, but downright filthy. The tables were covered in dirty plates with caked-on streaks of food, opened cans with the lids pryed up and fluted edges exposed, and cups with the hardened sludge of coffee at the bottom.

In the sink, pots and pans were piled and a dried dishrag was curled on the counter, also littered with food and cans, but also with batteries, a coil of fishing line, and a torn dog collar.

He pushed her forward and let go—she slammed into the couch and sat down hard on a pile of newspapers. He shut the door behind him and turned to her. What am I going to do with you?

He wasn't handsome like Billy, not with that black hair, his bony body, the bad skin, but there was something about him that made her skin pinprick under his gaze.

Maybe he likes me, she thought, and felt stupid for the thought. He'd kidnapped her. He wasn't a good guy. It didn't have to matter if he liked her or not. She looked around the room—maybe there was a way out. A large window or a back door, probably near the bedroom.

He leaned in the doorway, his thin shoulders wide, his face shadowed and craggy. His black hair fell into his eyes and he pushed it away.

My parents are going to wonder where I am, she said. I have people expecting me.

Good—let them wonder and expect.

He looked at her for a while longer until she had to make him stop.

Can I at least clean up in here? She asked. It's a pigstye.

He laughed. Sure. Do what you need to. Make yourself at home—you'll be here for a while. And don't even try to leave. It'll be worse for you if you do.

He sat down as the girl made a racket stacking pots and pans on the floor, filling the sink, and scraping plates into the trash. At least she was occupied.

What would he do with her? It had been a stupid idea, he knew that now and wished he'd just let her go. But he'd gotten scared and thought of prison, and when he thought of prison he flew off in all directions, not knowing where he was going until something stopped him. He'd had a dog as a child, a dog he'd called Goldy or

Brownie or some name like a color. When the dog saw a gun, it would go crazy—it would go in circles and whine, its head close to the ground. He was like that dog, made so stupid at the thought of prison that he couldn't think and ended up doing idiot things like this that could really land him in prison. Kidnapping. Jesus Christ.

Of course, this wasn't much worse than what he had already done in robbing the general store.

That was different, though. The Richardsons were in on it, and that meant that he'd get away with it. All he needed was enough money to get him out of town, get him an apartment in Keno and a job, and he wouldn't have to do stupid shit like this anymore.

But the girl, what would he do with her?

She lifted a soapy knife from the sink, long and serrated. He watched her wash it carefully, run it under the tap, and place it in the drainer blade-down, as his mother had taught him to do, to keep anyone from getting cut on accident.

The answer to his problem came easily. He hardly had to plan anything, didn't have to play it cool or lead her on like he thought he would. Connie wasn't the tough girl she'd seemed to be in the woods with all of her kicking and shouting and talk. In the end, she was like all the other high school girls he'd managed to get into his trailer, though younger—he wished it wasn't like that, but it was what it was.

He watched her as she cleaned the kitchen. She seemed restless, probably afraid to sit down, afraid what he'd do next. Did she think he was some kind of sex pervert? That he'd jump on her as soon as she stood still?

She was a pretty girl. He couldn't help but notice it.

After she wiped her hands on the one clean dishtowel he had, which was really a torn piece of a tattered bath towel, and looked around the room for something else to do, he motioned to her.

Come sit down here and let me tell you why I made you come here.

Connie wasn't usually trusting, but she liked something about James. He made her think of her uncles, men who were quiet with their affections but would surprise her sometime with an impromptu hug or gentle hair tug. Washing the dishes had calmed her; she wasn't afraid anymore. If he were going to kill her or do something serious, then he would have done so already. She was wary, but not afraid.

She sat by him on the sofa, keeping at least a foot of space between them.

I'm sorry I had to do this to you, he said. He looked down at his hands, which he laced and unlaced. He didn't meet her eye but stared down like an embarrassed child who could not meet the eye of a parent who had caught them in a lie. He glanced up at her and then moved his eyes quickly back down: she was watching, her eyes wide.

I was afraid of what you might say. I've been in jail before. You can't imagine what it's like there. I got beat up almost everyday. By the cops. By other guys. I got this scar. He pointed to a thin white line from the underside of his chin up to his earlobe. It was true—he had gotten this scar in prison. He'd gotten it from a guard, who had forced his face into the floor of his cell while he was fighting with another inmate over something. He couldn't remember what—prison was like that, full of petty arguments that mattered in that small, confined place but outside it dissolved like so much smoke.

She didn't say anything, but her face softened. Her mouth relaxed.

I was afraid you'd tell, he said. The sheriff, that fucker, has it in for me. I'd be back there for longer this time. I couldn't let that happen.

I wouldn't tattle on nobody, she said. You didn't need to say nothing.

He shook his head. I couldn't know that until I knew you better. Now I do, and I know that's true.

She nodded. He spoke to her as though she was an adult, and though the bruises on her arm still hurt, she felt sorry for him. He wasn't that different from anyone else.

12

Colleen lived in a double-wide almost hidden by the trees and bushes around it. The siding was streaked and dirty and branches pressed against the walls, blocking light from the windows. There was no yard, really, but a place where the road wasn't and the driveway wasn't. A peeling sticker on screen door said *No Solicitations.* Before the door, a dreamcatcher, leather-wrapped and intricate, swung lightly. Emily reached up and touched the feathers that hung from it.

When Emily knocked, Colleen came to the door, saw Emily, and nodded.

Come inside.

The air in the house was hot and still, the windows shut, but no air conditioner going. Though an overhead light was on, Emily could barely make out the outlines of photographs on the walls and furniture. A dusty glass globe covered the bulb, eating away at the light. The couch, covered with a crocheted blanket, lay like a sleeping animal, shapeless and hot. Inside, another dreamcatcher hung, this one with a chunk of jet woven in the web.

Colleen told her to sit on the couch, and Emily felt itchy even before the fabric touched her skin. Colleen left and Emily heard the sounds of water beating against metal. She'd put a kettle on.

She came back and sat down on the couch next to Emily.

These dreamcatchers are beautiful, Emily said.

Colleen looked up. These are real ones, she said. Not that crap over at the store in Keno. My momma was half Chippewa. She gave us these before she died. I change the feathers.

Emily nodded. I didn't know you would believe in things like this. Like dreamcatchers, Emily said.

Why not?

Because of Pastor Richardson. All that witchcraft stuff he was saying.

Ha. Pastor Richardson doesn't know everything.

Emily nodded.

I knew you'd come over here eventually, Colleen said, mercifully cutting Emily's attempts at small talk short.

What do you mean?

You want to ask me the details. I figured you'd find out what happened eventually, or at least the paper's version of it, if you didn't know it already, Colleen said. Do you know already? About what happened to your mother?

She went missing. I know that much. I found that in the papers.

Missing. Not sure that's what I'd call it.

That's all I know. Emily kept her lips tight. Colleen was almost smiling, pleased with herself. Emily told herself not to get offended, not to be upset. She needed what Colleen knew.

The papers said she was missing for two days. That she didn't remember anything that happened. That's all I know, Emily said.

Colleen shook her head. Things weren't the same then. The papers didn't say everything. You had to be careful.

The kettle screamed from the kitchen. Colleen went to the kitchen and came back with a cup of black tea in a cracked mug, the tag hanging from a string down the edge of the cup. She'd filled the tea with milk, which dulled it to the color of hospital walls.

So, Emily asked, do you know what happened to her, what happened really?

I only know what Frannie told me all those years ago, Colleen said. And you couldn't trust Frannie to say things outright. You had to read between the lines

Colleen looked at Emily. No offense to your people, she said, but with Frannie, you never knew where she stood.

13

He had only to listen to her, to offer, and she took, and she was soon leaning toward him, laughing, every last bit of tension released from her body. She liked to drink hard liquor already, something rare with girls her age. She took her whisky straight from a paper cup and only sqeezed her eyes shut hard as it went down and made a sucking sound between her teeth. He couldn't help but be impressed.

My mom drinks it, she said. I've been sneaking it for years. It helps me sleep. Helps me stop thinking.

She told him about school and the girls she didn't like and how her parents made her wash dishes when she came home every night and how her parents and brothers and sisters were nothing like her.

They don't care what they do, you know? They don't care about anything, she told him. They wake up, they clean and cook or go to school, they come home, they drink or play cards, then they go to sleep and do it all over again. It makes me sad to see them. I don't mean sad like I cry. I mean that it makes me wonder why they bother at all.

At this point, she was drunk, and James watched her speak without interrupting. She was a sweet kid—loud, full of those petty concerns that girls had (boyfriends, parents not understanding, all of that), but there was something James liked about her. He wished he could trust her, that he could just let her go right now and not do what he had to. She was changeable, her moods going from beaming to dark as she spoke about her mother and lowered her eyebrows and made the surface of her face small. As she talked, and as he gave her more sips of whiskey, a little at the time so she wouldn't fall asleep or throw up or grow suspicious, he grew more unsure of what he was about to do. But it didn't matter, he told himself, as he watched her bow mouth moving. He had to do it. It wasn't like he was going to kill her or anything. It was nothing she wouldn't get over. Part of him wanted to, of course. She was pretty, well developed for a girl her age, nobody he would kick out of bed anyway. The more he drank, the more he both admired her and wanted her and wished he didn't have to do what he was about to do.

You're lucky you're not in school anymore, she said. And you're lucky you're not a girl.

Oh yeah? Why's that?

Because girls are mean to other girls, not like boys. Some girls say I'm a slut, that I sleep with people. But I don't. She looked at him intensely, her eyebrows draw together. I've never done that before.

He nodded, pouring her more whiskey so he'd have an excuse to look away.

He handed her the cup. She smiled.

Later, after he had told her more about prison (true, but exaggerated) and about his own childhood in Heartshorne (mostly true, if edited — not to exaggerate, but to minimize), he said it was late. She should come to the bedroom and go to sleep.

I can't, she said. He had taken her hand and she'd let him, but she pulled away when he said bedroom. I'll sleep out here.

You can't sleep out here, he said, touching her hand again. You take the bedroom.

Once she got there, it wasn't difficult. She was already red-faced, nervous. He kisssed her and he felt her buckle. It was almost audible, like a piece of board breaking. She required only slightly more petting, more talk.

Afterwards, she cried and said she was sorry, she didn't do this kind of thing usually, it's only that she was so tired. He comforted her until she fell asleep, and when she did, he left the bed and went to the kitchen.

The light of the refrigerator lit up his body in the dark kitchen—he hadn't bothered to dress. A strand of Connie's hair was stuck to his inner arm. He picked it off and let it drift to the floor. He took out a beer and sat on the couch.

You're a bastard, he told himself aloud. You should go to prison. She's young—too young, almost a child.

He finished his beer and took another and finished it. He drank until he was ready to sleep and could feel nothing but warmth and the pleasant, dragging numbness of the beer.

He was a bastard, but he'd survive, and he wouldn't go to prison again. That was what mattered.

She woke alone in the bed in only her underclothes. Her head hurt—it felt as though her skull had shrunk and could no longer hold what was inside it. She ached between her legs and the muscles of her inner things had been stretched. She ached everywhere.

She hoped that he had left, that she wouldn't have to see him, but she soon heard him rustling in the kitchen. She pressed her face into the pillow.

It was right that she hurt and was sick. She should be. What would Billy think? She had practically climbed into bed with him.

He'd been so kind. She couldn't remember exactly how it had happened. First they were talking, he was giving her only small amounts of alcohol, very small, and then she'd been in the bed, rolling around. He'd ripped one of the buttons off of her shirt in haste and she had laughed. What if I'm pregnant? She imagined herself showing up at school each day, her stomach growing gradually too big for her clothes, everyone speaking about her behind her back. But that wouldn't happen—her mother would pull her out of school and keep her home until the baby was born. Then no more school. She'd work at the laundromat like Kelly Sigler, a woman who had just turned 18 and had a four-year-old daughter. She looked older than her age, pinched and miserable, dragging her dirty child around the laundromat as she collected the coins from the traps and peeled the lint from the dryers.

Connie pressed her face into the pillow harder, until her nose hurt. Maybe she'd be run out of town like James' other girl. Everybody would know. Billy wouldn't want her. Nobody would.

She had only James now, this man she barely knew who she'd seen trying to rob a store, who'd been in prison.What would Momma think when she took him home?

She imagined, the whole time, that at least she'd have him. He would see the seriousness of the situation. And he must like her.

Otherwise, he wouldn't have sat up all night with her, he wouldn't have treated her so kindly, would he?

If all he'd wanted was sex then he would have just taken it. He could've done it at any time.

She dressed and walked into the hallway. James stood at the stove making coffee. He was shirtless and barefoot, his hair disheveled. Connie had dressed neatly and smoothed down her hair, the appearance of respectability important to her now. It occurred to her in a small, funny flash that she finally understood the song *Will you still love me tomorrow?* It was a good question. She pulled her skirt down, buttoned her blouse up as well as she could with the missing button, but she could not stop feeling naked. She stood in the hallway for a few minutes, leaning against the wall, which buckled slightly under her weight. She didn't know what to say. She hoped that he would say something first, invite her over for some coffee. He said nothing. He kept his back to her until she walked into the kitchen and stood by him.

He didn't turn. She felt the room go hot, her palms sticky, her stomach tightened as if preparing for a physical blow. She opened and closed her fingers. He was ignoring her.

What am I going to do? She asked aloud. I mean, she said, feeling already how stupid her questions were, but unable to stop herself from asking them, what do you want me to do now? She spoke to his back, close to tears now. What did she even mean to say?

He turned, his face composed, not angry and not happy.

I imagine you should go now, he said. Your family is probably waiting for you.

Connie's face crumpled like a child's, and James had the urge to tell her that he was only joking, she could stay, she could live with him. But that was foolish. He let the urge go and instead busied himself by screwing the lid to the coffee back on the wide-mouthed jar, turning from her as her face contracted and reddened. It was easier not to see her upset.

She was young and she'd survive, he told himself.

I mean it, he said. You'll be fine. Just forget what happened here. Forget everything you saw and everything that happened. You hear me? You can tell them whatever you want—make something up—but I'm not part of it. You never saw me. You never went here.

She looked at him. You want me to leave?

He nodded. I want you to leave. And you can't come back. Not ever. Nobody can know you were here.

She felt it bubbling up, that old anger.

She remembered what he had said the night before, the tremor in his voice, how his face went hard when he talked about it.

I'll tell what you did, she said. You're a bastard. I'll tell everyone what you did. And they'll take you to prison like they did before.

His sympathy blinked out suddenly, an old bulb popping while still in the socket. The ride to prison flashed before him. He'd been arrested four summers ago, in August. They threw him in the back of a van with metal seats, oven-hot, the smell of sweat and booze ripe on his own skin and clothes. He was literally making himself sick with his own smell as he sat in the metal chair, his arms bent uncomfortably behind him. He remembered the flat, ugly building coming toward him through the bars in the window, a place that loomed gray against the blue, cloudless sky, the shrubs and grasses dead around it from the late-summer drought.

He wouldn't go back there. And like that, he was himself again, hard and small and interested only in survival.

You tell, and I'll tell, he said. And it'll be worse for you than me, let me tell you that.

If I tell, everybody will know. It'll be all over school, how you came over here, how you got drunk and came to bed with me, practically dragged me into bed. I'll say you said you were eighteen. I'll say you lied to me and then tried to get money out of me. Drank all of my whiskey while you were at it. I bet Billy wouldn't like—

She turned away from him and threw open the front door, beating her fists against the sticky latch of the screen door until it popped and she left ran down the steps, twisting her ankle sllighty on the last step, but running anyway, despite the limp.

He didn't have to bring up Billy. She didn't even remember telling him about Billy. She'd probably said something last night, in that blur of slurry talk and kisses that she could hardly remember. The thought of Billy waiting for her by the General Store, worrying about where she was and thinking she'd abandoned him, made her flush with shame. She ran as hard as she could until the salt in her mouth and tears and mucus at the back of her throat choked her and she went down on her hands and knees and threw up.

14

Colleen smoked. Emily hadn't smelled it on her clothes before, but this was probably because her clothes carried other dominant smells—Icy Hot, peppermint, and cheap polyester yarn. Colleen smoked Swisher sweets, those skinny, brown cigars, and their smell filled the house with cherries.

She held the cigar between her fingers and leaned forward.

Frannie loved your Mother, you should know that, Colleen said. She wished she could take Connie for herself, she told me so. Your mother's parents were nothing to get excited about. They worked your mother, and all the kids, like dogs.

Emily knew those stories. Connie waking at dawn to make breakfast for her young brothers and sisters while her older brother went to work with her father, a job he'd gotten at sixteen, when Connie's father had decided he'd had all the school he needed and that it was time to contribute. It wasn't so much that Emily hadn't believed the stories as that she hadn't paid attention to them. The contours were so familiar, as were the rhythms of her mother's voice when she told the stories, that their content had largely gone ignored. They were just another set of stories her mother had told to memorialize herself, to make her life seem more beleaguered than it had been. Emily had not thought of the stories as being related to real events. They were anecdotes pointing to Colleen's victimization, a theme that Emily had already grown tired of by Middle School.

So, Colleen said, when Connie went missing, it was Frannie who made a stink about it. Your grandparents couldn't be bothered.

She went to the courthouse and insisted that Connie wasn't just off partying, that she wouldn't just up and leave like that, she was a responsible girl. Still, nothing much happened. They searched the woods around the school and found nothing. Still, even that wouldn't have happened without Frannie.

When your mother came back, Frannie was the one who nursed her back to health.

I thought she was fine when she came back. Emily said. I thought she wasn't hurt. That's what the papers said.

Colleen laughed, a short, dry sound, and blotted out her cigar. She wasn't physically hurt, but she was hurt in other ways. She couldn't talk, for one thing. She just stared, her eyes big like this. Colleen opened her eyes wide and and thrust her head toward Emily.

I didn't know your mother well—she was too young—but I went to school with Frannie and talked to her over at the store where she worked, a general store that burned down years ago over by the Free Will Baptist. She was sick when she told me about Connie. Your aunts and uncles all had their moments, and Frannie wasn't any stranger to running away. She'd made off with the youth pastor was she was sixteen, but she came back after a week, saying he was a pervert, that he'd wanted her to do things in the bedroom that she'd never even heard of. Let him tie her up and all that.

When your mother came back, I thought at first she just keeping her mouth shut because she was afraid. Girls who disappeared for days and didn't say where they were were probably in one place—out with some man, having more fun than they should. But Frannie said this was different: your momma seemed scared, as though she'd seen something she couldn't even understand. She didn't say she couldn't remember, the papers had that wrong. She said she didn't know.

Emily sipped her tea when Colleen paused, though it had grown cold and bitter. She imagined her mother as Colleen painted her, wide-eyed and too afraid to speak. It didn't seem like the woman she had known.

15

Connie knew where she was: Near the lake, and from there, she could get back to the road. She could hear it close by, the vague sound of water against rock.

Her stomach felt empty, yet filled with something heavy in the place of food. She didn't want to eat. She didn't want to think. She didn't want to go home yet. She was close to the part of the lake where the shore had washed up many tiny pebbles. The shore here hurt to walk on barefoot, so it was usually empty. She made her way toward it. She needed some cold water against her face.

She emerged from the trees and was exactly where she'd though she would—beyond the shore, on the pebbly beach where broken, black trees stood in the water, tipping and rotted but still upright and sharp enough to tear a hole in the bottom of a boat. To her left, Connie could see the bridge and the highway. She was close to home.

She crouched by the edge of the lake, cupping her hand into the surprisingly clear water. In the middle, it grew murky, a blue/brown mixture that you lost your hand in after just a few inches. Here, the water was clear like river water.

She splashed it on her face.

She didn't understand what had happened with James. He had treated her well, he had fed her whiskey, he'd listened to her. And then, the day after, he'd told her to leave. Why? So she wouldn't tell on him. So he wouldn't have to go to prison for trying to steal some rolls of quarters and dollars from the general store. As if she would tell such a silly thing anyway.

He didn't have to do it. That was what made her angry. He could have let her go. She would've been with Billy that afternoon, instead of him. She would've woken up in her own bed. She would've had something to look forward to. Now, she couldn't think of her life beyond this moment in the woods, her hands and knees dirty, her underwear sticky.

She closed her eyes, feeling the water drip from her lashes and down her cheeks, though she was well past crying now, having gotten it all out back in the woods. She was not the kind of person who enjoyed indulging in a good cry.

She wanted to go back and shout at him, hurl something heavy at him and make him feel it, but she also wanted to be far away from him, at home in bed, listening to the sounds of her mother in the kitchen slamming and yelling.

She cupped lake water in her hands, splashed it on her face and poured a handful into her mouth, though she knew she shouldn't:

her mother had warned her against dirty lake, the insects and germs inside it, the worms that went into your mouth tiny and emerged in great ropes in your guts, turning you into a skeleton with a hungry worm inside. Her stomach, empty, rumbled.

As soon as she noticed the ache in her stomach, other symptoms followed. Her skin became hectic, hot and sticky. It wasn't just the heat of having run through the woods—it was as though her skin had its own source of heat just below the surface.

Her head, too, began to fog. She forgot, for a minute, where she was, and panicked, her hands searching her empty pockets. But then she remembered, remembered everything intensely, her thoughts red-tinged and beating against her skull like physical objects. She could not control them. The memory of James pulsed in her head and she imagined her forehead bulging. She pressed her thumbs into her temples to relieve the pressure. She'd read in a history book about fossil remains of people with holes drilled in their skulls to let the devils out and wished in that moment that she had a small hand-drill to do the procedure to herself, the devils inside her were so insistent.

She did not know how long she sat there, the sickness running through her. She tasted salt in her mouth and wanted to tear off her skin, it felt so tight against her muscles and bones.

I'm sick, she thought, but the anger swept her up again in waves like fever. She bent over, her stomach rioting, and threw up a stream of amber liquid: she'd had nothing to eat for hours and nothing to drink but liquor and water. The water made me sick, she had time to think, before she felt a burst of energy in the form of heat prickling at her arms and face. She stood up, shaking her head, tearing at her arms with her fingernails to relieve the itching.

She had to go back to James. She had to show him what he had done to her. But what had he done? The question clattered in her head and dissolved. There wasn't room to ask why she had to go back or why her head felt as though she had stuffed it with cotton or why her skin prickled and went from goosebumps to slick to itch or why it felt as though every hair on her body was standing on end. She felt the urge to move back toward James' house as well as the urge to stand still and vomit as well as the urge to roll on the ground and put out the fire that seemed to pour from her skin.

Just go back. Show him.

Another voice, smaller and more basic, a sound that seemed to come from the base of her skull, said *go back and show him and tear him apart.*

She began to run. It felt good to run. It calmed the sickness in her stomach and gave the heat direction. She was close to the small clearing, where she could just see the edge of his trailer-house through the trees. She moved through the woods now as an animal did, through any impediments instead of around them, jumping over fallen logs and running straight through branches, the sharp sticks and thorns tearing at her face and chest and bare arms and legs. But her body did not have the animal agility it needed to keep going like this through a dense forest littered with fallen trees and branches. Her foot caught in a bundle of exposed roots and she toppled over. She had enough time to turn her face away from the rock she knew she would hit and shielded her temples with her hands.

The rock glanced the back of her head, hard enough to make an egg-sized bruise. She didn't feel in pain in that moment, but instead a great desire to sleep. Her stomach settled and her skin cooled. She closed her eyes. The anger dissolved away.

16

Colleen sipped her tea and made a face at the bitterness.

I don't much like this stuff, she said, but I read it's good for you. Fights cancer and all that.

Colleen set the mug down on the end table, a bare, chipped thing decorated only with a bone-colored cordless telephone, fingerprints smudged around the receiver, and a photograph of a young girl, maybe eight or nine, in a cheap frame, the layer of fake gold covering the frame peeling away.

Here is everything I know, Colleen said. Frannie told me after your mother had been back for a few days, after she'd kept her mouth shut for so long everyone figured it was just a case of girl being afraid to make a fool of herself, Frannie told me she knew what had happened. She was the only one who Connie had told.

Emily leaned foward. What? What was it?

The old woman smiled. She probably didn't have much opportunity to tell stories, to leave somebody in suspense like this. Emily wanted to shake her. It wasn't just a story, was it? A real woman had disappeared and come back. A real person had died shortly after. A real woman had lived the majority of her life afraid, moving from trailer to trailer, from job to job, never believing she was wanted or worthy of whatever she had managed to get.

But Emily only nodded, encouraging her. Colleen didn't know everything that had passed, all of the sad, lonely rest of it. Her hands shook as she held the cup. Her eyes had the opaque glaze of cataracts. Her joy in this was small and sharp and ugly, and Emily was too tired and sad to feel much beyond pity.

It was a man, Colleen said. But it wasn't like everybody thought. Your mother hadn't run away with one. A man had forced himself on her. Had left her so scared she hadn't dared to tell anyone. Beat on her a little bit, too, that's what Frannie told me. Or so she told Frannie, eventually, after Frannie wouldn't take no for an answer.

The man who did it was James Blackshaw. The young man who was found shot, thrown in the lake, soon after. You probably saw things in the newspaper about him when you were doing your searching.

Emily set down her tea. She had a quick image of her mother, the first time Emily went out on a date, telling her to be careful, pressing a long cylinder of pepper spray into her hands. Connie had been shaking, then. Emily had taken it as more proof of her paranoia, her inability to trust that kept her away from any semblance of a normal life, but it had been something more. Emily wished then that she could go back and respond with more empathy then she had when she was sixteen. Then, she'd only rolled her eyes and walked away.

But what does this mean? Emily asked. What's the connection? Are you saying my mother killed somebody?

Colleen shook her head. That girl was hardly in a state to go to school for weeks, let alone kill somebody. She didn't have to do it herself, of course. She had family looking after her. Colleen leaned into the sofa's back. It was a too-soft, enveloping kind of sofa that made Emily feel as though she were sinking down into the fabric when she leaned back.

Back then, people took care of each other, Colleen said. We didn't need to get the police involved, bring them in just to the let the son-of-a-bitch who done it go free because of no evidence or because he's kin or a good friend of the sheriff. Nowadays, you aren't allowed to take care of your own business anymore.

So you're saying my family did this—Fran, my grandparents, somebody in the family?

Colleen shrugged. Honey, there's no telling who did it exactly. It didn't work like that, just one person walking up to someone and putting a bullet in their useless head. Families had their friends in town. Families stuck with their own kin, people who understood what needed to be done and how to do it. All I know's that once Frannie knew the man and the story, it was only a matter of time before that boy either disappeared or turned up dead.

In her day, Frannie was a force, Colleen said, her eyes glittering. You couldn't just push Frannie around. She got things done. Colleen nodded, smiling. You couldn't get anything past Frannie.

17

Connie woke with her left cheek pressed into the ground. Her ankle burned and felt swollen. Her arms and throat stung from scratches.

She remained on the ground for a few moments, unsure exactly where she was. She didn't want to rise while that fever still had her, made her run back to a place she didn't want to go and do—what?—something that would splatter her with blood. The word *blood* echoed in her head and she felt the last prickles of the fever flare and die. It had wanted her to kill James, to take out her anger on his body.

It had wanted her. What was *it*? Her head felt swollen and slow. She gritted her teeth and tried to determine where she was and how she had gotten there.

But the feeling, that burning violence, was gone now. Her stomach felt bruised, as it did after hours of vomiting. She placed her palms on the ground and lifted herself up to her knees, then stood upright.

She heard, in the distance, the sound of men talking, their boots crashing.

They're looking for me, she thought, but she didn't want to be found yet. She was still in a fog. The thought occured to her, as though whispered by somebody else; *you aren't ready to see people yet.*

She made her way back toward the lake, though she remained in the woods, skirting the sound of sloshing water. She followed it until she reached the road.

A rare police officer out on the highway picked her up by the general store as she tried to stumble home, the hunger and thirst slowing her, her cuts stinging, her head throbbing from pain and heat. It didn't occur to her to stop at anyone's house, to say where she had been and what had happened. She only wanted to go home, a place that she usually wanted to be as far away from as possible.

The police officer recognized her from the flyers in the post office and urged her into the car, where she lay in the backseat, her knees pressed against her stomach.

When her parents held her, hugged her hard, her mother crying (had she seen her crying before? The woman's face was usually as immobile and dissatisfied as a frown cut into rock), her father, even, choking on the sounds of her name, the first thing they asked was *where have you been? What happened?* Should couldn't answer. She opened her mouth, but the words wouldn't come, so she simply shut her mouth and shook her head until they stopped asking.

The more she tried to remember anything that happened after she had left James', the foggier and more fragmented it became. Had she drunk from the lake or just splashed the water on her face? Had she stripped down and swum in it? This didn't seem likely, but she had an image of herself in just her underpants, wading into the water. Why had she fallen? She had a lump at the base of her skull. She remembered the fiery feeling in her face and hands, the desire to *go* and *do* without knowing exactly why or what she'd do when she got there, but why had she woken up on the ground?

She only knew that something had taken over her body, like how the old people in the church sometimes spoke about the devil entering somebody's body if they suddenly had seizures or acted in a way that didn't become them, such as the music minister running away with an eighteen-year-old girl from the choir. It was like a devil had been in her body, emanating its heat and anger through her, replacing her own thoughts and intentions with his.

But she couldn't say that, and the words didn't seem quite right. It wasn't a devil so much as the desire of a devil, something pure and bodiless without any real direction. James had seemed almost incidental to the anger, a handy thing to hang it on, but her desire to go to him and make him bleed had been irresistible. If she hadn't fallen, she would have done it, too. So she had no words to explain what had happened and she couldn't mention James. She had nothing to tell them.

When she finally spoke, she told everyone that she had woken up in the woods, covered in scratches, and remembered nothing from school that afternoon until the moment she woke up. She pointed to the purple and green bruise, egg-like and throbbing. She didn't remember getting the bruise, she said, and she didn't remember where she'd been.

•

She stayed in bed for days. Her family insisted she lie down until the bruise on her head had faded and the cuts on her arms had healed. It was the first time she'd been encouraged to rest since a childhood bout with the chicken pox. It had the opposite effect it should have—she had nothing to do but the think of the night she'd spent with James (it had only been one night! It seemed like much more and loomed so large) and the morning after, and everthing after that, which was considerably less clear.

She sometimes caught herself thinking of what she might say if she went back to him. She might tell him what had happened to her, the anger that had boiled up and how she'd almost run back to his house to do something crazy—break a beer bottle on the porch and cut his throat, for example—and how her falling had saved them both. Would he see then how unkind he'd been then? Would he ask her to come back?

She'd replay scenes in her mind, scenes of him aplogizing, getting down on his hands and knees after wiping his hands on his jeans, asking her to marry him. He'd push the hair away from his face as he knelt down and try to tuck it back behind his ear where it would escape the moment he looked up to see her face and hear her say—

But this was stupid, Connie thought, unable to entertain such desires that she knew to be idle. He'd been fooling her. It was stupid to expect anything different and stupid to want him to want her. Did she want to live in a trailer in the woods with a guy who stole cash registers and ate straight from cans without even bothering to heat the food inside them? Whose greasy hair hung in his eyes? Who probably hadn't even graduated from high school? Why would she even bother with such a boy sober?

As she rested, she grew angrier. Instead of scenes of apologies, she imagined herself older, in possession of a husband and a job and a house away from Heartshorne, visiting the trailer by the lake where he still lived, growing older and balder as she grew more beautiful.

Look what you gave up, she'd say, making a show of wiping the bottom of her shoes on the tattered mat before his door.

Frannie was the most curious of all of her family members. She had time to visit and keep Connie company by bringing magazines and cigarettes to the cramped bedroom. She worked at a convenience store during the day and was a waitress in Keno on Saturday nights. When she came, her frizzy hair piled up in a tight bun, her cats-eye glasses flaring away from her face like wings, she'd throw open the windows.

Shit, I'm going to suffocate in here, she said, and carried her stacks of movie magazines to the bed, where they would both spend hours smoking and paging through them.

Frannie wanted to know what had happened, and she didn't believe that Connie couldn't remember. Connie's parents had been strangely silent around her, as if she were now damaged and they must be very careful not to break her completely. Connie imagined that they thought something so terrible had happened to her that she couldn't bear to tell or honestly couldn't remember. They thought she'd been raped, probably, and she had only barely missed the sheriff insisting that she be checked for rape. She insisted she had been alone. She was surprised that her mother had agreed; nobody would "poke around down there."

It was just a fainting spell, she told them. This was the new story. The doctors checked her blood, she was cleared as healthy, and they released her. She had started bleeding a couple of days later, to her relief. Maybe it could all be over if she just kept quiet and waited.

Frannie, though, wanted to know everything. What was the last thing Connie could remember? Could she really remember nothing? At first her questions had been innocent, the simple questions that everyone asked that Connie could easily avoid or evade or flat-out lie about.

She told Frannie that she remembered walking through the woods on her way home after school, then, suddenly, she woke up in the woods. That's what she'd told everyone else. But Frannie wasn't satisfied. It took her two weeks to chip away at the truth, or part of it.

She figured Connie was hiding something. God knows Frannie had hidden things from her parents when she was Connie's age, though it was truly a more innocent time then and there was less to hide that didn't become quite evident in a few months anyway. Still, Frannie had hidden things—long car rides with boys, staying in places she shouldn't, drinking when her parents thought she was studying.

She imagined that something had happened to Connie that she didn't want to tell. She'd come home with an egg on her head and scratches. Something had to have gone wrong.

She hit on something close to the truth by accident.

You know, she said casually, paging past a five-page spread of Elizabeth Taylor in pancake makeup and a black wig, you know, if a boy hurt you, you can tell me. If he did something wrong, you should let me know. I won't tell. I know how it is.

Connie had not planned to tell. Fran had suggested boys before, but she hadn't come out and said it like this. And something about the way she said it made Connie look up, surprised, and then made her eyes fill, which startled her into lowering her head into her hands. She hadn't meant to react so strongly, but once it started, she couldn't stop.

Is that it, honey? Was it a boy? Did he beat you up, is that where the bruises came from?

Connie couldn't stop crying. The days she'd been back, she'd had to lie so long. It didn't come naturally. It was a relief to stop. She would only tell a little and swear Fannie to secrecy.

He treated me so good at first, she managed to choke out, sniffling and wiping the edge of her quilt against her nose and eyes. Frannie nodded, her face hardened into the look she got when she'd decided something and had fixed that decision tightly in her mind.

Your aunt Frannie is like a mule, Connie's mother would often say. She can't be moved once she's decided something. If she hates you she hates you forever. If she decides she loves you, she'll do anything for you.

Connie would remember this later, long after Frannie had left that night and Connie realized she hadn't told the story right at all, though Frannie had nodded and patted Connie's hair and said *I know honey, I know, let it all out.* As Connie cried and said that she'd belived he cared for her, that he'd been so sweet, that she'd been so surprised when he'd been so cruel, *such an asshole,* she'd said, and Frannie had nodded vigorously, as though the word couldn't contain everything that he was.

Connie hadn't ever said, though, that she'd gone to his bedroom. She didn't explain that the scratches and bruises weren't from him. She hadn't been possessed enough to say anything coherent with Frannie there holding her head and urging her to cry and telling her that he was a jerk, that he should pay. She realized later that night that Frannie probably thought he had beaten her. Worse, that he had raped her. She ran the words over in her head later, extracting each combination of words that would Frannie to that wrong conclusion.

At first, in the days after she realized that Frannie had taken it wrong, she planned on telling Frannie the truth, that he hadn't forced her into anything, but he had been unkind. But how could she explain the bruises and the cuts?

And wasn't it better for Frannie to believe that she'd been (the word made her feel sickly, made her face redden) raped? It was best Frannie thought her a victim and not a common slut (she knew she was—girls who gave in so easy were, but she could change, she wouldn't be a slut anymore, not after this).

But still, at first, she did not imagine that Frannie would do much of anything about it. What could be done? She only hoped that Frannie would keep her mouth shut and let it all go away.

18

Colleen shrugged and sat up in her chair. She was tiring, the hard glint fading from her eyes. Soon Emily would have to leave.

So you think Frannie got the boy killed? Because he did—something—to my mother?

Colleen shrugged. She was coy again, unwilling to repeat herself. All I know is the boy ended up dead, she said. Frannie wanted him dead. I don't know what happened in between. All I know is that we used to take care of ourselves. Not like now. She shook her head.

Emily remembered Mr. Rodriguez's name in the newspaper, his suicide, and the death of the girl. Do you think the murders happening now are happening for the same reason? She asked. Somebody trying to get back at somebody else?

Colleen squeezed her eyes closed and made her mouth prune tightly. It didn't happen that way in our day, cutting people's throats in their own homes, and that girl with two children found all cut up on the shore of the lake. Colleen shook her head again. When somebody needed to be gone, they deserved it. We made sure of that. And we didn't make it something awful that a child might stumble on.

Emily felt she should say something, defend the idea of justice and sanity and civilization, in which people were entitled to a fair trial. But Colleen was an old woman, certainly, and entitled to her opinions and her prejudices. Emily's stomach churned anyway. She should have let it go, but her mouth wouldn't let her.

But does that go along with what they preach at your church? Are you allowed to just get rid of people you think are guilty?

The old woman looked at her sharply. Emily had made her disdain too clear. She felt the air change around her. She wasn't just a curious out-of-towner. She was judging, thinking herself above them all. She'd closed herself off to Colleen's help now, she could feel it.

Colleen pressed her lips together again.

Pastor Richardson is a good man, but he doesn't understand how it works sometimes. And neither do you.

Emily nodded. I didn't mean to suggest—

You think we're a bunch of idiots, down here killing each other willy-nilly, no reason at all?

Emily shook her head. No, of course not.

The old woman leaned forward. Let me tell you, when somebody here dies, it's for a reason. You think we can trust the law to do it? If we could, we'd be happy to let that happen. But they're easy to buy. They have kin, like everyone else, and they want to protect them. You can't trust them to do something when one of their own is in on it. And everybody's kin to everyone.

Except now, she said, these new ones, these young people, these women found all cut up. We don't do it like that.

In the old days, it was clean and quick and they deserved it. This isn't like the old days, she said. This is bad. And we don't know how to stop it.

19

James and the Richardson brothers had divided the money up evenly among the four of them. After all of that effort, it wasn't much, 100 dollars each, hardly enough to buy beer and pay the bills and get a new pair of boots. But it did give James of month of free time before he had to find work again. He could find work. That wasn't a problem. The problem was that the work made him want to kill himself by the end of the day. He could fill potholes in the heat, standing out amongst the fresh blacktop in a hard hat, shoving the hot goo down into the breaks in the concrete. He could haul logs. He could even be a handyman, a free laborer offering his services where they were needed to mow lawns or mend fences. It was just that those jobs made him miserable. Not miserable so much as angry. By the end of the day, he could barely stand to do anything but drink and curse the people who had hired him and stand under the shower to wash away the sweat and stink of tar or pieces of woodchips from his hair.

It seemed like such a waste of time, this going to work everyday and coming home and doing it all over again. Maybe it was worth it if you had something to come home to besides the stink of your own dirty workclothes and the dishes and the dogs whining from under the porch and the pounding in your head from last night's drinking. He had a kid somehwere, but the girl he'd knocked up wasn't the kind of girl you could settle down with. He didn't know what she'd done with the baby. She had cut herself with razors in hidden places (her ribcage, her upper thighs) and told him she had, sometimes, imagined running out into the road in front of a log truck. He wondered about the baby, but knew it was better off living with somebody else. He wasn't fit to be a husband and didn't want a wife. But it made life lonely. He didn't know what else there was to want to make life worth showing up for.

He remembered Connie storming from his house, her face all red, an angry child, almost: it made him sick to think of what he'd done to her when he thought of it. So he didn't think about it. He drank instead.

He was drinking the last of his whiskey, thinking that he should probably just go to sleep afterward (what would be the point of staying awake now?), when he heard the car pull up. He figured it was someone he knew, maybe Rick, who sometimes came over to drink and play cards or drive them both out to the bar by the highway, the one with the country band that did Hank Williams covers and a dancefloor that James was never going to get on, dancing seemed like such a pointless way to draw attention to yourself.

He set down his glass and opened the door. He didn't have a chance to see who they were—and maybe they were wearing masks, he wasn't sure, maybe just hats pushed down so they shadow fell on their faces. It was dark out anyway, and he was blinded by the glare of the headlights. He put his hand up against his eyes and said Who's— before somebody grabbed him and then another pulled his hands behind his back and bound them with handcuffs (he knew the familiar click and the heaviness of the metal on his skin). He thought it was the police until they put the stocking cap over his face and wound the tape around his throat and the fabric to keep it secured. The police didn't do that. There were laws against this kind of thing. It isn't the police, he thought at first with a surge of happiness, and then, he realized that this was even worse.

I'm going to die, he thought, already choking on the fabric that pressed against his nose and mouth. He fought the men, though they had caught him by surprise and had already bound his arms and ankles. He thrashed his head, feeling the muscles in his throat tighten and strain. He kicked with his legs tied together and wriggled in the confines. He could not hold a thought in his head. He felt his bladder close to giving. The cotton dried his mouth and he couldn't get it out without use of his hands. He imagined with each breath that he would choke, but his body kept breathing.

They put him in a truckbed. He recognized the metallic clunk his body made when he hit the bed and heard the roar of the car's motor echoing through his ears. He rolled himself over on his back. He pressed his head against the truckbed and tried to catch on the grooves to pull up the fabric over his face, but he felt a quick thrust of something solid and square to his ribs. The pain flared—his ribs were broken. He tried roll back on his other side, to curl himself in closer to his body, but the pain would let him do anything but kick his legs feebly.

Stay still, you little fucker. He wasn't alone back there. He felt his bladder give and no longer cared. He pleaded with the other person in the car, a voice he didn't recognize.

Please let me go, he said. Let me go. I didn't do nothing. I can give you money.

He didn't register what he said completely before saying it. Everybody thinks of the same silly things when they're gonna die.

The man didn't speak but jabbed an object into James' broken ribs, probably the heel of his shoe or a bat. James tried to move away and hold back the sickness, but couldn't: he vomited from the pain and choked on it, unable to escape the fluid filling his nose and mouth.

The truck stopped and the man inside it pulled him up by his bound wrists and threw him from the truckbed. He landed on his elbow and heard the crack as he felt it, a pain like heat moving liquid up to his shoulder. He screamed repeatedly, though the screaming only made the men hit him, this time in the face, though the pain registered as movement backwards, as he fell again, breaking something else.

His mind, knowing now that he was beyond what a human being can take, let his eyes close and his mind dim and his body become a faraway throbbing. He didn't felt the press of the small, metal circle at the back of his head. He certainly did not feel it go off.

20

Connie heard about his death from the newspaper, which her family usually didn't buy—what's the point, her mother would say, when you can just ask what's happening and somebody tells you for free? But the newspaper was folded neatly on the kitchen table when Connie woke up at eight AM, earlier than she had in weeks, and came downstairs fully prepared to look everyone in the face and no longer be the invalid, the girl recovering from cuts and bruises and a big hole where her memory was or whatever else had happened that she could not or would not tell.

Her mother had made oatmeal. She stood in front of the stove, stirring the mess with one of the many wooden spoons that filled the drawers. The kitchen was bright and hot already, the windows up and curtains blowing. Connie took a cup from the cabinet and put the kettle on.

Can I help, Momma? Need me to make the toast?

Her mother turned and pushed her hair away from her face and tucked it behind her ears. She'd had long, dark hair for as long as Connie could remember. It always seemed to be falling from whatever knot or twist she'd made to hold it.

She was beginning to look old. She had never seemed youthful, never beautiful or fresh, but had seemed solidly middle-aged for all of Connie's life—her breasts and hips matronly, her waist thick, her face broad and plain and unwrinkled. Now, Connie could see crow's feet around her eyes and wrinkles in rings around her throat. She was growing thinner, the chest of her dress sagging where it used to burst.

Her mother shook her head. No toast today. Your brothers used up the last of the bread last night when they came in late. You can get out the milk, though.

Connie placed the bottle on the table, the glass sweating.

Connie wanted nothing more than her old life back. This

was the first step, doing something normal and small. Her old, miserable life, the one she'd complained about so often. It seemed very small and precious now.

Her mother stood over the steaming pot, cursing under her breath when the bubbles pooped and burned her hands. She didn't seem to notice Connie in the room, didn't marvel at her return to the normal world.

So maybe it was over. Her life could resume again. She'd go back to school. People would forget.

The newspaper sat by the milk jug. Connie smoothed it out so she could see the front page. A young man's face was on the cover. The photo lacked detail. It could have been almost anyone, the picture being mostly shadow. But she knew who it was immediately—the hair as dark as the eyes, the severe line from just below the cheekbone down to the chin.

She touched the picture. Above it, the headline said *Young Man Found Dead*. It took her a moment to reconcile the picture of a man she'd known alive with the headline. It had to be him.

Her stomach dropped and her knees gave. She sat down so heavily on one of the rickety kitchen chairs that her mother turned and scolded her.

Connie, don't plop down like that. Mind the chairs or you'll be eating from the floor.

Connie nodded, not hearing. She read the story. It was sketchy and said little about the murder. That's what it was, murder—he'd been shot in the head and then thrown into the river.

A former inmate of McCallister maximum security prison, the article said, incarcerated for armed robbery, just six months out. Drifter. Estranged from his family.

Probably some trouble with drugs or alcohol, the sheriff said in the article. He was well-known as a thief and a drunk. Its a shame that such a thing should happen to someone so young, but I can't say that he'll be missed, the article reported in the sheriff's words. Connie had seen the Sheriff in the newspaper, a thin, balding man with a craggy face much like James' had been. Connie read the quotes, hoping to see some glimpse of the James that she remembered. His mother and father did not send in a comment, nothing to say that he had been a son, once, a baby, perfect in the ways that all babies are perfect. She searched for some hint that others understood that he had been a person. But she could find not a single kind word. Not a single mention of something he had done that might make him less than the black words on the page—former inmate, armed robbery, drifter, estranged.

•

Connie waited for Frannie. She'd called her that morning right after breakfast, waking her from her late sleep after the night shift. Frannie was the only one who knew about James. Frannie grew angry quickly: Connie had once seen her throw a glass jar full of pennies at her mother when Frannie was drunk and her mother had said *Frannie, why don't we make a pot of coffee for you, get you sobered up?* And Frannie knew people. She loved talking about her connections, the men and women in town who she knew who were important. She knew where to buy the purest everclear, where to go to get a new license plate for a car if you needed to ditch the old one fast, and where to get televisions for cheap.

Connie's mother had hinted that Frannie had connections beyond electronics and alcohol. She worried that Frannie was going to *get a reputation.*

Frannie arrived smoking a cigarette, her hair up in a messy bun.

Before she could speak, Connie shook the newspaper at her. Frannie set down her magazines and purse. She nodded.

You saw it, that boy's death.

Connie nodded.

So what do you think of it? Frannie squinted and began to unpin her hair.

Connie set the newspaper down. Do you know what happened?

Frannie smiled. The smile made Connie's stomach turn, and she feared she'd begin to cry if Frannie didn't say something soon that would soothe her, that would let her know that it was just a coincidence.

Now why would you think I know about something like that? Looks like the boy made somebody angry. She dropped her smile and unwound her hair, which fell in a coil down one shoulder. She began to separate it, breaking up last night's hairspray.

Looks like he was probably asking for it, she said.

Connie set the newspaper down. Her throat closed up. She

looked down intently at the pattern of her blanket, following the zigzags of stripe until she felt she could lift her eyes.

She wouldn't cry, not in front of Frannie. There wasn't any point. She'd have to explain everything if she cried—she'd have to say she wasn't raped, just treated badly, that she didn't hate James (hadn't hated him: was everything in past tense now that he was dead?), and that Frannie had gotten somebody killed for nothing.

Family was all she had now. James was gone, and she'd never had him anyway.

Looks like it, she said, when she finally looked up. A few tears slid down her cheeks, but that was all. Frannie came to the edge of her bed and sat down.

Listen, Frannie said, you don't need to feel bad about this. You didn't have anything to do with it, okay? You didn't know nothing, you didn't do nothing, and you don't know nothing now, you hear me? There's nothing to know.

Connie nodded. She swallowed until the tightness in her throat passed.

Frannie put her hand on Connie's knee. I love you, she said. Nothing's gonna happen to you again with me looking out for you.

•

For a couple of weeks, things were quiet. Connie went back to school when the bruises faded. People treated her differently, but not as she had expected. They treated her delicately, as though she were very sick and only appeared well. Her teachers allowed her to bring home the work she had missed. She wouldn't fail this year, but it was close. She came home and did homework each night until bed until she had made up everything she'd missed in the weeks she was out. Before, she wouldn't have worked hard—being held back didn't scare her. But now it did. She wanted to get away, and if you failed school, you could never get away. The careful, distant way that people moved around her made her feel lonely. This wasn't her home anymore.

Billy nodded to her in the hallway, and once he spoke to her after school, explaining why he hadn't called, why he hadn't visited.

You know we can't anymore, he said. He didn't meet her eye. Whatever we were doing before, that has to end. My mom, she, she just wouldn't let me, you know?

She knew. He was kind, but whatever they had had before, that undefined thing, was over. She had not expected anything else. Something had happened to her, everyone knew, even if they didn't know what, and whatever had happened had made her unsuitable for him. She understood that, though she couldn't have articulated it. It was understood the way that James Blackshaw's death was understood—something had happened and now the world was being set right, even if it hurt.

She did not doubt that the night she'd spent away from home, and what had happened in that night, meant that she must somehow pay. Now that James was dead (it was her fault, she had no doubt about it, though she didn't know how it had happened and hadn't wanted it to happen, it was her fault), she willingly

237

took whatever unhappiness that Heartshorne decided to give her. It seemed only fair.

Suddenly, she was a quiet girl, timid even. The girl who didn't take bullshit, the girl who pushed first in a fight, that girl was gone. Connie pulled her hair back tight so that her face was open and the skin thin around her hairline. Her skirts were well below the knee. She was always too warm in sweaters and sleeves.

•

The rule is that you don't speak about it. You don't brag about it. You don't threaten anyone with things you should not know and give details of deaths that you should know nothing about. When Frannie told the man at the bar who pushed her against the wall and pressed the his sharp hipbone against her stomach that he would *end up like Blackshaw* at the bottom of the lake, a hole in his head, and when she went back inside the bar, crying, saying that he had tried to *force her*, she was drunk and hardly knew what she was saying. *Motherfucker will end up like Blackshaw,* she told the room as she rubbed the makeup from under her eyes and re-buttoned her blouse.

People heard her. In a different town, her words would have gotten her arrested and questioned until they extracted the answers they needed. In this dive bar, the problem wasn't what she had done or arranged to be done, but that she had broken the rules about how to handle such information. What if word traveled out beyond Heartshorne?

When Frannie left the bar, she knew she had said too much. She hoped nobody would talk. She hoped it wouldn't get back to her family.

But it did. Frannie got an anonymous call the day later, saying that the sheriff's office was going to give her a call soon, that she best prepare her alibi. Connie's mother got a call asking if she'd heard of Blackshaw, if she could explain her whereabouts on the night of his murder. Her father, at work, heard that Frannie had talked. He heard that some people wanted to get to the bottom of the murder. Even Blackshaw had a few friends, and it only took a few friends to get the police involved, even for a no-good person like Blackshaw, a person who was better off at the bottom of a lake.

Of course, they all had alibis, they were all somewhere else that night. But still, it was too close.

Connie wasn't given much notice. She never understood quite how word traveled. Her parents called her to the kitchen. Her brothers and sisters had all cleared out. They said that they knew what had happened to her, and that Frannie had run her mouth about the Blackshaw boy, making it unsafe for them to stay in town. They said that the family was moving.

It's not good to keep you here, her father said, with what with what happened and all. It's not good for your brothers and sisters. We don't need the police down here. We don't need any trouble from Blackshaw's family or friends or any of those prison people he knew. Her father spoke quietly but firmly. She did not argue. He didn't look at her. Her mother kept her lips pressed together.

She seemed angry, though she continued to treat Connie carefully, as she had before the knowledge of what had really happened, though her lips remained shut.

They didn't say it, but it was clear that the whole thing was her fault. They had to leave Heartshorne because of her.

As they packed their belongings—everyone except Frannie came along, even her older brothers and sisters—her mother managed to say few words to her, nothing more than *label the box "fragile"* or to shout at her for folding the linens sloppily and not along the seams that had developed over the years from folding and ironing and folding again.

•

They moved to Kansas, a nondescript town and a smaller, more dilapidated house than they'd had in Heartshorne, where good land was cheaper and easier to come by. They felt like strangers in Kansas. They missed the hills. They were not Midwesterners by nature, not friendly, not religious, not interested in their neighbors or the local football team. The flatness made them feel exposed and lonely. They didn't understand neighbors visiting with food and asking questions about where they had come from, why they lived where they lived, and what the children hoped to do when they grew up. It seemed nosey, sneakily unkind.

Connie's father died of heart failure after working for ten more years for the telephone company in Coldwater, Kansas.

He died almost a year to-the-day after his retirement, for which he received a plaque and a cake, delivered to the house with his name spelled on the front. He had not worked long enough to earn a pension.

In Kansas, Connie began to think of herself as always on the verge of leaving. She wasn't there, really. She moved through school and jobs and dates with a detachment. She wasn't unhappy. She didn't miss the girl she had been before she had met James Blackshaw, that girl who had been lost somewhere between the school and the general store. That girl was gone, so why mourn her? She'd been stupid, anyway, and had been too innocent. Look where innocence had gotten her.

Connie would not be innocent. She wouldn't be caught in a place like Heartshorne again. Because she was from there, a daughter of Heartshorne, it was right that she had been punished. But no place would own her now.

She was completely free.

21

Emily emerged from Colleen's trailer into the heat, the change so sudden and unexpected that she gulped the air and was afraid that she might not be able to catch her breath.

She held her stomach. Am I breathing? It didn't feel like air, exactly, but like the prickly stream of forced motion that came from a automatic hand-dryer in a public bathroom.

She had left her windows down in the car, but it didn't help —

inside, she felt her skin damp and burning. She rolled up the windows and turned on the air conditioner.

She switched on the radio and listened to a song about a woman who finally decides to divorce a man who isn't good to her. She woman sang that she was now free to go out at night and *free* to watch the sun rise.

Emily listened to the lyrics carefully, trying to think about anything but what she had just learned.

By the time she had left Colleen's, she had somehow worked her way back into the woman's good graces. She'd asked about Colleen's children and grandchildren and her work at the textile factory (now closed) in Keno.

Come back sometime, Colleen had offered, placing her bird-like hand in Emily's hand. Her kindness, as strange and sudden as her anger, confused Emily. Emily nodded and promised that she would.

In the song on the radio, the woman's repetition of the word free became a shout, and the instruments in the background responded by rising in volume. A guitar shrieked as the drums pounded and the entire movement of sound became more insistent in agreeing with her voice. Yes, freedom.

Emily discovered that she was crying when she felt the tears slick the steering wheel.

•

Jonathan sat in her living room, on the carpet instead of the couch, where he never seemed quite comfortable or knew exactly how to sit. On the floor, he crossed his legs and sat upright. He shuffled his cards deftly in a few movements of his hand and set down the deck between them.

Okay, what would you like to ask?

Emily set her glass of wine on the carpet. She'd been nervous all afternoon after speaking to Colleen, but also at the thought of seeing Jonathan again. But he had not allowed her to be nervous. He had come to her and let her rest in the smell of his clothes, which didn't smell of soap but of something clean like cedar and his skin underneath, slightly salty. She told him the story that Colleen had told him and he said exactly the right thing:

That's fucked up, he said, and gave her a hug.

Emily looked at the back of the cards. The edges were rough and in some places the paper separated away in layers. He had used the same deck for years, he told her, though he had dozens of others which he used for himself.

What do you ask yourself?

He had shrugged. Anything. Anything I don't understand and need help with.

Can I ask the cards about something that isn't just about me? Emily asked. I mean, something bigger, something that I can't control on my own, with just my own choices?

Jonathan looked down at the deck. You can ask what you need to know about the situation. He looked up and gave her the lopsided, nervous smile he gave her (and maybe everyone? She didn't know him well enough to know yet) when he was about to say something he wasn't sure about.

Is it about the town? He asked. Your family? The whole thing? Because I can only tell you things directly about you and your choices. I can't explain somebody else's behavior.

Emily nodded. She pursed her lips together. I want to know what needs to happen to make the murders stop, she said. I want to know if I have something to do with it. If I can help.

Why? He asked. How could you stop it?

She shrugged. I'm from here, she said. This is the only place I can call home. My mother left because something terrible happened and she never had a home again. If I'm going to stay here, I want to help make it right.

He nodded and picked the cards up again, shuffling. He stopped and cut the deck.

Okay, he said. Here's what the cards have to say.

PART THREE

1

The Harris twins had just arrived home from school when Frank saw them. The boy still wore his backpack. The girl's was on the ground, bright pink and plastic reflecting in the sun. It was the hottest time of the day, just before dusk and after an entire day of sun overhead. He wondered how children could play in this heat, how they didn't just fall over with exhuastion.

They were taking turns on the tire swing. They were about eight or nine, maybe ten. They still played like children, though from the car, where he had parked with his window down, he could hear the boy shout words like *stupid* and *die*. The boy, in between turns, was playing with a toy water gun, pointing it at his sister on the swing and at something beyond her.

Frank liked these two children. They had spark. He liked the children with spark most. He had the twin emotion of excitment, a palpable fluttering in his stomach, and sickness at his excitement, which also bloomed in his stomach as heartburn. He swallowed down bile and composed his face. He couldn't appear suspicious to them. He had to be friendly, but not too friendly. He had to get them to come with him, otherwise, it would be messy, it would be partly ruined, like the time before, when the child had bit him in the shoulder when he was driving and he'd had to let the kid out after threatening that if he told, he'd come back and kill the boy's whole family.

These ones were trusting. He stopped his car in front of their house and asked if their parents were home. He knew they weren't, but just in case some other adult was lurking around, he had a plan. There was a dead cell phone in his pocket and a story about having to reach his wife, who was in the hospital up in Keno. It wasn't much of a story, but he figured the details would flesh out if needed. He performed well under pressure.

When he asked them to get in the car and show him where the next gas station was, they both agreed, arguing about who knew how to get there better. Before they went to the store, though, Frank told them he needed to stop back at his house, he had to get something important. They agreed; it was an adventure, one they'd tell their parents about when they got home.

He knew the dilapidated trailer from his own childhood. His uncle, James, had lived there, and when he had died, the house had gone to James' sister, Frank's mother, who had stayed there off and on when she got tired of his father's drinking. It was close to the lake, but far enough in the woods that it was hard to find if you didn't already know how to get there; the woods around Echo Lake still had mystery, despite all of the houses that had sprung up around them. The old driveway to it had long been grown over, and the trees sloped over it, hiding it from view. But he knew the markers by heart.

It was the kind of place where even the loudest screaming would go unnoticed.

He kept them for as long as he could stand it. They became sluggish. They were dirty and started to smell. The way they flinched when he came in didn't thrill him; it simply reminded him that yet again, he'd gotten himself into a predicament that could only end in getting rid of them. And that was the hard part.

He hated doing it every time. The joy was in getting and keeping, not in disposal. But he was starting to worry, and they were so tired, so unhappy. Nothing like the children he'd met that day after school. He brought a wheelbarrow, bound their hands and feet, and covered their eyes. They cried, weakly, but he was not worried: there was nobody around for miles.

He could not stand to hit them or hurt them in a violent way: he held the children's heads under the water until they stopped moving. He bound them both together, weighted them with a cement brick, and rowed them out in the canoe he kept tied up to a tree by the shore.

He looked out across the lake, which shone dully in the heat. He was drenched in sweat, sick to his stomach, and wanted nothing more than to get rid of them.

He had never done this before, had never left them in the lake. He had usually taken them home, back to Arkansas, where the nearby Ozark mountains were deserted enough to hide most anything. But he didn't want to drive all that way with them; what if he got pulled over? What if he panicked and revealed he was hiding something and they made him open up the trunk? He'd only done this twice before, and each time, the drive back had been hellish. It was safer just to be done with them here.

He had to row a while before the lake was deep enough to drop them in. He was far from houses, far from other shores, and it was early in the morning—the sun was just slipping up and the sky gray. He threw the block in first, and when it hung heavy, he slipped the bodies over the edge of the water. They dissappeared, bubbles rushing up for a few moments until the water was still again.

His uncle had died here. He'd been found shot, floating in the water. Frank sometimes wondered if he had been killed for being something like Frank was: a monster, the kind of person who deserved to be shot in the head.

Frank waited a while, watching the sun come up. It didn't seem fair that the children, who had done nothing, would not be able to see the sunrise. It didn't seem fair that he was still here, alive, when they were gone, their parents knowing nothing of where they were, hoping they might come back home when they were, for certain now, past hope.

As though responding to his thoughts, he felt his boat rock; the water was rippling, sending him back to the shore. He saw the mist on the water more clearly now, the sun visible above the mountains. It was greenish and heavy, a sickly-looking dampness.

His mother had not let him swim in the water here and would shout when he waded out farther than his knees.

It's not safe here, she said. It's dirty. Sometimes it's even poison. You heard about the mist?

He had not.

It rises up and makes you sick. Possesses you like. That's the old story, and I don't doubt it.

His boat rocked so vigorously that he started to row back, afraid it would send him crashing back to the shore. He shouldn't be out here, visible to any passerby, anyway.

He rowed back, tied up the boat, and washed up the room where he'd kept the children.

Maybe, he thought, I'll stop soon. Maybe I should burn down this place and make it harder for me to come back here. This was the place he always went when he felt the need coming on. It was part of the need. If he destroyed it, maybe the need would diminish.

But he wasn't ready yet. He washed his hands in the sink and got in his car and drove back to Fort Smith, where his wife waited and asked him how his weekend had been and how many fish he had caught and thrown back.

2

Levi had not slept well since Frannie's death.

He had not known her well, though in a small town it was impossible not to know everyone in passing. He had sold her candy bars during his senior year in high school when he had to sell a box of a hundred to raise money for the senior trip to Dallas. He remembered her in particular because she had bought half of the box. At that time, she'd been a well-preserved forty or so. She wore her hair long and straight, in the style of the time, and had traded her cat's eye glasses for the large, colorful, plastic frames that everybody wore in the 70's. He had known her then only as the last member of the Collins family and one of the few single women of her age. She had no children, which was rare, and he'd heard rumors about her his entire life. She was a lesbian. She was barren. She had multiple boyfriends up in the city, who she visited over the weekend. But you can't believe everything people say about other people.

Frannie's death kept him awake at night. He had nightmares about it. In the dreams, he saw her death in detail—the dark slice in her throat, the blood pouring down on her flowered nightdress, the sounds she made as she woke and clutched at her throat and how the blood came out in gushes with her heartbeat, first sluggish and then streaming when she tried to scream and couldn't.

When he woke up from a dream, he would stumble into his kitchen for a glass of water and, out of habit, an ibuprofen, though he didn't usually have a headache. It seemed he should take something for the dreams, which were like a pain, and ibuprofen seemed harmless enough for him to take without worrying about addiction (he was afraid of addiction, of anything that might take the place of God in his heart). After he had placed the pill bottle back in the cabinet and washed the glass and dried it and placed it back in the cabinet, he would crawl back into bed and pray until the images went away.

He remembered the first night he'd dreamed of her death, though he had not known it was hers that he had dreamed of at the time. He remembered it well because it was the night she'd been killed, before he'd heard of her death at all. That night had been the worst—he'd woke with the images of her death fresh on his mind, as though he'd been there. He distinctly remembered the feeling of blood streaming onto the thin skin of his wrist, how warm and thick it had been. That night he'd run to the bathroom to vomit in the toilet. After he'd stripped off his soiled pajamas and scrubbed the toilet clean, he stepped into the shower and stood under the hot water, letting it beat against his back, for at least a half hour before he was tired and clean enough to crawl back into bed and sleep. He woke the the morning after that with a genuine headache, and so the habit of ibuprofen began.

When he heard the news of her death later that day, he didn't tell anyone about the dream. Maybe it was a message from God. Maybe it was Satan, trying to make him believe he had some special powers, trying to temp him. He had been raised to believe that psychic abilities were real and were from Satan, not God, who did not allow anyone to have sight into the future. It could be a coincidence, too. So he had not spoken of his dream.

•

The morning of the all-church meeting, the day after Emily's visit, he took two ibuprofen, his headache real and insistent. He did not complete his usual routine. Each morning he usually did calisthenics—the same set of exercises that his father had taught him as a child, when his abundant energy had found nothing to tame it (he was hopeless at sports and they lived out in the country, away from easy access to roads or sidewalks for biking). He did five sets of 15 jumping jacks with 25 push ups, sit-ups, and squats between. After his regimen, he took a shower, and after wiping himself down (careful attention to the webby skin between his fingers and toes as well as behind his ears) and drying the shower (the wet was how scum grew, how the tiles turned black and had to be scrubbed clean and the little flecks of dirt chipped off and got into the bathwater), he would dress and comb his hair and brush and floss his teeth.

That morning, though, he broke his usual pattern. The dream was different this time. In it, he was not merely viewing Frannie's death; he was participating in it. His hand sawed her throat. His shoes were splattered with blood, and he saw himself coming home and placing something in his garage. Instead of doing calisthenics, he went to the yellow toolbox in his garage and opened it. Inside, a woman's hairnet was hardened in a knot, stained black.

He took the hairnet in his hands and brought it inside. He set it on the table, but he couldn't stand to look at it, so he went upstairs.. He hurriedly brushed his teeth and dressed. He combed his hair down with water and looked at his face.

Everything was changed now. It was all over, this good life he had created.

When he sat down to write his message, visions of the woman's blood came before him, so bright and present that he couldn't look at the neat rows of words without seeing the gash in her throat.

Eventually, though, he managed to write something. It was mostly action that he expected from the meeting anyway. Action that the whole town (or at least the people who were coming tonight) could partake in was what was needed. Words didn't have the impact that actions did, especially not here. So all he had to do was provide words that would motivate them, make them fearful enough to move, make them act. Levi couldn't get everyone to come. There were the hill people, those who didn't even come down to take their children to school or find wives and husbands outside of their close-knit clans. And there were those who went to other churches, like the Southern Baptist church on the other side of Heartshorne or even the Methodist all the way in Keno. Some, of course, didn't go to church at all, for whatever reason, be it disbelief or backsliding or shame, and he couldn't reach them. But he'd heard that more people were coming than ever before—nonbelievers and believers alike, all concerned about what was happening to the town.

Heartshorne wasn't what it had once been. The homecoming parade used to be the highlight of the year—young women were crowned princesses and placed on floats, and the Homecoming Queen wore thick makeup that dripped from her face in the heat, but she'd smile anyway, waving at people in the crowd who she had known since childhood, people who loved to see one of their own elevated, even if it was only on the back of a pick-up truck. People rode horses and held up the American flag along with the Oklahoma flag and flags of the local tribes; the Choctaws, Chickasaws, and Seminoles. A marching band would follow up the rear, wearing their heavy wool outfits and stomping in the horses' excrement, not minding the heat or the crap on their shoes because everybody was there to watch them play, and so they played. Those days had ended slowly and gradually, twenty years in the making. Levi didn't understand quite why it had changed, but he imagined it had something to do with young people moving away. If high school students got through their high school years without getting pregant or dropping out, they usually left—it only made sense, the jobs being elsewhere and life being sleepy and unchanging from year to year.

Those who stayed became trapped in the everyday march of life from school to work to school again. Jobs no longer paid for much but the basics. They did not have time to organize the rental of dozens of horses or the buying of a genuing tiara for the homecoming queen and princess. Things wound down.

But why was it different now, when this had been the familar pattern of life from year-to-year in the past? Had young people always wanted to escape, but previously been unable? Did they make elaborate homecoming floats in their garages or front yards and have children and buy boats because there was no other choice? Levi didn't know: he had never been one of those young people who wished to be somewhere where his life could have been louder and brighter and more distinguished from the lives of others. He had never wanted that regular life of children and family, either. He was content to be who he was right now— somebody responsible for the part of life that really mattered and lived: the spiritual life. But the thought pained him now, the spiritual life. How could he be an example to anyone now?

He had only wanted to please God

(That's why you have to do this tonight, he thought, what you want isn't what you need, that's why you have to)

and to be of service to the public.

He finished the short speech left a note to himself on the bottom:

Tell them everything.

There's nothing else to do, he said aloud. It's over, but make it clean. Give it over to God.

He wondered if this was the last day in his house, his last day free. He wondered why he didn't go to each room and kiss the floors, why he wasn't more afraid. He stood up, unsure what to do with himself. He went to the bathroom, where he washed his face for the second time that morning, and then scrubbed his underarms and reapplied deodorant, placed a fresh undershirt under his button-up shirt, and came back down to drink his single cup of coffee before leaving to the church for administrative and visiting duties. He would work up until he could no longer work, until everyone knew and he could no longer be the only person he knew how to be: Pastor Richardson, man of God, shepherd of souls, doer of no harm. Today would be no different than any other day until he told them. Up until the end, they would know him as the man they thought he was, not the man he really was.

3

Emily lay next to Jonathan and listened to the soft sound of his breathing and the pound of rain. It was torrential, the kind of rain that she associated with movies about missionaries trapped in tropical climes, the tin on their roofs pinging as if small rocks were pouring from the sky. She didn't know if her roof leaked: she imagined she would find out soon. But she couldn't worry about the rain today. It was an accompaniment to his breathing, a sound that lulled and hummed and reminded her she was here, on earth, in her aunt's home, and happy, not with her throat gaping open like her aunt or a bone-ragged hole in her head like the woman who had died on her lawn. Jonathan didn't snore, at least he hadn't yet, but only gave off a constant damp, windy noise, which soothed her instead of annoyed her.

But how would she feel in five years? It was impossible to know. She didn't want to allow herself that brief time when most people imagined that everything about their lover was perfect, the only person in the world that they would never grow tired of. It was a silly idea, one she knew only brought unhappiness. But what if? she thought, as she tried to shut her brain up and make it listen to the rain. What if she never grew tired of him, and he never of her, and what if he would stay with her in this big house, cleaning the gutters and keeping raccoons out of the big plastic trash barrel by her mailbox? Would that be happiness, then? Would they live like adults, waking up in the morning to go to places where they were expected and coming home to each night together? It was probably too early to wonder about this. She should enjoy what she had in the moment, she knew, but it was hard for her to allow herself momentary happiness.

As she listened, the rain stopped almost as suddenly as it had started and the clouds began to clear. She saw the gloom lift slightly, and then a piece of blue. The window brightened, heating the room—that rectangle was filled with sun so sharp and direct that it hurt to look through it, and all she cold see now was light. The sun must have been outside their window directly, hanging like a yellow button in the blue. She sat up, letting the blankets fall from her. Light slashed across her chest, warming her skin. She could see from the window now, the sun angled away beyond the frame. Outside, the trees leaned in, seeming suspended in the heat and mist, each leaf sharp and clearly delineated in the otherwise hazy air.

It seemed strange that she lived in such a place, a place where the plants overran the things man made to contain them, where the landscape from afar looked impossible, like a 19th century illustration from a fairy-tale, a forest that a maiden or child would have to enter for the story to begin. Emily had taken a class about fairy tales in college, and now she couldn't help but see all fairy tales as the patterns her professor had put on the chalkboard, each one boiled down to a simple formula: the pattern of abandonment, perseverence, and return, or the one of hierarchy challenged and then hierarchy restored. The world of fairy-tales was one of basic fears, of a parent's hunger overcoming parental love, of the world not working by the laws that it should, of an undesirable (the crippled, the ugly, the deformed) gaining power and using that power to punish others.

The night before, Emily had told Jonathan everything she'd learned about her mother from Colleen. She'd told him about the death of James Blackshaw, how he'd probably been killed, how Frannie had caused her family's exodus from the place they'd lived for several generations This was after she'd asked about the murders, after he'd given her the tarot reading, after she had let him take her to the bedroom and after sex. She had lain naked, red in the heat and from the rub of their skin together, her throat rashed from his cheek where he'd pressed against her throat, her knee throbbing from where she'd slammed it against her night table.

So now he knew everything. He did not seem surprised. He only nodded as she spoke, interjecting only for clarifications. She'd cried, but he had not acknowledged it, which was the right thing to do in the moment. She had not been asking for acknowledgment.

It's isolated here, and I don't just mean geographically, he said after they had dozed for ten minutes or so, cooling their skin, and woke again. People don't leave unless they have to or very much want to. They keep to themselves, that's what people say. It seems almost wrong to come into a place like Heartshorne and tell people who they can and can't kill. You sign an agreement if you're born here—

You can't sign agreements when you're born, she said. You don't agree to being born at all.

He sat up in bed, his head against the wall. He only shrugged and did not explain himself.

She loved this about him, how he wasn't afraid when she or anyone disagreed with him. He didn't rush to clear away the hurt or confusion or anger.

Maybe this was yet another thing she would hate about him later. She imagined an argument, her trying to get some reaction, wanting to shake him up, and him merely setting back, swallowing, closing his eyes before he began to say something completely logical.

I just mean, he went on, that as soon as you are born, you are born into a place where these are the rules, as clear as the rules that the everyone else lives by, just different.

Emily had nodded, sleepy from the sex, from the reading (the readings drained her, the way he did them, how he demanded her to contribute in figuring out what the cards meant and why), and she had not argued.

Now, as she lay in bed, she thought about her mother again. Whatever had happened to her (and she'd never know, would she? This was what happened when a person died—they took everything that only they had known or could know with them) had made her the person that Emily had known, a person who she had never quite been able to love beyond the basic love of necessity and guilt.

Jonathan stirred, first blinking, his eyes closed for long intervals. Then he pulled her close to him and breathed into her throat.

I'm free today, he said. What should we do?

4

That night, it had rained so hard that the plants with closed, hard petals were forced open, their inner pollen released and drowned in the muck. The flowers that had bloomed all summer were pummeled and smashed. It rained so hard that pools of water formed in the low places on dirt roads, making some impassable, trapping men in the houses they hated, the women they loved or had once loved angry and chain smoking, the children unable to leave for school, the children trapped in houses they hated with mothers who drank and slurred and watched beautiful women and men on television shouting at each other or living in places that the children had never seen and could hardly imagine, the children afraid and angry but also desiring to pick at the wound that made the mother cry or shout or even hit, and the women trapped in the houses they hated, with the children that they loved and so could wound, with the men they loved and who wounded them with their indifference or the liquor they bought instead of bread, and the people who lived alone and the people who lived in ways that Heartshorne would not approve of—men with men, women with women, there were a few of them, lying low. They were more afraid than usual, paradoxically fearing the inability to leave the homes they'd thought of as sanctuaries from the pressures of the church pot luck or the staring eyes at the general store. It was terrifying to be stuck.

The town muddied and the trees grew bright like jewels, the rain a glaze and the humidity so thick nothing could dry. Pools of dead leaves and drowned worms reeked when the sun came up.

And the lake rose. It had raised an inch by morning, when the rain stopped and the skies cleared momentarily before the next torrent would begin.

5

As she made coffee, she watched the enormous puddle in her yard shimmer and shift, the droplets hittting it in slanted waves. It had started raining again lightly. The yard was littered with buds, branches, and stray pieces of trash which caught in corners and around anything that . At the table, Jonathan sat with the paper, which he had fetched from the convenience store down the road, along with a package of stale honey buns and a pack of Swishers Sweets.

Do you smoke? She'd asked after he came in and set the objects down on her table.

Would she have to think of it, soon, as our table? She did not know how she felt about that. He placed the paper and cigarettes and sticky honey-buns, their crusted sugar hardened to the cellophane in a dried film, down on the kitchen table with such certainty, not a hint of reluctance, as though it were his house in which to figure out where things should go. She wanted to pick up all of the objects and put them in different places, just to remind me that he didn't have the right to decide where things went, but she stopped herself.

He shrugged. Sometimes. Let's share some tonight, outside, he said. They're sweet.

She nodded. She used to smoke recreationally, at Eric's gigs, though she only filled her mouth with smoke and blew it out. Smoking had been something to do with her mouth when she had nothing to add to the conversation, which was often. Eric's friends liked to follow their own thoughts down rabbit holes, arguing the ability to be effortlessly cool without trying to be cool, debating who fit the bill and who didn't. Johnny Cash was cool but Radiohead were not, because even stupid people liked them and knew at least one of their songs—Creep, probably, a song that even regular people thought was about them, the kind of loser anthem that people who were decidedly non-losers in the regular world had adopted as their own and therefore ruined. They spoke at each other, not to each other, each trying to dazzle the other long enough to make them stop and listen to the clever or complex thing dancing along the surface of the monologue, or at least that was how it had seemed to her, in the background, chewing on the filter of her cigarette and waiting for Eric to wear himself out trying to be heard. It was an exhausting way to live. She had given up early on the competitive aspect of it, content to watch the others try to best each other. It made her sad to think of them now, still trying to make somebody listen but never stopping to listen to anyone else.

She touched the pack of cigarettes, brown and slim. Sure, she said. She wondered if he was a stress smoker. Was this his version of stressed?

She looked at him in his gray, long-sleeved shirt, ragged holes in the cuffs where he'd poked his thumbs through, his jawline at a constant two-day shadow. He crossed his legs easily at the knee, on black sock thinning at the ankle so she could almost see his skin beneath. His eyes were deep-set, giving him the appearance of being tired until you knew him and saw that it was an illusion. He folded his hands over one knee, and then on his lap, moving his hands in a circular motion to warm them. He carried himself with a compact elegance that appealed to her: he did not throw his body around as some men did, needing to prove themselves worthy of the space they inhabited. His movements were efficient and catlike; he folded and drew his limbs back into himself.

Do I have something hanging out of my nose? he asked.

No, she said. I was just. I don't know. Admiring.

He gestured to her and she walked over to him and sat in his lap.

What do you want to do today? He asked.

What she wanted to do was stay at home, curled up with Jonathan, not worrying about what was happening outside or about Levi's meeting that night.

I don't know, she said, rising from his lap. It was too comfortable there, too easy to sink into and forget.

She poured the boiling water into the french press and pumped the water up and down, blackening it to the color that Jonathan liked and that she was getting used to.

She had to go to the meeting that night. It wasn't that she wanted any kind of spiritual guidance and it wasn't that she felt she owed it to Colleen or Levi or anyone else. She felt she had to go, that missing it would mean missing something important about her mother and Frannie and everything. It was a rare, strong gut feeling. Emily had thought herself generally devoid of helpful intuition, completely free of the twinges and signs her mother identified everywhere: a feather floating on the porch might mean that she shouldn't leave the house that day, a spider in the bathtub meant unexpected money, or she's see a premonition of kitchen curtains streaming fire across the flammable wallpaper and turn the car around only to find that she'd left a kettle on a still-hot burner, the smell of melting aluminum permeating the house. Emily had never had a premonition in her life (if she had, perhaps she would have seen Eric's womanizing coming, though perhaps it had taken only common sense to see that, something Emily was also missing). But now, she felt the need to go that night strongly, an urge as obvious and easy to relieve as the urge to sneeze.

I want to go to that meeting tonight, that church thing, she said. She didn't turn to watch him. Would you come along?

Of course. She turned to bring him the carafe and poured a cup of black coffee. He grabbed the mug, folding his long fingers around it.

It's hot, she said, imagining him dropping the cup, scalding himself, the pieces of pottery nicking them both. She did not have intuition, but she had inherited the ability to anticipate elaborate disaster scenarios, a far less useful talent.

I'm fine, he said, and leaned back in his chair, crossing his legs again, looking as though he lived here, really belonged here, as if anyone could.

•

The night before, he had suggested a simple three-card reading.

What does Emily need to know about the murders in town? He said as he shuffled.

This card is the problem, he said, laying down the two of swords. In it, a young man held two swords, balanced equally, blades crossed.

This is the benefit: The Tower. Her old friend.

This is the solution: The Wheel of Fortune. Emily noticed, this time, the man below the wheel, pressing himself as flat as possible to avoid being crushed by its enormous, wooden weight.

So, what does it mean? She asked.

He laughed and looked up at her. He had already commented on her Tarot face, rapt and expectant like a child waiting for the rabbit to jump from under the hat.

She knew that he wouldn't simply answer, and he didn't. He looked at the card. He shifted the two of swords slightly so it overlapped the Tower.

What do you see? He asked her.

The two of swords were completely balanced by the boy (or woman? Somebody ascetic and ungendered, a figure in a black robe with a black cap over his or her hair). Behind the figure and the balanced swords, the sky was gray and heavy and a peephole of a moon seemed very far away.

These two things that could kill this person, the two swords, they are balanced, she said. The balance has come from discipline, from keeping things tightly organized. She liked this idea, this boy/ girl who could hold something deadly and make it safe as milk.

How long can the boy hold up the swords?

Forever, she said. He could hold them up forever. A storm is about to come, but he's smiling. He knows he can hold them up.

Why is this a problem? Remember this is a problem card.

Emily thought of Colleen, how sure she was that the town was usually right. The people who had to die had had to die. These new deaths were different—unplanned, unsanctioned by whatever body (the people, their silence) had sanctioned the previous deaths.

So the problem is that things could remain as they are—the swords that kill might stay balanced, Emily said. The storm comes and the boy's just standing there, not moving, not changing.

Emily looked up at the roof, which was slapped with rain.

He nodded, looking down at the cards. When he read, he didn't move his attention from the cards and her responses. He could not be distracted.

So the problem is that things might remain exactly as they are, he repeated. The swords can be held up forever. Even a great shaking up might not move them, not if somebody doesn't make that boy move.

Emily nodded. So the boy has to decide to move. Or something so big he can't help but move has to happen.

Jonathan nodded. After a pause, he moved on.

So here's the benefit: The Tower. What do you see?

She'd seen the card before, but she tried to look at it again, to see something she didn't already know. She saw a group of people in brown and black capes, their thin, white hands clasped together, their pinched 18th century faces narrow and greenish, gathered below a falling building, too afraid to move away from the rubble, too afraid to use their sense.

Something happening that's beyond control, she said. She could almost feel it, then, a wind so severe that it could knock a building over, a wave of energy that they had to simply watch destroying their tower. Something so big, bigger than the storm coming—or maybe the storm coming in full force, will bring the lighting that hits the tower that will move the boy with the swords. She moved to touch the card next to it, that girl/boy with his look of complacency, no fear of being cut.

Maybe the lightning will hit the swords like a lightning rod. She paused, not sure what she meant, but she kept speaking anyway. He had taught her this trick: don't freeze up, just keep talking, explaining, noticing, and something interesting will come out.

What happens will be so big, people can't help but look at it. They can't hide, they can't put it into order and understand it: they have to look. They will be forced to look.

So is it coming, he asked, or does it need to happen? Does somebody have to make it happen, or is like a natural disaster, something that you or I cannot control? Jonathan looked up at her, breaking his concentration on the cards. Remember, this is the benefit. Do you mean this needs to happen, that it will happen, or that you somehow have to make it happen?

Emily shook her head. The card grew dark and mute, just pictures on cardboard. She felt suddenly silly.

I don't know.

Ok. He touched the third card, The Wheel of Fortune. What do you see?

She didn't know this card, not like The Tower (her card, she liked to think, with all of that confusion and collapse and people with nothing left but prayer and dumb staring).

The people are moving, everything's moving, she said. The creature—person—on the bottom is the only one being crushed. He's afraid, but he doesn't realize he'll spin up to the top soon and the creatures above him will be below. Everything is moving and you can't hold it still.

She looked at Jonathan. The boy can't really hold the swords *forever*. He can hold them for a while, and then the wheel comes down on him and he has to let go.

Jonathan pressed his lips together. So what will happen to him then?

He'll cut himself.

Jonathan nodded. So he'll cut himself. He'll fall to the bottom of the wheel. He'll have to drop his swords and might cut himself and maybe even somebody else. But it's good that the swords fall—it's the balance that's the problem. But something will shake him up from that complacency. The wheel will swing and he'll be on the bottom.

So the question is, does somebody else spin the wheel? Do you have to throw that lightning that breaks the tower? Is this something that you are supposed to do?

She looked up. Why would it be me?

He shrugged. You seem to care. You seem to think you need to do something. Does anyone else care?

Everyone cares, she said. Pastor Levi cares. Even Colleen cares. Everyone cares.

Jonathan had flared up a nascent sense of pride of place. The feeling was strange and thrilling. She wouldn't speak badly of it, now that she knew it was her own. The pride surprised her and made her even sicker. She did care. She cared about this place. But she wasn't really from here. She felt silly; how brazen, to think that she would be the one to save the day.

People care, she said again. They just can't see from the outside. I feel like I'm both from the inside and the outside. My mother came from here, and so it's inside me, but I don't know this place.

They paused for a moment, listening to the sound of the rain, which had regained its torrential power.

She shook her head and busied her hands by pointed to a figure farther out from the scene than the others in the Tower card. The figure was kneeling, his hands on the ground, his head uplifted to the sight before him of the tower cracked and tumbling and bodies twisted from falling a great distance.

I'm this person, Emily said, covering the figure completely with her finger. I'm there but not quite there. I can see what's happening, but I'm not part of it. Look, this person is about to run, but only after they've bowed to whatever is happening. They know it's terrible and important and but also that they should run as far as possible in the other direction.

Jonathan nodded. So it's right to run?

She paused again, running her finger over the man on the ground.

Pull me another card, she said. What do you call it—a clarifying card.

He nodded and held the deck in his palms for a moment before halving it.

The six of swords, he said, setting it down before her.

She'd had this card before, in her previous reading.

Water, she said. I have to cross the water. In the card, a woman held her wrapped-up child in a boat, six swords in a bundle at the back of the boat and a man at the helm, moving them through a storm.

What does that mean? He asked.

She shrugged. I think I need to do something for myself, I have to cross the water. I need to worry about my own Tower before I can take care of anyone else's.

•

So you really don't mind coming tonight? She asked over her shoulder.

He nodded, looking up from the paper. He lifted it so she could see the front page, the second headline down from the first.

FREE WILL BAPTIST CHURCH TO HOLD
TOWN MEETING ABOUT MURDERS

Looks like it's the biggest event happening this weekend. He
smiled, folding his hands over the newsprint. I think it's a good
idea that we go.

She opened her mouth, but he had already turned to the paper.
He went to the comics page, where he found the word puzzle he
did daily. To sharpen his mind, he told her, and she had an image
of him as an old man, completing the puzzle each morning over
coffee, his hairline receding, his face lined and rough and no
longer quite the face she knew. But his mind would be sharp.
She wondered if she would still know him then or if he would be
a memory: maybe she'd remember him like this, young, still a
stranger to her, mostly, drinking her coffee in her small kitchen.

6

Levi asked the church party committee to set out tables full of
food—marshmallow-covered sweet-potato slices, carrot cakes
with cream cheese icing, fried okra, chicken-fried steaks laid
out in slices, a whole tub of white gravy, biscuits, tater tots and
ranch dressing, fried chicken, macaroni and cheese made with
50% velveeta and 50% cheddar (which was Colleen's specialty).
and two enormous plastic bowls full of pink ambrosia, the chunks
of fruit suspended in pink-stained cottage cheese. Despite the
dampness of the ground and the yet-again impending rain (the
sky was heavy but ambiguous in intent, still grayer than the blue-
black of imminent rain), he expected a large crowd. The rain had
kept everyone in for two days, flooding the roads and swelling the
creeks up past the barriers. Now that the rain had stopped and the

ground was only marshy, not soaked, people wanted to get out of their houses, to open the windows and be in the outdoors.

Inside, his mind rioted and his stomach roiled, but he was surprised at himself: the whole morning and afternoon, his hands had not shaken and his voice had betrayed very little of his fear.

I am a practiced liar, he thought. I have been practicing deception for my entire life. It's no wonder that even my body knows how to deceive.

He placed the hairnet in the cabinet below the podium, on top of a stack of King James Bibles they had taken from the pews once the NIV came out. The people here had never liked the King James. They thanked him profusely the when the church finally made the switch. Levi missed the cadences of that archaic language, though. How could he abandon *As the hart panteth after the water brooks, so panteth my soul after thee, O God* for *As the deer pants for streams of water, so my soul pants for you, O God?* The first sounded like a cry out to a lover, the second like a perfunctory bit of metaphor, clumping along in dead, toneless language. But he had exchanged them, and since he prepared his lessons for them, he now read the newer version in its flat, obvious language and sometimes could not remember what he was missing.

Soon, he'd be able to read whatever he wanted. He imagined himself in the cell, reading his King James. So much time. No responsibility to anyone but God.

He took his NIV and went to his study. In this moment, he needed words that they could all understand.

Emily and Jonathan arrived early.

Where's Pastor Richardson? Emily asked a young man who was pouring drinks at the end of the table.

He went to his study to prepare, he said. The boy had acne along his jawline, the kind of acne that would scar him for life and leave his face lightly pitted, the texture of a palm after being pressed hard against gravel. His hair was slicked up in spikes. Emily watched him and the other teenagers, a group of them gathered around the ambrosia, the girls making faces at the clots of cottage cheese clumped along the edges of the glass bowls. She watched Jonathan spoon sweet potatoes onto his bowl and felt how delicate humans are—to think that something so soft and flimsy as sweet potatoes soaked in sugar syrup could keep us alive. It seemed strange that these perfumed and sauced and cooked to mush collections of colors on our plates could really be the fuel of life. It should take something more substantial to keep humans alive, she thought, like oil, or minerals.

The church, small, only two stories, was tall from her perspective, seated below at one of the long tables. Emily half-listened to Jonathan explain to a youngish deacon in a plain white shirt and black slacks that no, he was not a regular churchgoer, and that he did know about Jesus, thank you. She looked away from the deacon, hoping that he would not try to catch her eye. She looked up at the sky. The small steeple seemed enormous, liable to fall. Emily couldn't keep her leg from making compulsive little kicks and jiggling her knees when she crossed them, so she put both feet on the ground and leaned her elbows on her lap.

Levi stepped out at the appointed time, spooned his food onto his plate, said hello to the people that required hellos. He nodded at Emily and the man she'd brought, a young man of around thirty who wore smart, wire-framed glasses and spiky, short hair. He wore silvers and grays and blacks and Levi found his stomach hurt to look at this man. This was the kind of man that Levi had admired from a distance for years. A kind of intellectual type, somebody who might bring a book along to a doctor's appointment so he wouldn't get bored in the waiting room.

He'd thought that Emily would be the barrier, the thing he would have to overcome in order to give his speech, to say the thing he had to say to make the town realize what it needed, realize that it needed a reckoning. But this man made his hands shake. Now, everything inside of him that he wanted to hide was close to being laid bare. And here was this new person, somebody he would have hoped to impress, here to witness the lowest moment of his life.

He could be in the presence of men who worked the oil fields, with their tattoos and their muscles and their hard beer guts and hair that peeked out from the edges of their ball caps: they did not do much for him. But this was the kind of man who made his knees weak.

In the moment, he was more afraid of this man than of what he'd done, what he had to tell them. The feeling was even worse, wasn't it? Not a heat-of-the-moment thing, but a stain he'd always had, something that couldn't be absolved away or cured by time.

He didn't look at Emily and the man. He turned his back to them and ate his food quickly. He ran through three napkins in his

LETITIA TRENT

haste, wiping up the loose confetti of coleslaw and bloody lumps of ambrosia from his lap. He imagined the teenagers noticed him fumbling, as lidless-eyed as they were, always watching for something to point out and repeat amongst themselves later.

When he finally finished eating and mopped away the mess, he nodded to the youth pastor, who was waiting for his signal.

When he stood up at the podium and looked out at them, he saw their faces opened—not just in the metaphorical sense, open to the Lord or The Word or open to his ideas and his thoughts. He really saw their faces open and their thoughts pouring out— Colleen, her knotted hands working beyond her control, hoping that the speech would be over soon so she could get home, he could see it in the pinch of her face. The teenagers were thinking of each other, of how to please each other by being the most God-fearing, by loving Jesus the most (soon, they would realize that other avenues were the best route to the heart, but for now, they seemed to be in a cocoon of safety). The families worried about themselves, their little units. They worried about their safety and hoped he had something to say that would make them fear less or help them to know what they could do. We are all so small, he thought, so concerned with our own safety, our own appearance, our own ability to impress. We don't understand that something larger than us might come and sweep all of that away.

Emily waited for Levi to speak. At the podium, he seemed larger, and she remembered the feeling she'd had at church, that he was better at what he did than she'd taken him for, that he had a natural authority that she hadn't understood. He was not just a lonely man who clung to religion for some anchor, a man who couldn't stand to keep a dirty dish in his house because of some pathology that religion served to escalate, as she'd thought before. That man dissolved as he stood before them. He looked out at the crowd, half-smiling, one hand casually on the podium, the other in his pocket. He watched them until they grew quiet. He made them wait for his words, and they waited in silence until he spoke, the only sound the shuffling of feet under chairs and the tiny clicks and clinks of plastic cutlery against cardboard and teeth.

He cleared his throat. He had only one piece of paper, which he had taken out of his breast pocket. The paper was lined and folded into a small square, which he unfolded and smoothed on the podium.

Welcome, everyone, he said, leaning forward, the staticky mike squealing lightly.

I'm happy to see so many of you here—people from the community, regular churchgoers, and newcomers to our community. We've had a church meeting about this subject before, but I thought it appropriate to work with our local community leaders to gather up more people, to work together to take back Heartshorne for the Lord.

But you might wonder why I invited people outside of church families, too. The community of people who do not attend, and even unbelievers. I've called you all here today. Levi paused and, for the first time, looked down at the paper he had smoothed out on the pedestal before him.

It's because this problem, what's happening, requires all of our attention. It isn't a chance event, not something that was visited upon us for no reason. And I think we all know this.

Emily wanted to turn to see the faces behind her. She could feel them staring and shuffling, no longer scratching at the paper plates with their forks.

Emily held her breath. He was going to bring down the Tower.

In this town, people disappear, he said. Probably more than in other places.

Emily sat up straight and touched Jonathan's knee under the table. He placed his hand on hers and squeezed.

People disappear and the police investigate and the circumstances are always mysterious, the bodies rarely found, the disappearances called runaways, deadbeat fathers and mothers, suicides. Drugs, now, are the most popular explanation.

But we know they aren't all just the lost, the wicked, the addicted, he said. We know where most of them are, and some of us know exactly how they got there. Levi pointed out into the driveway. But Emily knew where he was pointing. The lake, which lay beyond the road, across fields, and across the main road, across Emily's property and through the woods behind her house.

Until now, I knew this and ignored it. Like the rest of you, I imagined that we were different, that this place had its own wisdom, a wisdom that worked to flush out trouble. I didn't think of what that meant or what it did to us as people. I didn't even think that it bothered God. I thought, in my heart, that God was on our side, that the world would be better if they let people work out their justice amongst themselves. I really believed this, folks. And I bet that some of you do, too.

A faint, but unmistakably disapproving sound came from a man at a table in the back. Levi looked down at his notes again, turning the single page and smoothing it down. He paused, running his hand along the page. Emily had time to glance backwards—everyone watched him. Only the smaller children remained oblivious, playing on the ground, some splashing their toys through the mud puddles that had gathered in the low points of the yard, something that surely would have concerned their parents if they had been watching. The adults, though, looked forward, watching Levi.

I didn't realize what it did to us until the deaths this year— the woman murdered in the yard, the children missing. Finally, people were paying attention. People were afraid.

The only difference between then and now, brothers and sisters, is that these murders are not just being quietly taken care of. They are out for everyone to see. Our secrets are in the open now and we don't understand them in the light of day. Make no mistake: these murders are against the will of God, but the ones before them were against the will of God, too. Levi stopped and rifled around under the podium. Emily's first and strangest thought was that he had a gun, that he would shoot them all and them himself, that she would die here, but then her mind came back. Why would she think this?

He pulled out a a hair net. The kind older women wore over their curlers before bed or cafeteria workers wore as they spooned helpings of mashed potatoes and cobbler onto into the portioned lunch trays at elementary schools. This hairnet was covered in black streaks, as though somebody had broken a pen and spilled the ink all over it.

I found this in my toolbox back home, Levi said. He made small, coughing noises and looked down at the podium. Emily held her hand up to her throat in automatic sympathy—He was crying.

I found this and I know what it is. He breathed in deeply. I know what it is because the Lord showed me in a dream. He showed me what I did and he told me the way. He said to admit it. To admit everything and to get on my knees and ask you all to admit it, too, for the crimes you have committed and the crimes you've allowed others to commit.

Emily could hear people speaking now behind her.

Pastor Levi, one of the young men in a Jesus T-shirt shouted from the back. Are you okay? Levi had stepped away from the podium. He unbuttoned his shirtsleeves and rubbed the edges of his sleeves under his eyes.

I am all right, he said. I'm better than all right.

He stepped forward, out in front of the podium, his shoes sinking into the mud.

I killed Frannie Collins, he said. And for that I should be punished. I urge anyone else who has committed a similar act to come forward and admit it to the congregation and beg God for forgiveness as I am.

7

On a particularly warm day in July, before Emily arrived in Heartshorne, Levi had finished his Wednesday afternoon sermon and had left the church almost immediately, saying he had a conference call with the women's crisis pregnancy center they had partnered with in Keno, the one placed right across from the only Planned Parenthood south of Tulsa, where he and the church bishops had stood in front of the doors of the church with poster-sized pictures of tiny, torn fetuses.

He was lying. He had no call to make.

That day, they had welcomed a new member into their fold—Levi had baptized Derek after several weeks of attendance. Derek was young, under thirty, and unmarried. He had come to Levi for counseling.

I want to commit myself to God, he'd said, but I have so many doubts. Levi had explained that doubts were natural and watched the young man's hands, how they rested on his knees and how he would lightly clutch the fabric of his pants when he spoke emphatically. He was clean-shaven and had slicked his hair back in what Levi recognized as a desperate attempt to seem older and wiser and more capable than he was.

I have such a hard time believing, he said. I have a hard time believing that a good God would say so many things that are harmless aren't allowed.

Like what? Levi had asked. Derek had admitted to drinking, drugs, the usual, nothing that shocked Levi. He had heard much worse from people who looked far less capable of mischief. And he had admitted to sex before marriage.

I don't think I can stop, he said. Drinking, I could stop. Pot, I could stop. But not that, not sex. Sometimes I want to, you know, I know it would be right. But I won't. I just won't. Levi had asked Derek to say more. He offered his advice if Derek wanted to come to him on difficult nights, when he felt urges to do something that he knew would separate him from God.

So Levi became his confidante. The young man would come to him and admit that he had urges toward his girlfriend and he wasn't sure if they were wrong or right.

Tell me about them, Levi would say. He arranged his face to be dispassionate, to be the face of a man above the petty concerns of lust, like a doctor before a naked human body, interested only in routing out the disease inside of it. He nodded and followed the lines of Derek's face as he spoke, noting if he had shaved or not, if his shirts were neatly ironed or disordered from haste or carelessness, if he wore an undershirt that covered the sparse hair at the base of his throat or not.

This continued until the night of the Baptism. Derek wore one of the baptism robes. He'd changed from his clothes in the church bathroom and wore only his underpants and a t-shirt under the heavy white robe. It smelled like moth balls and was yellowed from years of use without washing. Still, he looked angelic. Levi glanced at him as he gave the short speech before each Baptism, a speech about committing your life to Christ before the community.

This is a whole new step in the life of the believer, he said. You are telling the rest of the church that your heart is with Christ, that you are willing to be a true brother and sister, a soldier for Christ not only for yourself, but also for everybody else in the congregation.

Derek stood in the hallway between the stage and the back rooms, his hands folded before him, listening.

The Baptismal pool was rolled out, a portable tub with wheels. Levi placed the stepladder by the lowest lip and held out his hand. Derek came forward.

The step was unsteady, so Levi held Derek's shoulder and he stepped into the pool.

He spoke the words he always spoke and then put his hand on the young man's chest.

For a moment, Derek looked confused, his eyes afraid—it must have been instincts kicking in, the part of the human mind that riots against anyone holding one's head underwater.

Close your eyes, Levi said. You'll be fine.

The man closed his eyes and Levi pushed his chest. He could feel his bone underneath the heavy fabric, imagined he could feel the young man's heart beating. He plunged his body down, and then his head, and whisked him back up again, holding him by the arms until he had recovered from the cold and shock and could stand up alone.

You are reborn in Christ, Levi said as Derek sputtered.

Thank you, he said. Thank you, Pastor, for giving me this gift.

After the Baptism, after Derek had shaken hands with the

congregation and had rested, tearful, in the space between Levi's elbow and throat, saying that he loved Christ, that he wanted to give himself to the church, that this was the best day of his life, Levi left.

He drove not home, but to the lake, to the place where he had swam as a boy, an unofficial swimming hole carved out of the woods on a rocky but shallow shore. Few people knew about it now, and Levi was careful to replace the mouth of the path with a tangle of fallen branches, as everyone else seemed to, since it was always there when he came here, covering the tracks in the grass.

In his glove box, he kept a pack of menthols. Cigarettes were a dirty habit, one that he couldn't stand in others, but he found himself buying a pack of menthols every time he ran out. They felt cleaner than other cigarettes, like smoking mint.

Smoking was the one vice he allowed himself, and he smoked here at the lake almost exclusively. It was where he came when his mind was confused and prayer and fasting could not clear it.

He parked his car in an empty parking lot for a convenience store that had mysteriously closed, as most new attempts at stores did around here. Only the oldest buildings were still standing, and they traded ownership between different families in town. Now, the store's windows were broken, the inside dusty and wrecked. The gas pumps had been vandalized, the plastic tubing ripped from the pump and strewn on the ground.

His hands shook as he lit the cigarette. It was getting dark— would be almost completely black outside in an hour—but he sat down on the flat, dry rock closest to the water. He knew his way out, and the moon was full anyway, leaving enough light for him to at least make his way back to the car and the wrecked gas station.

His stomach churned. He listened to the sound of his body reacting with curiosity. He had left church because his hands wouldn't stay still after he had baptized the boy (the man, the young man. That was the trouble, of course. If he'd really been a boy, there would be no problem), his stomach angry and churning loudly, his brow sweating. He had watched Derek, wet-haired and smiling, standing at the front of the church, shaking hands with each person in a row, and he had had to leave. What was in his head seemed so incongruous in that simple, holy place, everyone else with their thoughts firmly in the right place. Oh, but his thoughts, they could not be borne in that place of God.

His loneliness in that moment, too, was unbearable. He was not often reminded of the things he could not have because of the way he was made. He would not have a family. He would not sleep beside another person every night. Usually, he could distract himself from these thoughts, remind himself that he was serving a far greater purpose, that he was giving up a sinful life of pleasure for a pure life of service to the Lord, but tonight, he could not stop himself from mourning his own missed opportunities.

You are a fool, he said out loud, the cigarette a red point of light in his hand.

He had become a pastor because he knew what it was to sin, to want what you should not have, and he thought that helping others would cure him of the disease in himself. This was not the first time.

If Derek had known what you were thinking when he described his nights with those women, Levi thought. The clutching and sweat and shame. Levi shook his head. He was worse than a sinner, he was a deceiver, just like Lucifer himself.

As a boy, Levi had not known himself so well. He thought he was just lonely and his desire for touch only the result of being the only boy, of having no cousins close to the family. He thought he wanted friends. Strange how when you are young, you confuse friendships and sex, you do not understand the barriers and the kinds of loves that would please God and the kinds of love that would anger God. Then, it had seemed quite simple: he only wanted people, anyone, near to him. He preferred other young men, but wasn't that normal?

But later, he knew, and he accepted, that it was not normal. Christ could forgive all things. As long as he did not give in, as long as he kept his intentions pure, he'd be cured. Levi lay smoking cigarette after cigarette until his throat burned. It had not been true. He wouldn't be cured, and he should never had thought so.

God had not made him to be cured. God wanted him to be what he was, a walking wound, to test him. He was like a saint, unable to touch people like others touched people, unable to let himself be free. And that was what God wanted. Maybe God had made him this way to keep him separate, to sanctify him for higher purposes.

The sky above him was completely clear, the stars pinpoints in the sky, the moon so bright it almost hurt his eyes. He imagined the creatures in the forest around him, the snakes coming up on the shore from the water, the possums in the woods and each rustle — which could be anything from a stray dog to a coyote to a panther — slinking through the darkness to find the soft place in his throat.

But he wouldn't move. He let the fear sweep over him and then recede. If he died tonight, maybe that would be for the best. He had prayed for forgiveness. He had done his duty as best as he could. Maybe he was reaching the point at which he was no longer useful to God, the point when he was bound to give in to the devil and ruin himself and the church.

The papers would have only good things to say about him if he chose now to end it. The young men he had counseled would say he had been like a father, the families that he had been their ally, the children that he had been kind. Nobody could say that he had hurt them. He had confided in nobody, made nobody an intimate in his troubles. He could disappear completely, only his public face remaining as a memory.

He smoked three cigarettes slowly and completely and then put the pack in his pocket, his throat sore. He walked to the edge of the water, where the rocks replaced the grass and the water sloshed up. He crouched down by the water and dipped his hand in, testing the temperature. It was cool, but not cold. He breathed deeply, the air thick around him and cooling, though he was sweating at the brow and a wide, dark stain spread around his underarms.

Fuck it, he thought, and even mouthed the words, though he could not say them. He took off his shirt and unbuckled his pants. He imagined what could be in the water, the snakes and tangles of branches, and slid his pants down his legs. He stepped out of them and took off his shoes and socks, leaving his clothes on the shore. He did not stop to fold his clothes. He didn't turn on the headlights to see what was in the water before him. He didn't shout and stamp his feet as he often did in the woods, when clearing an old path, to scare the snakes and armadillos away.

Let come what will, he thought, before he stepped in and then jumped, his whole body taking the shock of the cold.

He emerged from the water shaking, fearing he would bite his own tongue as his teeth chattered, and walked away, naked and barefoot. He ignored the car and walked past it into the woods, where there was no path, no way to know where he was or where he was going. But he knew where he was going—how? He tried to wrangle his thoughts, to pin them down and make them his own again, but they swam in front of him. He felt almost apart from his body, like somebody watching himself as he entered the darkness of the woods and dodged the branches, moving quickly on his way to somewhere, but where? There were plenty of houses out here, scattered along the dirt roads and tucked away down long driveways.

His body tore through the woods, one green branch whipping across his chest, opening a small, weeping gape in his skin.

And then, he saw a light, a window within the frame of a house. He moved toward it, his head buzzing. He worried that his car would be found, he'd be seen stumbling in the woods, and the worries joined the cloud of thoughts already in his head, the sound growing and needling into his skull like a dentist's drill.

He broke through the trees and touched the cool siding of the house. It was real. He could faintly hear the sounds of television from inside it.

Somehow, he had to get inside. But why? The question was far away from his ear and did not mean much to him. He went around to the front of the house, his hand brushing the dirty siding, tracing the windows.

The door was not locked. Inside, a woman sat in a chair. She did not move and her mouth was opened, her head leaned back.

His mind buzzed. His stomach tingled and began to churn and heave. He saw his feet move him into the kitchen.

She's going to be upset when she finds you here, the words buzzed in his head. She'll call the police. What will they think? His hand picked up a knife from the block of wood where she kept a large collection of knives, probably something she'd bought from QVC— it seemed new and never used, the handle lipstick red and the blade bright as a knife in a model kitchen.

He wondered what his body would do with the knife right up until the moment that his hand slid the blade across her throat, pulling her head back hard as he did so. Her hairnet came off in his hands. He looked on as the blood shot across his hand, his bare chest. The woman first tried to raise her hands to her throat, but quickly stopped, her hands dangling heavy when they fell.

It's too much blood, he heard some part of himself say, and he noticed the black gushing from the gashed place in the woman's throat and felt something rise up his esophagus and burn. He turned away and the sickness cleared.

His legs carried him out the door and back the way he came. He threw the knife into the water once he reached the lake, put the scrap of fabric in his pocket, and stumbled back to where he'd started. He washed his hands in the water, scrubbing the blood from under his fingernails, from his chest, which was bare and scratched. He went back to where he had left his clothes in a pile and put them on quickly. By the time he got into the car and turned the ignition, his mind was clearing. But clearing wasn't the right word—it was filling up again, after being cleared, a blank. He didn't know why his legs ached as though he had traveled a distance, why his hands were damp and pink from scrubbing, why his mouth was salty and his stomach unsettled. He remembered diving into the water, the cold, the sludge under his feet, and after that, only static until he was in the car and driving.

When he got home, he undressed and emptied his pockets of their contents. In the dark, he did not know what the hairnet was. He put it away in the garage, in the yellow toolbox he rarely used. He didn't know why he had kept it or why he had put it where had, but his mind was so aching and tired, his body so exhausted, that he did not question it until later, when he remembered the woman's blood flowing into his hands and her wet gasps and needed something to show for it, to prove that he was not the man that everyone believed that he was.

8

In moments of great stress or fear, Emily tended to go outside of her body. Instead of feeling her own reactions when upset, she imagined how other people would react. How would people in a Western film react, for example, versus people in a drawing room in a Jane Austen novel? What exactly would be the appropriate response to this kind of news, anyway? In the world of ideal responses, what would she say to a man who claimed that he had killed her one known living relative?

She tried to reconcile the Levi she knew with the dead great aunt she had not known. She did not love him as she would family, but she liked him. He was kind, if strange, and too religious, of course, but there were worse sins. She should be angry, disgusted, horrified, she decided, but she wasn't. She watched the scene unfold, unmoving, as the space around her began to fill with the sounds of bodies rising from chairs, a kind of crackling and whisk of fabric.

Jonathan touched her knee, squeezed it hard until she turned to look at him.

Are you okay? He asked. Talk to me, Emily.

She turned away from him and looked back up at Levi.

Now, Levi was weeping, his hands over his face. His body collapsed onto the podium and the microphone squealed and rustled against his lapel.

She turned to Jonathan again.

Did you hear that? He asked, then shook his head. Of course you heard it. What do you think? What should we do? He spoke in a whisper. She turned her hands palm-up and turned from him again. It was too early to plan what to do. What could they do?

I need a minute, she said. I can't really talk about it yet.

She looked behind her, at the confusion. The children were still on the ground, some still playing, but most had caught the last moments of Levi's speech—the ones old enough to understand were tugging at their parent's shirtsleeves, some crying.

A man stood up. Like Levi, he was excessively neat, his striped shirt unwrinkled at the shoulders and collar. He was younger than Levi, had more hair, and sat at a table with a woman and three children. His family, Emily imagined. He was the youth pastor, she overheard, the second-in-command.

Pastor Levi, he said aloud, addressing both the podium and the crowd. It sounds like you've had some kind of shock, but I can assure you, what you say is not possible. He faced the crowd now, clearly making an argument to them, not Levi. Why would you harm an innocent woman? What could make you do this? The man shrugged with exaggeration, scanning the eyes of the crowd. This is not the Pastor Levi we've all known for the last fifteen years, is it, folks?

Most people nodded. The men who were standing began to sit down. Somebody else had taken charge. Emily could feel the tension diffuse, the people in the room sitting and letting any weight fall from their shoulders. Here was somebody to take that weight.

Emily felt her hands opening and closing in her lap, her fingernails pressing the palm's flesh.

I'm not sure why you think this has happened, Pastor Levi, or why you believe this dream, but I'm here to tell you that I know what kind of man you are in your heart. This is not you. You did not kill Frannie.

Another man, this one toward the back of the room, stood up. Greg's right, he said. You didn't do this thing, Levi, and we can get you the help you need.

Levi lifted his head. He lifted the hairnet. What about this? If I didn't do it, what about this? Why do I have it?

Greg shook his head. There's some explanation, brother Levi, some reason, but you didn't do it. You didn't do it.

Greg turned to a group of teenagers and motioned to them. Go up to Pastor Levi and help him down, he told them. Two boys separated themselves from the group—they both wore matching shirts advertising a Youth March for Life in Keno. They stepped up to the podium and took one arm each, steadying Levi.

Come down, Pastor Levi. Come down and rest, Greg said.

But I did it. His voice was softer now. Believe me. You all know about dreams: they aren't all foolish. God gave Joseph dreams that were true. God gives dreams, like he gives everything else. I did it. You know I did it. And it was the lake that made me do it. It knew I had so much hate in my heart. He wiped the tears away from his face with his wrists. Despite his words, he let them budge him from behind the podium, let them walk him, slowly, down the steps and into around the edges of the crowd. Frannie's hairnet lay on the podium, light, liable to be blown away if a small wind blew.

Emily watched his descent, her legs jittery, her hands pressing moons into her palms. For once, she felt her body working, not her mind, as Greg stepped up to the podium to explain that Levi had been under so much pressure lately due to the murders, that he had overstretched himself in his bereavement work.

He has taken responsibility for this terrible crime because his mind is tired and, like all of us, he wants answers, Greg said. And because he loves this town and the people in it, he's willing to take responsibility—but this is not true. I know with all of my heart that this man is not capable of such acts.

Greg's voice grew more forceful as he spoke. The more he spoke, the more he began to believe himself. He began to swell with the truth of his words, with the logic, with the nods of the people listening.

Emily stood unsteadily, not turning to acknowledge Jonathan's whispered Emily!, resting her hand on the plaid print of the tablecloth.

 The crowd nodded and said Amen. The crowd decided that they would not believe what Levi said.

Hello! Emily shouted. It was a stupid way to start, nothing like what she should say, but her mouth opened and the simple greeting flew out.

You know me, she said out loud, turning to see the people behind her. Frannie was my great-aunt. I didn't know her. But I live here now. This is my home, too. Her chin wobbled, and she feared her voice did, too. She pushed forward anyway.

No matter what really happened, I know one thing. You don't want to know the truth. You don't want to know really happened.

Why don't you want to know the truth? I know you care. I know you want this to stop, but it won't stop until you do something about it. Until you decide to listen.

She opened her mouth, her face flushed, and shouted: WHY DON'T YOU WANT TO KNOW THE TRUTH? What do you have to hide? A child began to cry from somewhere behind her, snapping her out of her moment of stupid, thoughtless bravery.

She put her hand over her mouth and thought she might be sick. She had not meant to speak. She'd never meant to say those things. It was all so confusing. It was too much.

Hey, Em—Jonathan began. He stood up and touched her on the shoulder, but she walked away from Jonathan, passed the rows of people who turned to watch her, and made her way to the back of the row of picnic tables, where the teenagers had set Levi down at Greg's request. She stood by Levi.

Greg remained at the podium. He was silent as she spoke, and then, when she was done, seemed to resume as though she had never spoken. He instructed everyone to clean up the tables, to go home and pray for Pastor Levi and Emily (who had gone through some *serious trauma today*) and to go home and get some rest after this trying day.

The teenagers looked up at her, afraid.

I have to talk to Levi, she said.

Pastor Levi needs to go home, Ma'm, one said, the taller, thinner one, with a dent in his chin and the look of a young man who would be able to sail through life on his square jawline and his blue eyes. He's not fit for talking right now.

Levi was hunched at the table, his hands in his hair, his face resting on his bicep, turned away from her. The boys held him with difficulty. He seemed to be shaking all over, a flap of escaped hair (once gelled down, now in wild clumps) moving with his body.

Emily ignored the boys. She went to the other side of the table, where Levi faced a tangle of short, vine-choked trees. She knelt down to meet his face, leaning against the vine.

He had his eyes closed tight, though water escaped. His usually tight, controlled mouth wobbled. Levi, she said. I need to speak to you.

He opened his eyes.

I believe you, she said.

He closed them again. She saw a shudder roll through his body and felt the faint clack of his teeth banging together.

I'm sorry, he said. It's true, and I'm sorry. I didn't know what I was doing—

I believe you, she said again, less firmly this time. She couldn't absolve him, but she also couldn't manage to hate him: she hadn't known Frannie. He was more real to her than she had been.

But what made you do it? She asked him. What's making this happen? It's been like this for all of the murders, hasn't it?

He raised his head and jerked his arm away from the boy at his left. Let me be, he told them. Emily and I have things to say to each other.

The boys stepped away, surprised by his sudden force where he had been only limp and accepting before. But they wouldn't have much time before somebody with authority came, the youth pastor or one of the tall, older men who served as deacons and stood like obelisks at Greg's side.

He leaned close to her. She could feel the heat and faintly taste the salt from his skin.

It was inside of me, all that anger. He said. But this place made it come out. It was the lake. The lake did it. It took what was wrong in me and pointed it at anyone who I came upon. It didn't matter who. It's the lake, he said. It's where all of the feeling gathers. It's like a bullhorn, an amplifier. It takes whatever you give it and send sit back tenfold. That's what happened to the others, they were like me—opened to receiving something ugly, feeling murderous anyway, confused, susceptible. It's like the devil, he said. It gets inside if you are weak. And I am weak.

You can't just bury things forever. I guess the water held all of that, and now it has power over us.

Did you see them? He flicked his head at the crowd, the families stuffing cups and plates in plastic trash bags and sealing the Tupperware containers closed. They didn't want to hear it. But they know it's true. They tell their children not to go to the lake alone, to never go to the lake after dark, but they don't say why. Maybe they don't even know why.

He turned to her, the skin around his eyes purple and blue, his mouth chapped and cracking. They're afraid. We've been doing this for too long. We can't stop now. It won't let us.

One of the deacons approached.

Thank you, she whispered. Thank you for telling me. She

stood up, and then hesitated, her hand still on the table. She knelt down again.

I forgive you, she said. She leaned in close enough to see the small pores in his nose, hear the little whistle of his breathing. I don't know what happened, or why, but I forgive you.

The words seemed to weigh him down instead lift him, as she'd hoped that they would. But really, how much could he be lifted now? Levi collapsed back into his own arms.

A boy stood by her side, his hands in his pockets, his eyes unable to stay in just one place.

Ma'am, I'm here to take you to see Greg, our youth pastor; he respectfully asks a word with you.

She imagined that the youth pastor had couched him to use those words exactly, *respectfully asks a word*. She felt sorry for the boy and smiled at him. His pale hair was cut so short at the sides of his head that she could see his scalp.

He wants to talk to you about Pastor Levi, those things he said about your Aunt Frannie tonight, things that must have upset you so much.

Emily nodded and stood up. I'd be happy to speak with him.

Happy wasn't exactly the correct word, but it would do for now, for this boy who was innocent and basically well-meaning in his ignorance.

Greg perspired at the podium as he fielded questions and families holding their now-crying children or shepherding their confused grandparents to the minivan or truck. He held a cloth handkerchief and mopped his forehead.

He shook her hand and asked the man who stood red-faced before him to wait a moment, he had something important to say. She watched the man reluctantly leave the podium.

Emily, he said, smiling at her in that practiced, directed way that she'd seen now only in preachers and salesmen. I wanted to apologize on behalf of Levi for his words tonight. I can't imagine how much they've upset you.

Emily nodded. She pressed her lips together, knowing they would make a harsh, fleshless line.

He says that he killed a member of my family, she said. Why shouldn't that upset me? And more importantly, why shouldn't I believe him?

Greg blinked and lifted the handkerchief to his head again.

I can assure you, Ma'am, that he had nothing to do with—

But how do you know?

He sighed and balled up the handkerchief. Ma'am, I can assure you—

You can't assure me of anything, she said. Why don't you believe him?

Greg looked down the podium, which had names carved into its rough surface. I don't believe him because what he says is impossible. What would possess him to do such a thing? There's no reason.

That isn't a good enough reason, she said. He admitted to it. He showed evidence. He knows what he did. Shouldn't we believe him?

Greg shook his head. You aren't from here, so you don't know, but Levi is not the kind of man who would do such a thing. We know who would do something like this: it's very clear, when you get to know the people around here—

I'm sick of this, Emily said. I'm sick of people telling me that I'm not from here, so I wouldn't understand. Maybe I don't understand, but I don't think I'm wrong. She surprised herself by turning away from him, by not even saying goodbye or waiting to hear what he had to say.

She went back to Jonathan, who remained seated at the table. An older woman from the church had seated herself next to him. She seemed to be telling him about the tragedies that had struck Heartshorne—the murders, the missing children.

And now our pastor, she said, shaking her head, seems to be touched. She pressed her forefinger against her temple. Touched in the head, I mean.

Jonathan nodded.

Can we leave? Emily said. The old woman looked up, alarmed, used to being deferred to. I have to go home, she said. I have to get out of here. Jonathan led her back to the car, where she realized, as she sat in the passenger seat and watched the sky open again and a downpour ripple across the windshield, that she was angry. She was shaking with anger. And she was not afraid.

9

It took Jonathan a half hour to get them home, though it was usually only a ten minute drive—he could hardly see through the rain pounding against the windshield. The dirt roads were flooded.

I won't be able to leave in the morning, he said. Can I stay the night again?

She nodded at the windshield. Of course you can, she said. I'd love for you to stay.

I'm sorry, she said, after a few minutes of silence. I'm sorry I'm not here right now.

It's OK, he said. We'll figure out what to do.

She turned to him and smiled. She appreciated his kindness, though it seemed like a silly thing to say. What could they possibly do about this? It was larger than the both of them.

Jonathan and Emily ate soup and crackers and listened to the rain pounding her ceiling. It did not leak, so far, though the rain was hard and constant and poured down the windows.

Why did everyone ignore what Levi said? She asked. Why didn't anyone stand up and say that he had to be listened to, that if he was guilty, then he should be able to confess and be heard? Jonathan didn't know.

Should we call the police? He asked, but she shook her head.

But why not? What are you waiting for?

What she was waiting for was the town to admit everything. That would be better than the police coming, taking one person and leaving nothing really unchanged.

I want them to do something, she said. They are like the boy holding the two swords, afraid to do anything because they might cut themselves. I want them to cut themselves.

They all knew that Levi had killed Fran, Emily thought, but they knew other things, too. They knew why her mother had left.

They knew how Mr. Rodriguez had died. The ones who didn't know didn't want to know and the ones who were still innocent were being taught how not to hear.

No, she said. Let's not call the police. Not yet. Let's wait.

Wait for what? Jonathan showed signs of tension in his mouth, a tightness that was new to her. He was upset. But she couldn't give in. An image formed in her head, the six of swords, the mother and child crossing the water.

She turned to him and placed her hand on his knee. I don't know exactly why, but I want to wait. Can you understand that? It's just a feeling. You trust those, right? Intuition?

He nodded. I just—

Let's wait, at least a day. Let's see what happens tomorrow.

After a quick dinner, they fell asleep early, just like married people. Only she didn't really fall asleep: she pretended, keeping her breathing shallow and regular until she heard his breathing become regular and his legs stopped their restless kicking. Soon, he snored softly. And then, when she thought he was deeply enough asleep to leave the bed without disturbing him, she felt that telltale heaviness that meant she was sleepy, too. She closed her eyes, just to give them enough of a rest to allow her to get up, to dress, to make it to the edge of the lake. But her body would not let her. She felt herself sliding into sleep, felt her thoughts branch out and multiply into absurdities, and knew that it was too late. She couldn't stop it.

•

Connie was a teenage girl. Her hair was whipped up in a bouffant and twisted behind her head with bobby pins. Emily could tell it was Connie because her eyes and mouth were the same as they'd been when Emily was a child, same as they'd been when she was older, even when she was dying. Her eyes were big, but capable of quick, suspicious movements. Her blue eyes were surrounded by pale lashes that Connie painted in blackest black Maybelline mascara, a purchase that had not changed in all of the years that Emily had known her. Her mouth was small but shaped like a bow. She'd been a beautiful girl. She wore a short-sleeved white blouse tucked into a knee-length A-line skirt, stockings and sandals. She had a lighter in one hand and a cigarette in another. The lighter was metal with a flip-top that you could open by jerking your hand downward sharply at just the right force and angle. Connie did this, flicked the flame to life, and lit the cigarette end.

My mother was cool, Emily thought. She was beautiful and she could light a cigarette like a femme fatale from a film noir, even at what, fourteen? Connie narrowed her eyes and pursed her perfect mouth at Emily.

So, what were you planning?

I don't know, Emily said. She felt awkward around her young mother. She was in her nightgown, a long t-shirt with a hole in one armpit that said OSU across the chest in garish, red letters. She was not cool and never had been.

Did you hear about the water? Connie took a drag and blew the smoke from her pursed lips. Did you hear what he said? The water makes you do crazy things? Makes you even more angry than you already are and turns you on the closest person?

Emily nodded.

So you were going to go out there as you are right now, so angry, stupid with anger?

Emily shook her head. I'm not angry.

Oh, I think you are. Connie narrowed her eyes again. She stepped forward and Emily resisted the urge to step away. This was her dream. She didn't have to step away. She stood her ground.

Connie took her arm. Listen, she said. She put out the cigarette under her heel. I know you are angry with me. You are mad that I never told you about this. Mad that I tried to make you hate this place. Mad that I died and was never the mother that you wanted to have, all of that. Connie waved her free hand in the air and rolled her eyes.

But guess what? Connie tightened her grip on Emily's arm. I was the mother you had, the only one. You don't get to choose. You don't get to tell me who to be, just like I didn't get to tell you who to be. It works both ways. I was your mother and I was a woman going to a shitty community college who found herself alone and pregnant, and I was a fourteen-year-old in Heartshorne, and a child in Heartshorne Elementary, and a baby on Frannie's lap and in my mother's arms. I was all those things. She let go of Emily's hand.

Emily looked around for the first time, seeing the scrubby brush that surrounded them, the cracked and dry ground. They were in Heartshorne. In the distance, Emily saw the school marquee, no longer electronic as it was when Emily last saw it, but crowded with black letters that the janitor changed by hand every week: *Harvest Dance*, it said.

You don't know what happened here, Connie said. Don't punish me for what you don't know. You can't be angry when you go out there, she said. You can't do it angry.

Emily nodded. She crossed her arms over her chest, suddenly cold.

You have to figure out how to love me.

The light changed then, a column of it falling from the blue, enormous Oklahoma sky, and Connie changed, too. She was an adult, at a kitchen table. A room enclosed them, the weather now outside, tapping at a small window to get in.

Sit down, Connie said. Let me help you.

•

Emily woke to the continuing sound of rain. Jonathan had wrapped the pillow around his head and kicked the blankets to the floor. Jonathan was so deeply asleep that she didn't even moan or break the hum of his snoring when she got out of bed and felt for her shoes and her robe on the floor.

In the kitchen, she drank a glass of water and watched the rain streaking the window. She switched on the porch light, which revealed a swamp, the road overflowing. She went to the hallway closet and took out her only jacket. It wasn't waterproof, but it had a hood. She took out her rain boots and a heavy flashlight which she'd bought before her road trip and had never used until now.

She'd reach the lake in just a few minutes if she went straight through the woods. She knew the way.

The rain pounded against her jacket, and though the flashlight was drenched and she feared it would short, it shone through the trees and rain. She had not imagined how peopled and active the woods would seem in the rain and how much what she'd learned about Levi and the lake would make her body revolt against her movements. She felt herself shivering, not from cold, but from some deep part of herself trying to keep her from going forward. She had to force every step.

She didn't look beyond the light or behind her. If she looked backward, she might turn back. If she paid attention to things that seemed to be moving in her peripheral vision, she might turn back. And she couldn't turn back.

She'd had another dream conversation with her mother. They were sitting at her new kitchen table in Fran's house, her own house now, at the gouged countertop. Connie was as Emily last remembered her—thin, her hair wispy with pink patches of scalp showing through. She lifted her hand to stir the milk and sugar into her coffee and Emily saw the bruises on her wrists from the IV's and the sticky, black edges of the tape that had held the tubes around her nose and mouth. She didn't shake, as she had at the end, and wore a light, white dress. Just before the end, she grew so cold, even in rooms heated to 80 degrees, and always needed a blanket around her chin. Even when she could still speak, quietly, but still coherently, her toes and fingers had already started to lose heat. Emily had found this particularly painful, insulting even. Connie's mind was still working; she understood what was happening even as she lost the feeling in her toes and fingers.

Emily, she said, stirring her coffee tan. Do you remember when we drove to West Virginia? You were eight. We drove together, just the two of us, and went to Black Mountain Caverns? Do you remember how I pulled you to me as the elevator dropped us down to the bottom? How scared I made you because I bruised your arm? It was because I was afraid, you understand? I was afraid that you'd be hurt. You struggled and pulled yourself away from me and out of my arms, but I held you tighter and I was angry with you, because you did not understand how afraid I was and how much I needed you to simply let me hold you.

Emily nodded. She did remember, but she remembered it differently. She remembered the elevator's sudden shift down and grabbing at her mother's clothes, afraid of flying off into the dark of the cave where the dim lights reflected off of what had seemed like sharp stalactites. Emily remembered fearing that she would fall from the elevator (it only had a bar, waist-high, keeping her from the cave walls). She remembered, too, that her mother had pushed her away.

Connie continued to stir, and then took another spoonful of sugar from the opened bag.

And do you remember when I drove you to school, the first day of first grade, and how you cried and I told you to stop, that you had to be a big girl? After you left, I stayed in the car, watching you as you weaved among the other children. Those other children, they didn't matter, do you understand? They didn't matter to me. You entered that building, dry-eyed after some sweet, young teacher showed you your new classroom, and I cried until my eyes were swollen and drove home slowly so I wouldn't wreck, I was so afraid of having you away from me for a whole day. That's how foolish you made me because I loved you and I couldn't help it.

She looked up, her under eyes purple and translucent in the sunlight of the room. Emily turned her head to see the light source—the kitchen window, opened out to the day. It wasn't raining anymore. It was noon, the sun full above them.

You have everything you need, she said. So stop it. Stop the anger. You think because you don't say it and are quiet and alone it isn't there, but it is. You aren't fooling anyone. Your mother knows you, even if you don't want her to know you. Let it go. Stop wanting what wasn't possible and want what you actually had.

It took Emily ten minutes to reach the water, she walked so slowly and carefully through the muck. She heard it before she saw it. The rain beating against the lake sounded different than the rain against the leaves—flatter and more insistent. Then, she hit a patch of soaked ground, and her boots were ankle-deep in water. She sloshed through until the trees ended and she reached what was once the shore. She was now knee-deep in water. The surface of the lake was black with little flashes of pale light where the rain hit the surface.

She took off the rain slicker and let the water hit her. She was soaked immediately. The water at her knees was as cold as river water, but she stripped off her clothes anyway until she was down to her underwear. She turned off the flashlight, leaving herself in darkness, and put it in the pocket of her slicker, which she draped in the shoulder-high branches of the closes tree. She waded out until the water reached her chest, and then she dove.

•

She was not the only one at the lake that night.

Levi woke from a dream he could not remember. He'd bitten into his inner cheek in sleep and tasted salt. He held the side of his face as it throbbed. Above him, the rain pounded against the roof.

Then, it all rushed back to him: Frannie's death, the community dinner where he had planned to lead his flock back to God, but had succeeded only in making a fool of himself and convincing nobody. The memory made his stomach churn. He deserved the pain. He had not been the man of God he should have been. He could not convince them of the clear, but difficult path of righteousness.

He sat up in bed. It was still raining. Levi stood up and dressed carefully, choosing his best suit and his best shoes. He wore a raincoat over his jacket and plastic boots over has shoes, a habit he could not break, despite what he was planning. Yet another piece of evidence pointing to the obvious: he was too wed to the body and its needs, to the things of the world, even in a moment like this.

Outside, his feet sunk into the lawn. The car would be useless— he'd have to walk.

•

Emily didn't allow herself to register the cold and slide of broken branches and slimy grass that brushed against her feet and thighs. She held her tongue back away from her chattering teeth and brought herself back in time:

Her first sleepover, at five, when she cried in bed until her best friend's mother (she couldn't remember the friend anymore, only the sudden feeling of all of the air being sucked out of her chest, the feeling of her throat closing up) made her get out of bed and marched her back to her mother's house, where she could not help but hiccup and cry until she was back in her own bed, Connie sitting by and smoothing down her hair until she could sleep.

In first grade, after failing to get a perfect score on a spelling quiz (the word *momentum*, easy when she thought of it, had momentarily escaped her), and after Tamara, the girl who sat in back of her in Math class, had tugged at her hair and said she didn't brush it, clearly, because there was a big knot in the back, Emily sat waiting for her mother to come get her for ten minutes after the last bell had rung. She'd watched the other kids leave the school and enter the buses (which had seemed happy, full of people talking and laughing and not frightening, loud, and tribal, as they had when was actually inside of one) or their parents' waiting cars and felt the bruise of self-pity growing. The world hated her. But then Connie drove up, just as tears were at the edges of her eyes, and said *get in, silly. I'm taking you out for ice cream.* The relief had been so sweet, so unexpected, that even thinking of that feeling brought up a sliver of comfort.

And, after her first middle school dance, when everyone else had matched up, boy and girl, until she was left alone, she had left the auditorium decorated with purple and pink crepe paper and the floor piled with glittering confetti and run home, a mile at least, Connie had brushed out her hair, set so carefully in the curls and pins hours before, saying only that she was happy to have Emily home, that the house had been lonely without her. She had not asked Emily why her eyes were red or why she'd torn a hole in the knee of her stockings and had not scolded her for walking in the dark at night.

Emily had more moments like this, ones she hadn't thought of in years: they ran in a loop, the memories fresh for being so scarcely used. Her arms began to burn, but she did not allow the feeling to penetrate her mind. She focused on the repetition swish of water past her ears and the thoughts.

She had loved her mother. The thought surprised her and she stopped, treading water. She had loved her mother and all this time, she'd thought otherwise. She was mistaken about her own feelings, which seemed impossible. But she had loved her. She had cried when physically separated from Connie, had sought her comfort, had been delighted, more times than she could count, at her presence.

I loved her, she said out loud, her voice no match for the rain, which still pounded against the water. I loved her.

•

He'd played in the lake as a child, as everyone else who grew up in Heartshorne had, though with caution: like everyone else, he had heard the rumors about the fog, had been rushed, suddenly, from the water by his grandmother and mother on particularly damp and misty nights. He didn't swim in front of his parishioners— after he became a pastor, he thought it a bit unseemly to go out in swimming trunks, his body exposed, the hair around his nipples and on his back showing to everyone. He had to keep an air of separation.

Perhaps that was why it had been so easy for the lake to take him. It spoke a language he didn't understand anymore but once had—like a child who knows Spanish at birth but speaks English now, who suddenly, upon passing a group of Spanish speakers realizes that he understands what they are saying. And so, the lake knew him, and he had not been able to refuse it.

The walk to the lake was quick, and in the pounding rain, he heard it long before he reached the water lapping into the leaves and sticks of the woods—it had risen far beyond the shore.

Much like Emily, he removed his clothes carefully and folded them at the shore. It had seemed important to dress well to bring himself to the lake, to show that he was still himself and not beaten, but now, the thought of sloshing in the water, his clothes dragging the twigs and branches, his body swollen and still grotesquely dressed like a live person, seemed silly. Better that he show himself naked now, showed that he understood that he would leave the world as he'd been brought into it. So he undressed and waded into the water.

It was cold, and his body recoiled. He moved slowly, inch-by-inch, wondering if it were better just to plunge in and get it over with.

Silly. This is the last time you'll have to feel the cold. Why think about it? Even now, at the end, he couldn't let himself go. He shook his head and dove into the water. The cold hit him—an enormous slap—and he began to swim, his body energized.

He planned to swim out into the middle of the lake until his body was exhausted. Then, he would dive down, swimming deeper and deeper. People drowned accidentally all of the time. Surely he could make himself drown on purpose.

•

The lake was still. She felt the burning of cold in her arms and legs, but also a throbbing in her head like something trying to get in through her ear. Her body could not take much more of this.

I loved her, she said aloud again, that's all I have. What can you do with that? What can you create with that? I won't give you anything else. She treaded water, the pain growing in her limbs, her body so cold she feared she wouldn't be able to make it back to the shore.

The rain continued to pound against the lake, making any small sources of light puddle and jump. Nothing would happen. She would swim back, warm herself in a hot shower, and then slip into bed with Jonathan, hoping that he had not noticed her absence. She wouldn't tell him what she had done; she had already decided that as she turned back to the shore and began to paddle back. Not unless he caught her coming in or had been awake and waiting, worried. She'd figure out then what to say, if it came to that. If he was asleep, then she'd explain the mud by saying that she'd had to go out and take a walk. She'd say that she couldn't sleep, which was understandable enough and part of the truth.

As she paddled back, imagining she could almost see the outlines of her jacket in the tree, the water began to move. Waves rolled around her, ducking her under and bobbing her back up again like a cork. She spit lake water from her mouth (it tasted like mud and grass and something metallic) and prepared for the next wave, jumping up with it. She could not touch the ground with her feet, though she had swam back toward what she believed was the shore (had she turned herself around? Was she paddling back out into the middle of the lake? It didn't seem so—the lights from the town were behind her).

The water was rising. It pushed her back as it rose.

She was a strong swimmer, but her teeth chattered, her arms felt burdened with weights. She kept swimming, fighting the push of the waves and the rising water.

Something from below the surface of the water rammed up against her leg, bruising it and stunning her so badly that she stopped swimming and dropped below the surface. The object, large and block-like, rose up, pushing her out of the way. She spluttered up, clawing, her arms and legs burning with the effort.

•

Levi swam quickly towards the heart of the lake, as far from the share as he could stand until his arms ached and he had to stop. He bobbed there, his feet far from the ground,

This seemed like as good a place as any. Levi held his breath and dunked his head. He dove downward, swimming hard to get himself so far down that he could not possibly make it back up in enough time. He meant to swim to the bottom, close enough to touch it, and then let go. He knew his body would fight him, would make him tear to the surface. He deserved that suffering. He only hoped he could resist his body's desire to live.

He had not gone far before the object rammed into his side, stopping his descent. Panicked, he fought his way back up, his side aching. He broke the surface of the water and saw, in the moonlight, that the lake was moving. It looked, too, like it was filled with bobbing objects. Coffins. The graveyard had come up again, as it had forty years before.

About fifty feet away, something struggled against one of the coffins. The water sprayed and a hand popped up momentarily before it fell back down into the water again.

Levi didn't think; he swam toward the person. He knew what drowning looked like, that desperate attempt to stay above water, the arms reaching up, trying to get enough leverage. Drowning people do not usually shout; they are too busy trying to stay alive. He reached the coffin and grabbed the flailing arm, hauling the person up and onto the coffin, which floated easily.

It was a woman, her hair plastered against her head. She was in her bra. Her skin was cold to the touch, her teeth chattering so hard that she could not speak.

Hold onto this, he said, throwing her arms onto the coffin. I'm going to go on the other side and balance, he said. We'll make it to the shore that way.

I don't know where the shore is, she said. The shore's flooded.

We'll make it far enough to stand, he said, and find your clothes.

He recognized Emily's voice.

•

The sky was slowly transitioning from black to gray—she could see the outline of trees and objects now, and the horizon over the lights of the town grew a murky orange. It must have been around five thirty in the morning. She held onto the piece of wood, one arm slung over it, and padded to the shore, where she could see her flashlight glinting in the pocket of her jacket.

Across from her, Levi kicked, propelling them forward. She was too cold to kick much, but she tried, though she could not feel her legs. She shivered uncontrollably, now too cold to speak. She wondered why Levi was out here—had he been following her? Did he mean to do her some harm? She didn't think so; why would he have saved her, then?

When they reached the shore, the water was knee-deep. Levi helped Emily down from the coffin and into the woods, where she had hung her clothes on a branch. They were damp, but better than nothing, and Levi helped her into them. His own clothes were somewhere else, probably spread across the water by now. He put the jacket over her head and helped her navigate her arms and head through the holes.

Are you OK? He asked? Do you need to see the doctor?

Emily shook her head. I don't think I was out here too long, she said. She was deeply tired. She simply wanted to go home and get into bed.

Levi nodded.

Why were you out here? She asked. They were making their way back to her house, where she said she could find him clothes. He was naked, but not shivering. She noticed, in the dim morning light (the sun had almost broken over the horizon) that he was covered in scratches. He held his right hand against his left elbow, pressing it to his body.

He shrugged. I guess I wanted to make my peace with this place.

She nodded. Me too.

They walked silently for a while.

I tried to die, Levi said, breaking the silence. I was trying to punish myself for what happened to your aunt. I wasn't brave enough to just turn myself in. I wanted the easy way out. But you were out there, too, and my plan didn't work.

Emily hugged her arms close to her body. It was too cold to think clearly. She heard Levi as though from a distance. She struggled to listen, to answer in a way that would be helpful to him.

You shouldn't turn yourself in, she said. You shouldn't do it.

I have to, he said. I told people I wanted change. I wanted justice. I can't only want justice when it's convenient for me.

She shook her head. This is different. She didn't know how. She only knew that she didn't want him in prison. What purpose would it serve? What justice would it deliver? Frannie would still be dead. The town would lose him. He would lose everything.

They approached the backyard. Emily felt a great relief at seeing the house, her back window lit from the light she had left on. She had never felt so much relief and happiness at coming home before.

I'll bring you something to wear, she said, slipping inside. She tiptoed into the bedroom, where Jonathan was snoring, sleeping heavily. She brought out a pair of pants, flip-flops, and an oversized sweatshirt.

I'm not sure if these fit, she said, but it's the best I could do.

Levi pulled the clothes on, grateful to no longer be naked in front of Emily. As soon as he was clothed, he realized how cold he had been. But the air was already warming with the sun, and it would reach almost 90 degrees by noon.

Don't do it, she said. Don't confess. It won't do any good, not now.

I don't know what I'm going to do, he said. But I'm done here. It's over for me.

Emily nodded. She wanted to stay here, to give him some words of comfort, to hug him, even, but she was too cold and too tired.

Goodbye, she said. And thank you for tonight.

He nodded. I'm grateful I was there.

He walked away, the plastic bottoms of his flip flops slapping against his feet. She never saw him again.

10

That morning, the sun emerged and the clouds cleared by eight AM. People tried to get to work, placing planks of wood across the mud puddles for the cars to slog through, though most called in—those whose phone lines still worked. Many met the sound of static when they placed the phone against their ears.

Word spread about the coffins. Some had washed up intact, just worn boxes, the hinges rusted closed. Some had washed up and rammed against the trees, busting open from the impact, and the dressed bones lay now in the mud in their silks and necklaces and ropes of long hair. Others had washed up on the road out of Heartshorne, spilling their contents onto the major road to Keno.

Other things had washed up, too—pieces of cars, shopping carts, years of garbage, and chunks of the waterlogged trees that broke apart from the surge of water. The county men came out to clear the road to Keno, while others took the back roads around the perimeter of the lake, which, though still high, had retracted from its nighttime levels. It was calm now, and few had seen the roiling and how the water had insisted its way over its usual edges.

The county men found the children early, as they were clearing the road that ran adjacent to the bait shop. Fishing line was wound around the children's hands and throats. They wore the clothes they had been lost in. The girl still had a purple plastic barrette in the remnants of her hair.

The man who found them covered them with his jacket and wouldn't let the others near them.

Stay away, he said, his voice gone soft and hard to decipher. They're sleeping.

This is what his co-workers heard, and afraid (they had a brief glance at the bodies before he had covered them, the color of the skin and the shapes of them familiar enough that they understood what they were, if not yet exactly who), they tried to talk him away from the children.

John, one of his friends on the crew, Martin, said, stepping forward. We've got to call this in. We aren't supposed to touch people who...people who wash up like this. Martin's mind flashed to a police procedural show that he watched every Tuesday night, one in which bodies were only coded information, nothing more. If he could put himself in that mind, like the police on those shows who walked around bodies placed on steel slabs, their heels clicking, he could help. He could lure John away and cover them up.

We aren't supposed to disturb the scene of a crime, he said. We might contaminate the evidence.

Shh, John said. Don't wake them up with that kind of language.

John had expected only to clear away the slimy boughs and branches tangled with plastic Wal-Mart bags. He had not expected the children, the Harris twins, though earlier that month he'd been on a search party to find them. During the search party, a slog through the muddy woods around the lake, he had not expected to find them. Then, he'd imagined they'd been kidnapped, taken by some angry relative or even a stranger. Somewhere distant in his mind he understood that they could have been killed, but that thought had been so far away, so farfetched, that he had never seriously considered it. They had disappeared miles away, almost in Keno. They had not, he knew, searched as thoroughly as they should have.

The only dead person he had ever seen was his grandmother, who had died when he was a child. He remembered her in the coffin, powdered and in a dress she'd only worn to marriages and graduations, her skin cold and her wrinkles hardened (according to his sister, who had bent down to kiss her on the hand—he had not had the guts to touch her). Since then, he'd been lucky—everyone in his family that he cared about or knew still alive, his job at worst showing him only a dog with its insides spilling out of its body on the road or dead birds, piles of feather and bone with pink, almost pretty entrails.

This was more than what he could understand. He liked children. His girlfriend wanted children, though he had urged her to wait and insisted on condoms, though she didn't want to use them.

It can't hurt to skip it just this one time, she'd say, though they both knew this to be untrue. How many babies had their friends brought into the world that way? He'd insist, though, citing his shit job, her desire to go to beauty school.

We can't afford a baby, he'd say, and he meant it. He just wanted to be ready. He wanted to buy his future children good swing sets, the kind you had to set into the ground with a cone of concrete, and he wanted to put them in clothes that would not shame them (he remembered a rare unpleasant occurrence from his childhood, when he had been called a white trash for wearing a jacket with a rip in the armpit and paint stain across the chest).

Seeing the children made something inside of him dislocate. He had believed in the goodness of the world, in children playing outdoors without parental supervision, in sunny days at lakes and drinking beer in the afternoon while you watch the children catch lightning bugs in jelly-jars. For most people, these things were no longer real or possible, but they were real for him here in Heartshorne. He loved living here, far away from places that made him nervous, like malls with expensive clothing stores, the mannequins headless and wearing asymmetrical pieces of fabric, restaurants with live music, and hushed museums filled with art that seemed, to him, like ugly affronts to everything that was simple and good. He had believed without irony that Heartshorne was the best possible place to be born in and the best place to grow up. The children here on the ground, the blue-blotching and brokenness of their skin, their arms and legs bound, their bodies swollen—this was not something he could understand. It was cold. They should be covered. This had been his first, stupid, thought—he had to cover them to keep them warm, though by the looks of the bodies they had not been warm in a very long time. He put his coat over them anyway.

He could not leave their side. What if they woke up, afraid, and did not know where they were?

They're sleeping, he said, and then again *they're sleeping*, believing suddenly that yes, this was possible. He could press his mouth to their mouths. He could make them alive again. Martin pulled him away as he began to cry, something he had not done since he was ten, since his grandmother's funeral. The men, knowing how much it took to cry in front of other men, looked away from him.

Something was happening that they could not understand. They held him and he hung heavy in their arms, his weight dragging down toward the ground.

Still, there was more.

What had been whispered about, gossiped about, even joked about, now washed up onto their lawns: frayed pieces of rope, tattered county boots with a plate of steel inserted over the toe, a single human hand still wearing a class ring, all remnants of acts that they had heard had happened, but most had not fully understood as real.

Before, it had been easy for people to disappear. They always had, drifting in and out, never heard from again, and how they disappeared, whether by choice, like the Collins family, or by death, like the many others, hadn't seemed so important. Like a working body, the town had flushed out what did not serve it, had sent antibodies to fight any sign of sickness. Now, those who had disappeared were speaking with their boots and ropes and remnants of bone and nobody knew how to shut them up.

11

In the early morning hours, after leaving Emily's house, Levi walked back to his own house, about two miles away, around the lake. He had sprained his elbow while swimming and the forearm was swollen, the elbow itself shooting pain each time he move it from its only comfortable position: pressed gently against his side, bent.

He didn't know what to do. He could turn himself in, but he no longer had the hairnet; somebody had taken it from the podium and probably destroyed it. Still yet, surely the police wouldn't turn him away if he came to them. He would tell them what happened.

He thought of Emily, telling him that turning himself in would be pointless. It would only serve to make him feel better and to shame the town. Despite what he had said at the meeting, people still thought of him as their pastor, as a man of God. What would it do to them to have him in prison? To have everyone know? He would shame them all by association.

Killing himself seemed stupid now. A momentary madness that he probably couldn't have gone through with anyway.

Maybe God had wanted him to live. God had put Emily there, had wanted them to meet that night. God wanted him to live.

Since he was a child, he had loved God. He had spoken to Jesus like other children spoke to imaginary friends. He had heard God's voice in his head at a revival in Tulsa, one record hot summer. He had been kneeling beneath a white tent, the air still and sticky and unrelenting, the preacher in the front in his gray suit, shouting that God would tell each person who he was in the Kingdom, what role he had to play, how he would bring the Kingdom of God into the world, and Levi had heard, just as they described, a still, small voice, telling him to preach. To preach the word to his small town. He had obeyed that word, and had never regretted it.

Levi stood on the porch of his small house, a house he'd owned outright for five years, he'd been so diligent about his money, so careful to never be in the position of losing something that he had loved, of always having security.

He'd lost all security now. And what did he have left?

He stepped inside, shut the door, and got down on his knees. He spoke to God as he had when he was a boy, not as a preacher. When he was done, he stood up.

He said goodbye to his house, taking only what he needed (his definition of need now refined — canned goods, his toothbrush and toothpaste, a few changes of clothes), and then left, touching the door before he left. The gesture seemed right, though he didn't feel anything electric beneath his palm to tell him that there was life here. His home now had the hollowed-out look of a recently abandoned house that had not yet fallen into disrepair, the grass still short and the windows still intact, but clearly without anyone inside it. Maybe this was how it had always looked, even when he had lived there. He drove away from it easily. He'd abandon the car when he'd gotten far enough away.

Leaving what he'd known was enough like death.

12

Emily woke groggy, her throat sore, her body aching. Her hair was still damp from the rain, and her socks were black and slick on her feet, so wet that they'd made basketball-sized rings of damp on her sheets. She peeled them off and observed her white, blue-veined feet beneath, looking vulnerable and flaky like fish meat. She tried to sit up, but her blood, hot and choppy in her head, rioted and set her back down. She touched Jonathan's bare shoulder and pressed against it until he woke.

I don't feel well, she said.

He looked at her wet hair, her exposed, pale feet. Where have you been?

She looked down at the bed; she had smeared the bed sheets where she'd slipped between them and her muddy hand prints smudged the edge of the blankets where she had pulled the covers up over her head.

I had to go out, she said. I had to cross the water and put out the fire, like the cards said.

She thought that what she said made sense—didn't he remember?—but the way he was looking at her made her stop talking. She sank back down into the dirty blankets.

It's too hot, she said, even as she tried to curl back into the head of her chest and belly for warmth. She was both freezing and sweating, her head a hot, heavy thing connected to the cold, plastic sack of her body.

Stay down, Jonathan said. I'm going to bring you water. Don't try to get up.

She no longer could get up, so she only nodded and sunk under the covers.

I'm lucky to have you here, she mumbled, though she didn't know if he was still in the room. I would have been alone if not for you. Alone like Frannie.

He came back soon and pressed something cold against her lips and the liquid fell into her mouth and slid down her throat, making her cough.

She could hear him speaking and felt the press of his colder hand against her cheek and forehead, but she could not respond. She was so tired.

Emily thought that this would be the perfect time for her mother to come back, for the dreams to return, but they didn't. She did dream, of course, just not as she had for the last few months, and when she dreamed of her mother, it was in scenes from her memory, her mother moving and speaking in the ways that Emily remembered her, but she said and did nothing new. Her mother did not speak directly to her anymore.

I miss her, Emily said once, as Jonathan woke her momentarily and placed a cup against her lip, the glass clicking against her teeth.

Shhhh, he said. Go back to sleep.

Somebody else was in the room. A woman, Emily could tell, because she could smell sweet shampoo and hear a rustling of hair.

Mom, she said, and then, embarrassed even in her sickness, tried to explain: I know it's not her, but I thought I'd see her.

Shhh, Jonathan said again. Just sleep. It's okay.

She dreamed of the lake rising, until it overtook Heartshorne, plunging it underwater just like the town that had been flooded before it to make the lake. She imagined herself floating up, her body washed on a new shore.

She dreamed of Levi, too. He was in the water, drowning, and she stood at the shore, watching him bob up and down in the black water. He was naked and she did not call to him, knowing he would be embarrassed if she acknowledged his body.

Don't come out to me, he shouted to her as he bobbed up and down. She thought of the poem *Not Waving, But Drowning* and remembered, maybe, that the poet had killed herself. Or was that some other poet? It could have been any number of them. Since Levi didn't want her to come, she stood at the shore, watching until he didn't come back up anymore.

Once the fever broke (a phrase she knew from Victorian novels) and she could sit up, she remained in a haze. Jonathan came in and out, bringing her broth and vitamin water. His sister had come from Keno, bearing medicinal teas, actual medicine, and other accoutrements of health: a humidifier, Vicks rub, and a mint candle made with natural beeswax.

Who has been watching the store? Emily asked, as soon as she could sit up.

Our parents.

How long have I been sick? How long was I sleeping?

Just two and a half days, he said. We weren't sure if we should bring you to the hospital: we thought we'd wait a day, see if you were feeling better. But what a day it's been. Look at the paper.

He unfolded it on her lap:

LOCAL PASTOR GONE MISSING:
Suspected Suicide by Drowning

Oh Jesus, she said, her hand over her mouth.

I'm not so sure he's dead, Jonathan said. No body found yet, and they've been dragging the lake. They mention what he said about Fran here, briefly, but they call it an "episode" and say there was no evidence to support Pastor Roberts' "extraordinary claims"—he pointed to a paragraph, but her head was still too clouded to read the entire article.

And look here. Jonathan pointed to the headline below it, accompanied by a photograph she'd seen before, the two Harris children.

HARRIS CHILDREN FOUND:
Two-month Search Ends in Tragedy

They were killed, she said. She couldn't bear to read the article past the first sentence: *A month of searching and a family still hopeful to somehow have their children home safe ends in tragedy after two bodies washed up in the Echo Lake flood last night.* She set it down on her lap. Jonathan sat at the edge of her bed, his face untroubled. She didn't want to be upset with him, but she was. She could hardly think straight, and he was filling her head with visions of drowned children.

You didn't have to show me all of this right now, she said.

I'm sorry, Jonathan said. He shook his head. What happened to them is terrible, but I wanted you to see this. He lifted the paper again, pointing to a paragraph halfway through the article:

The discovery of the Harris children is only one of the mysteries uncovered by the Echo Lake flood. Physical evidence from the James Kirkland, Luke Medders and Douglas Morrison missing persons cases have washed up in the flood. Although the physical evidence has been badly damaged by the exposure to water, the presence of these items give police a place to focus their investigations and new leads.

Things are changing, Jonathan said. That's what I wanted you to see. I don't know what happened, or why you were out that night, or even it is somehow had something to do with you—he pressed against Emily's cold hand then, hard, and looked her in the eye—but something's different now. This newspaper is saying things it wouldn't otherwise say. Thing are coming out into the open.

He stopped speaking as Claire entered, wearing a black, long-sleeved shirt that went down to her knees and black stockings. Claire was as beautiful and remote as she had been the few times Emily had met her. She was the kind of person who, upon meeting somebody new, offered a limp hand and smiled, briefly, before pulling herself away.

Claire, Jonathan said. Tell Emily what Mom and Dad said.

It was such an effortless exchange, but it almost made Emily tear up. They were cozily familiar, he and Claire. They loved each other and shared things. They had two parents who they visited on holidays and talked to on the phone and even visited out of the blue, just to see them. Emily could hardly imagine it. Claire sat at the edge of the bed and smiled at Emily.

They said they've never seen anything like it. They can't remember hearing so much talk about missing persons, about investigations. The FBI has come to investigate the Harris twins' murders—it fits a familiar profile, or something. Other children have been found over in Arkansas. People don't usually talk like that around here.

Dad has a friend on the Keno force, Jonathan said. He let it slip about the FBI thing.

So what does it mean? Emily motioned toward the glass of water, which she now desperately needed. Her tongue felt enormous and covered in fuzz.

It means something might actually happen. The murders might end. They might figure out who did it, and they can stop. Jonathan reached over and grasped the glass of water, passing it up to her as she struggled upright into bed.

Emily laughed, spitting water onto the quilt. The lake did it, she said, wiping her mouth and dabbing at the covers with the sleeve of her nightgown. Don't you remember what Levi told me? He said that the lake made him do it.

Well, no matter what Levi thought, it's been happening since before then—those other guys, the ones in the article, they happened before all of this, Jonathan said, tapping the surface of the newspaper, where a few grainy faces shaped a square above the article. The murders left out in the open are new. The ones that happened that nobody ever talks about, those have been happening for a long time. People never used to say these things out loud. A year ago, that boot they found would've just been thrown back into the lake where it came from.

Emily nodded, though her eyes felt heavy and she fought sleep. She knew that she should be happy. Of course, Jonathan was right. This was what she had wanted, but it didn't feel like enough. The children were still dead. Her mother was dead. Frannie was dead and the person who might have killed her was also probably dead, or at least gone. Whatever had happened to her family so many years ago was buried. The people who knew anything were dead, and those still alive weren't talking.

What do I want, then? She thought.

I have to sleep a while, she said, patting Jonathan on the hand. Thank you, she said. You two have been sweet.

They were sweet, but they, too, weren't enough. What did she want? She didn't know.

•

When she felt well enough to go outside, a week later, Heartshorne seemed like a completely new place. The temperature had dropped twenty degrees, finally, and the leaves on the trees, though still mostly green, had become dark and limp and curled into themselves. Frost had gotten them while still green, Jonathan explained, and this caused them to roll up, exposing their lighter undersides. The grass crunched beneath her shoes, dried and fragile from the long, hot summer.

Everything looks tired, Jonathan said, doesn't it?

Emily agreed. She was wrapped in a sweater and Jonathan's coat, a stocking cap on her head and her cold hands tucked in the fur-lined pockets.

Are you cold? he asked, and she was, but she shook her head.

I'm going to go walk around for a while, she said. Feel free to go back in. Or you can go home, if you want to. I'm sure you want to see your store again. I'm going to be OK.

He had been at her house daily for the last two weeks, feeding her when she was too weak to get out of bed, bringing her magazines and books to keep her busy.

He nodded. I'll run out to the store. That's a good idea.

She didn't take the road, as she had led him to believe she would as she waved and watched his car drive away. When he was out of sight, she went back to the house and to the backyard, which had both grown up and been cut down since she'd last seen it. The grass, tall, had been battered down by the rain and bowed, yellowing at the tips. The yard was still littered with fallen trees from the storm. She stepped over the branches and into the woods.

The way to the lake was not long. Now, it was almost silent, few birds and only the enormous sound of her shoes cracking and breaking the twigs and branches littering the forest floor.

The lake was completely placid, only the slightest of movement of the water against the land. The shore had revealed itself again, now dotted with exposed driftwood, still black and slippery. She crouched down by the water and let it wash across her hands. She buried her fingers in the sand, pushing her hand down into the muck as far as it would go. She pushed her hand until she couldn't push anymore, until she hit rock or something submerged.

She imagined that she was touching the bedrock of the town, a piece of rock extending from the edges of Keno to the Painted Hills, a plate of rock that everybody lived on, sending down the small vibrations of their feet to mingle with the larger rumblings of semi-trucks and cars and four-wheelers and the even louder pounding of earth moving equipment tearing up chunks of red dirt and constellations of root.

Her hand in the sand was so cold, she could no longer feel the rock below her fingertips. She eased her hand out and washed it clean in the lake while looking out at that calm expanse. The broken trees that had once stuck out had been cleared away by the flood. The lake looked normal, now, like a place you could safely dive into.

This wasn't true, though. She'd read the paper that morning, which had reported that the bodies and caskets washed up had been re-buried, though there was no way of knowing who they had been. The trees were cleared away, but the report claimed that only a fraction of the coffins had come up. When they'd dragged the lake for Levi Richardson's body (never found), divers had found other remains, submerged in the mud, as well as remnants of houses and even cars, rusted and in pieces but still there at the bottom. They could always come up again.

PART FOUR

Connie had packed her clothes and brought her paper-bag covered schoolbooks back to Heartshorne High. She'd left them stacked outside of the office in a grocery bag. She had not bothered to say goodbye to any of her teachers once her mother told her about their decision. She had told some friends goodbye, but few, since she'd lost track of them in her weeks away from school, and more importantly, had lost interest in them. They were so young. Now, the relationships she had cared so much about seemed petty. She could feel, even before her parents had formally announced it, that she wasn't meant to stay in Heartshorne much longer. She'd been disconnecting herself already. The few girls who came over seemed to want nothing more than to gossip. They wanted her to give them details about where she had been, about what had happened to her, and tried to lure it out of her by telling her the rumors.

We heard that somebody kept you captive, they said, and that you remember bits and pieces. Is it true?

She would only shake her head. I don't remember anything. It's like on some nights when you are so tired that you fall right asleep without remembering anything and then open your eyes and are awake and can't remember sleeping. That's how it feels. Just a big blank.

This was completely opposite to the truth, which was somehow easier than making up a more plausible lie. This was how she wished it had been, at least. A big blank.

After she had finished packing most of her books and clothes, her radio and records, she walked to the lake. She reached the edge of the lake, at the spot where she and her brothers and sisters had played as children. It was still a parking place, where teenagers came to make out, the grass dead and pressed down into the car tracks, but the town had set up a picnic table and a trash can which was never changed, so the trash overflowed the can and scattered on the ground around it. She sat down on the dry ground and took her socks and shoes off.

She had once imagined that she would always live here. She thought she would be like her teachers or her friends' mothers or her own mother—a husband amongst the young men at school and, eventually, children and a job watching or teaching children (these were the only jobs that women had, as far as she knew, and though she didn't much like children, she thought that this was where she would work, too) or no job at all except for a house and a family to keep her busy. Like her mother, she might spend her days doing laundry and cooking and cleaning all day, waiting for everyone to come home and undo it all, and then do it all again before bed.

She stepped into the water with her bare feet, letting the lake mud squish between her toes. Usually, she ran out to the rocky point in the water, hating that soft, squelching feeling under her feet, but now she figured she should sit here and take it—it was her last time here, probably, and it couldn't hurt. She let her feet sink down into the mud until she could only see the beginning of were her foot sloped down from her ankle. She closed her eyes.

She took a piece of paper from her pocket. On it, she had written two sentences. She read them again, pleased with their finality. The lake was the one thing gave Heartshorne its borders: it was a big, watery limit, a body that almost everyone in the town had entered. It struck her as funny, the phrase *body of water*. They had all joined with it at some point, leaving behind their skin and hair and other bodily fluids. The lake held as much of them as anywhere else. It seemed the right place to leave her resolutions. She had to close the place up behind her.

That way, she could leave, and the past could close up behind her like a zipper. She touched the surface of the words, slightly raised from the lead of her pencil:

I will never tell the truth about James.
I will never come back here.

She took the pages, her words printed on them in bold, and ripped it up, slicing her sentences in half, and then the words in half, and then each strip and piece of paper in half until she had tiny pieces of confetti. She threw them into the lake, where they grew wet and dark and disappeared.

ACKNOWLEDGMENTS

Infinite thanks to everyone at Dark House Press, particularly Richard Thomas, Carrie Gaffney, Jacob Knabb, and Victor David Giron. I can't thank you all enough for getting behind this novel.

Thank you to Alban Fischer, cover designer, and Helena Kvarnström, for providing the amazing cover photograph.

Thanks always to my dear friend Kyle Minor.

Shout out the Tel Aviv Writer's group, who warmly welcomed a bewildered newcomer to Israel to the group and saw early drafts of this novel. In particular, thanks to Naomi, Alex, Kate, Greg, Anna, and Alona. I know I'm forgetting a few others!

Thanks to Michelle Herman, who first encouraged my prose writing.

Thanks to MacDowell Colony & Vermont Studio Center for the solitude and the good meals.

Thanks to Chris Wells & K.D. Lovgren, two excellent readers, writers, and friends.

Thanks to the McMurrian/Strange/Trent clan for my yearly dose of Oklahoma and tales of Sardis Lake and local murder.

Lastly, thanks to Zach Trent, for being the most supportive and loving person I've ever known.

LETITIA TRENT

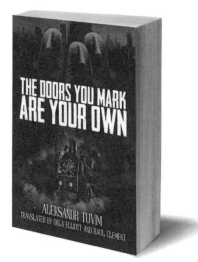

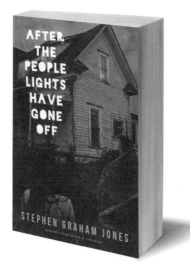

WWW.THEDARKHOUSEPRESS.COM

DARK HOUSE PRESS

Published by Dark House Press, an imprint of Curbside Splendor Publishing, Inc., Chicago, Illinois in 2014.

First Edition
Copyright © 2014 by Letitia Trent
Library of Congress Control Number: 2014942039

ISBN 978-1-940430-03-4
Edited by Richard Thomas
Cover photograph by Helena Kvarnstrom
Interior photo © Lisa Valder/iStock
Designed by Alban Fischer

Manufactured in the United States of America.

www.thedarkhousepress.com
www.curbsidesplendor.com